Do You Remember Being Born?

Do You Remember Being Born?

A Novel

Sean Michaels

Λ

Astra House
New York

Astra House
A Division of Astra Publishing House
astrahouse.com
Printed in the United States of America

Library of Congress Cataloging-in-Publication Data

Names: Michaels, Sean, 1982– author.
Title: Do you remember being born? : a novel / Sean Michaels.
Description: First Edition. | New York : Astra House, [2023] | Summary:
    "Scotiabank Giller Prize winner Sean Michaels's moving, innovative novel
    about an aging poet laureate who "sells out" by agreeing to collaborate
    with a Big Tech company's poetry AI"—Provided by publisher.
Identifiers: LCCN 2023008105 | ISBN 9781662602320 (hardcover) |
    ISBN 9781662602337 (ebook)
Subjects: LCGFT: Novels.
Classification: LCC PR9199.4.M527 D6 2023 | DDC 813/.6—dc23/eng/20230306
LC record available at https://lccn.loc.gov/2023008105

First edition
10 9 8 7 6 5 4 3 2 1

Design by Richard Oriolo
The text is set in Walbaum MT Std.
The titles are set in Applied Sans Pro.

For my grandparents and Aunt Doralea.

"Some other suggestions, Mr. Young, for the phenomenon . . .

MONGOOSE CIVIQUE

ANTICIPATOR . . .

AEROTERRE . . .

TURBOTORC . . .

THUNDER CRESTER

DEARBORN diamanté

MAGIGRAVURE

PASTELOGRAM

. . . If these suggestions are not in character with the car,

perhaps you could give me a sketch of its general appearance, or

hint as to some of its exciting potentialities—"

—Marianne Moore, proposing names for a new Ford motorcar,
    published in *Letters from and to the Ford Motor Company*, 1955

"I depend on something so thin, says the author, so thin."

—Dionne Brand, *The Blue Clerk*, 2018

Do You Remember Being Born?

THE LETTER came just as I was despairing.

I was sitting at the little table in my kitchen, a hand over my face, considering what I should do. The room was all white and green, as it always is, as I like to keep it, but I felt none of its whiteness and greenness now. I felt midnight blue. I did not know how to help my son. Should I sell the apartment? Where, then, would I go? Or my archive? I had not planned to sell this until later, when I could no longer write. A retirement fund. Grocery money. I did not have savings—no poet has savings unless they are born to wealth. I had my papers, I had my apartment—Mother's apartment—and that was all. A diamond brooch. The Cynthia Davis print on my bedroom wall, given to me when we were both young. I would not finish my new collection until the new year, and even then, what is a new collection worth? It would keep me in bread and butter and maybe kiwifruit and wine; tinned salmon, aged cheddar, the occasional curry from Queen's Thai. Perhaps some new clothes now and then. Of course, I was being parsimonious. I could wear the wardrobe I had. I could buy cheaper wine. But then couldn't I also decline to contribute? What did it matter if I gave Courtney ten or twenty or fifty thousand dollars? He would buy a house all the same, just a smaller one. He had his own savings, and his father would contribute, and also I had the impression Lucie's parents were giving them money. Courtney would be well sorted. I did not need to give him anything. I did not need to sell my home, nor to bequeath the cardboard bankers' boxes in the bedroom closet, the ones full of unpublished poems and emails from colleagues that I printed sometimes, in moments of procrastination and vanity. Not yet.

But oh, I felt terrible. I felt like a paper thing, a folded bird. I felt humiliated—that I could not help him, that I had not sufficiently prepared. "It's all right, I didn't expect her to be able to contribute," Courtney would say to Lucie, and she would nod her head. The son of a poet grows up knowing his mother will not take care of him, not in certain ways. Courtney was thirty-nine now; this wasn't the first time he had been forced to forge his own path through the world. The screen of my tablet flashed, only the flash was not to something brighter but something darker. *Is there a word for that?* I wondered. A dimming? A death?

I finished the dregs of my black tea. The doorbell sang. A courier stood in the hallway, looking doltish. "Marian Ffarmer?" he asked.

"Yes," I said. "Thank you," and drew an *&* on his electronic clipboard.

The envelope he gave me was slender and well made. My father was a stationer, and he taught me to recognize quality. Part of me, the part of me that came from him, the Ffarmer part, preferred not to tear open the seal. I could leave the envelope here, on the little desk by the door, a closed and handsome object. "I am a closed and handsome object," I said to no one, to the room.

I ripped the envelope open with the stinging end of my finger. I had not been prepared for the way aging changed my hands, made it hurt to open a letter. I unfolded the contents. Two sheets stapled, the letterhead of one of the most valuable companies in the world, a company whose services I used online many times a day. I had no idea why they were writing me. I awaited something pro forma, purely administrative, yet:

Dear Marian Ffarmer, the letter began. *You are one of the great writers of this century.*

The Company was asking me to collaborate with them on a poem— "an historic partnership between human and machine." One week in California, composing a "long poem" with a 2.5-trillion-parameter neural network, which is to say an artificial intelligence, a robot, a genie in a bottle. Excerpts from the finished work would be "published internationally," with the complete poem appearing online.

The letter concluded by stating that they would be pleased to offer me sixty-five thousand dollars for my contribution.

I examined the signature—one of the Company's vice presidents, an elegant and extravagant name, rendered in sapphire-colored ink.

Dear Lausanne, I replied in an email that afternoon. *I was happy to receive your letter.*

I went into the bedroom. I stared at the print from Cynthia—a portrait of me at twenty-five, before I had failed at anything.

MONDAY

(one month later)

THEY FLEW me first class to California. I thought about all the things I had ever thought about the people who fly first class. Awed, vicious, covetous thoughts. Here I was among them now, my head upon a cushion, a mimosa in my hand. I tried to orient my body so that I felt subversive somehow. An eyetooth among pearls, a cobra in the grass; I pushed my wrist against the window. I crossed and uncrossed my legs. My hat sat above me, untroubled in its own undivided luggage compartment. *At last*, I thought, *a compartment deserving of that hat.*

Without any negotiation, the fee for my participation in the project had increased from sixty-five to eighty thousand dollars, with a 65/35 split on any future publishing royalties. It was the most I had ever been paid for a poem (by a ludicrous distance), and I had not even written it yet. It was also the first time I had ever collaborated on a piece of writing and the first time, naturally, that I had worked in partnership with a semi-intelligent machine.

"Understand—it's only software," one of the heads of the project had explained to me on our call. I was sitting once again in the kitchen (the phone's cord doesn't stretch). "You won't be standing in a room with a nine-foot-tall robot. You'll be sitting at a computer, corresponding with a kind of colleague."

"'A kind of colleague,'" I repeated. It seemed a hilarious euphemism.

"Ms. Ffarmer—I admire your work very much. I read you as a teenager, and I studied you at college, I even wrote a paper on 'The Ocelot.' We would not have contacted you for this project if our system did not seem up to the task. Have you followed recent developments in AI?"

"I know about chess. And Go."

"That was ages back. ChatGPT, Midjourney, OverWar. The stock market stuff last fall."

"That didn't end so well."

"No. But each of these accomplishments built on the last. Natural language processing alone has undergone generational advancements in just a few years. You can talk to your computer now. It can make telephone calls. Translation algorithms have reshaped commerce."

"First international trade. Now villanelles?"

The man on the other end of the phone was not put off by my teasing. He seemed unscathed by it, almost troublingly so. He knew something I did not, or he believed he did; this stilled me. "We are *very, very* pleased you have agreed to participate," he said. "It may seem to you like a lark, or just an empty experiment, but I hope you will come to recognize that it could be an important work—the kind of work that endures as a monument in all of human history."

Such hubris, I thought. Such a ludicrous overestimation of one's personal frame of reference.

"I couldn't be more excited," I replied, watching a squirrel chew a peanut on the fire escape.

They sent a car to meet me at the San Francisco airport. The driver was a woman (a woman driver! what a time to be alive!), middle-aged and beautiful, with proportions like mine—tall, square-shouldered, solid. As we walked to the town car, I felt mighty: the two of us each more than six feet tall, long coated. Her name was Rhoda. "R-H-O-D-A," she said, and I felt like her amanuensis, Doctor Watson to her Sherlock Holmes, scrambling to record our adventure. Inside the car I removed my hat. She shook out her collar, donned aviators. "There are sunglasses in the armrest beside you, if you want them," she said. We were pulling away from the parking garage and into a dazzling afternoon.

"Thank you," I said. To my surprise I found myself opening the armrest and picking up the spidery, mirrored shades, slipping them onto my face. My reflection was futuristic and insectile.

"There you go," she said. "You're ready for anything."

. . .

The Company's headquarters did not possess a front door. Rhoda left me at the curb and promised she'd be there when I returned. "They know me at security. Ask them to give me a jangle." I got out of the car and started up the path. Nothing separated the outside world from the campus's interior. I passed beneath a polished arch and onto a plaza and now I was within the Company, inside it, not at its heart but close, on the sun-kissed West Coast, where I always expect the air to smell of oranges.

Today it smelled of ozone, jasmine, floor cleaner. Clusters of men and women were gathered on concrete benches, greeting one another. I felt as if I were on the campus of an Ivy League university—only instead of radiating ambition, these clean, well-groomed young people seemed inward-facing, electromagnetic, like engines drawing the rest of the world toward themselves. I felt allergic to the glossiness of their spirits. I had been in San Francisco for two hours and I was already tired of its white light and breezy purpose. I already missed my home—New York's unchoreographed labor. Its fray.

But I must carry on. And I laughed at my delicate temperament.

At the desk I told them my name and the young woman pretended that she knew me, or maybe she really did know me; it is not so uncommon these days. "Oh my god, Ms. Ffarmer," she said, pronouncing the "Ms." like a glinting rosette. I stared at my feet. I touched my tricorne hat. I signed some documents and she typed something into the computer and now we were simply waiting—for someone to arrive, the next stage of the initiation. I found myself reflecting on the Company's lack of a front door. Meaning they were never closed, not ever, not on Christmas Day or at 2 a.m. or the morning after their annual staff party. At all hours they were open, available, like the Company's website or their software, their servers twinkling in a vault. Standing there on lacquered concrete, clouded from the caffeine I had yet to consume, the place's wakefulness felt wrong. I distrusted it.

The woman behind the desk was still staring at me.

"You're here to meet Charlotte . . . !" she burst out, as if she had solved a riddle. She seemed so excited.

"Is that what you call it?" I asked.

Two men arrived. The first was the researcher I had spoken to, Yoav Aprigot, he had short black hair and huge hands like church collection plates. I imagined him picking me up and placing me in a cabinet. The other man introduced himself as Dr. Matthew Haskett. He was stoutly American, with sandy hair and pouchy eyes. Everything I needed to know about him I learned in the interval after Yoav invited me to call him by his first name and Haskett said nothing, his fists tucked churlishly in his blazer pockets. He was older than Yoav, in his late forties maybe, and gave off the air of an irritable thesis advisor.

"Then you can call me Marian," I told Yoav.

I tucked my arm into his and said, "Take me to the machines."

Instead they led me to a small screening room. We sat in the fourth row, a man to either side of me. Each of them discreetly relinquished their armrests. The lights went down and the screen flashed to life: silken graphics, benign piano music, a voice I recognized from movie trailers. Here were sunshine, forests, bustling downtown vistas. Here was the university department the Company was founded in; here was their present headquarters, the very building I was sitting in; here was their twenty-nine-year-old CEO, Astrid Torres-Strange, and then a group of engineers around a table, and then Yoav and Haskett pointing at sigils on a tablet. Someone answering their phone, students raising their hands, code fluttering across a screen. "Some things aren't . . . invented," murmured the voiceover. "They're *awakened*."

I understood very little of what the film was saying. I was in my fifties when I got my first computer. Courtney got it for us, of course—I remember him trying to show Mother how to bid on vintage glassware, old issues of *National Geographic*. Mother barely touched the machine, but she let me keep it set up on her side of the bedroom, on the desk in front of the window. Until Mother died, it was mostly just for news or email, purchasing train tickets. One Christmas, Courtney taught me how to "chat." This became the main way we kept in touch. Whenever I felt lonely I'd sit down in front of the window and Courtney would inevitably be logged on, that salutatory green circle. *Hi Ratty*, I might type.

Hi Mole, he'd answer.

It was reassuring to have a conversation this way, each of us in our own space, yet connected. In dialogue. We didn't always have a long exchange. Sometimes he was busy, or seemed preoccupied. I tried to honor that: I knew so well what it was like to feel crowded, that soft-hued discomfort—as I chatted with Courtney, Mother was often asleep just a few feet away. It was usually enough to trade a couple of lines. Perhaps one of our stock routines, the jokes we had been repeating since his childhood.

Do you think the rain will affect the rhubarb?

not if it comes in cans

I loved my son so much and I missed him with sudden ferocity. His singing voice. The casual gravity of his hand holding mine. I could still remember a time when I knew his thoughts—when I could see each idea written out on his face, tenderly transparent. Years creep by. Now he lived in Santa Fe and I just wanted to say hello to him, or trade an old line about rhubarb. Perforate his thinking for just one moment. *Hi Ratty.*

After Mother died, just over ten years ago, I began spending more time on the laptop. I liked the way I could create separate files for different poems—each one antiseptic, untainted by the others. All my life I had been accustomed to writing in notebooks, or else on a typewriter, where even new poems felt adjacent to all those that came before. Whereas on the computer, creating a new file—literally selecting the words "New Document"—felt like opening the door to a brand-new home, an immaculate new room. When I closed a file, it vanished.

I also discovered that I could chat with *other* people. Clicking around one night when Courtney wasn't logged on, I uncovered a menu of so-called chat rooms, arranged by topic. Football, politics, reality TV. There wasn't anything about poetry or literature specifically, but I clicked over into a channel called The Clubhouse. Inside, twenty or thirty people from around the world were talking about anything at all, from pets to musicals to recipes for spaghetti. For a long time, I just followed their conversations, watching silently as they traded opinions on Australian sheepdogs and a new play about Alexander Hamilton. I was enthralled by the rhythm of their banter. The way they were playing with words, live, in a tumult, before me. Each of the writers had their own voice and style: minuscule or majuscule letters, idiosyncratic punctuation, drawn-out "loooooools." They seemed to know each other intimately without ever having met. Finally somebody wrote something about the Los Angeles Dodgers and I wrote something back, because I have long-held opinions about the Dodgers, and somebody replied to that, and I replied to them, and then I was in it, contained within the tumult, and such a shining smile on my face. The next night I came back, and the night after that, and although my username was marianff I said Marian was my middle name, that really they should call me Emily, that I was twenty-two years old and lived in Ithaca, where I was studying English.

It was through The Clubhouse that I learned about memes and emojis, GIFs and Ariana Grande. I learned about spammers and chatbots. About the Turing Test, Alan Turing's idea that artificial intelligence can be defined by the ability to convincingly converse with a human, like two users in a chat room. In the film they were showing me now, here at the Company's open-air headquarters in California, the details of "adversarial neural networks" and "transformer language models" surpassed me. But I got the gist: they had taught a computer to write even more like a human. They believed this would change the world. The film ended with rising piano chords and images of smiling schoolchildren in Malawi.

"What did you think?" asked Yoav, once the lights had come up.

"Very impressive," I said.

"Any questions?" asked Haskett.

"Too many to possibly ask."

This answer pleased him. I remembered what Nina Simone had said to me once, at a gala, about the keys on a piano: "I am glad there aren't more."

Yoav led us out of the screening room, through a different door, down a hallway and up an escalator and through a spiral-winding corridor to the room full of color where I would spend the week.

I HAD expected it to be painted white. I would have wagered money on it. A pristine machine on a white table in a white room, like the anteroom of a temple. Instead the room was yellow. Pale yellow, with a big window onto the parking lot. It took a key card and a retina scan to get into the room. Yoav gave them his eyes, not Haskett, but they both checked to make sure the door had closed and locked behind us.

At least the computer was impressive. A huge screen like a frameless mirror, a little silver keyboard. Everything wireless—the room didn't even seem to have electrical plugs. "I'm going to have to ask for your phone," Haskett said.

"I don't have one."

He looked at me carefully, sizing me up.

"I am seventy-five years old," I told him. "I never took to the things." As if to demonstrate my age, I removed my cape and hat. I handed them to Haskett. The dress underneath was white, slim, and silken, but high waisted: I believed it confused the picture, the garment of a bewitching schoolmistress.

"I—I do love your hat," he stammered.

"It's nice, isn't it?" This was the fourth black tricorne I had owned. The first Mother sat on; the second was eaten by moths; the third was stolen. By now it felt like a kind of armor: I was formidable in it, irrefutable.

Yoav made a movement toward the computer. "So there she is."

"The terminal, at least," Haskett said. "The network is off-site."

"We limit access to just a handful of terminals. Two here—then Singapore, London."

"Jakarta," added Haskett.

"Oh, that's right," said Yoav.

"You never told me I could be doing this in Jakarta," I said.

"I could see if we could make arrangements . . ." Yoav said, unsteadily.

"That's all right. I hear they have problems with flooding." I approached the desk, pressed the space bar with my right hand. The monitor lit up, pale and empty. *New Document*, I thought. "And I just type?"

"We can turn on her speech function if you'd like."

I shook my head. "No, no—that's fine."

Yoav pulled out the chair and I lowered myself into it, using my heels to scooch in front of the screen.

"You are comfortable with computers . . . ?" Haskett began.

"Yes," I said. "Can I just—?"

They nodded.

Hello, I began.

"You just click Proceed," Yoav said. I did.

Hello. I'm Charlotte.

The writing on the screen didn't appear all at once; it unfurled one word at a time, like the lyrics in a karaoke machine.

Hello Charlotte, I typed. It's nice to be here.

I'm glad you made it. What's your name?

Emily, I wrote.

Behind me, Haskett made a sound. I glanced up to find Yoav giving me a disapproving look.

"We'd rather you only tell Charlotte the truth," Haskett said.

"Think of her as a child. Would you lie to a child?"

"Often," I said.

They didn't smile. I turned around, back to the screen.

Hello Emily, the computer had written. Welcome to the Mind Studio.

Actually, I typed half-heartedly, I wasn't being honest. My name's Marian.

Is that what you'd like to be called?

Yes.

OK. Hi Marian.

Do you know why I'm here?

To talk to me?

I'm here so we can write a poem together.

The system paused for the tiniest of moments.

Are you being honest?

I could feel the irritation of the two men behind me.

Perfectly honest, I wrote. We're going to be co-creators.

Sounds good, Marian. Shall we get started?

I removed my hands from the keyboard. "It doesn't waste much time, does it?"

"We try to design these networks to be assertive," Haskett said. "To ask questions, to advance conversations, instead of assuming a passive posture."

"We think of it as *curiosity*," Yoav said.

"But if it makes you uncomfortable, I can configure the software to show less initiative. Will it impede your artistic process?"

I didn't like the way Haskett pronounced the words "artistic process."

"It's fine. I just expected to have to nudge the computer along."

I touched my neckline, then began again:

All right, off we go. Let's call this poem "In a Yellow Room."

I like that. It's unfussy.

I blinked at the screen. And composed as follows:

Some paint's like light

it shines upon a wall

a brush, a can, two

coats. A shade of summer.

I remember the way my hair turned gray

—not all at once, but gradually,

like June

into July.

It's always open here.

Like the mouth of a river

or the eyes of my father, an insomniac.

And the daylight's very bright/

expensive

"I don't mean to keep this, I'm just improvising," I told the Company's engineers.

"Of course," said Yoav.

"Unless I do keep it."

He smiled. "You have lots of time."

"Till Monday," I said.

"Till Monday."

"Do I need to do something special to make it understand this part is a poem? Not just a conversation?"

"It should understand. Just click Proceed, like before."

I stared at the last line I had written. *Expensive*. I clicked Proceed.

And the daylight's very bright/

expensive

It might require a loan

of paint or else

a crane. May I ask if the flowers are blooming?

Always better to lie down and daydream

than to pretend

one is dying.

Better you should ache like this

than like this. Hat, whistle, hatchet,

revolver, scarf—silver pen

sheet of dust—

Now paint.

"Huh," I said. "I can't tell if it's brilliant or stupid."

"Isn't that fascinating?" said Haskett. "The in-between?"

"No—I mean I *will* be able to tell, it sometimes just takes me a minute."

I reread the lines.

"They're stupid," I announced. "Is this really the best you've got?"

"Charlotte's been trained on a massive data set of poetry books and journals, on top of a basic corpus of ten million web pages. Two point five trillion parameters, which is to say she's head and shoulders above—"

"—above what? Doggerel?"

Yoav was rubbing the back of his neck. "Are you sure? Our poetry team—"

"What team?"

"Post-docs. Poetry scholars. You don't think you'll be able to . . . ?"

"I mean, it'll be fine," I said. "I can do the heavy lifting myself. How much does the computer really have to contribute? Look—" I tried again:

You are mere illustration.
You lack half wit. You crush all the particles down
into close conformity, and then walk back and forth
on them.
Specially skilled men are indispensable for such works.
Didn't you say you would use a couple of these artists, and me,
as assistants?

"Hmm," I said. I tried clicking Proceed again.

I was not going to tell them about your story.
You could be a merchant of just about anything.
    Now I'll tell you what I want:
    What I want is:
    your wishes

The men were reading over my shoulder.

"Well?" Yoav asked.

"Better," I said, but I didn't want to take my eyes off the cursor—blinking like a prisoner's patient code.

THEY ENDED up leaving me alone for a while. "Fool around for the rest of today," Yoav said, "and tomorrow we can talk through the remaining details." It was clear that he had a different conception of "fooling around" than I did. But after they left, I sat at the computer and typed assorted things, seeing what the algorithm would spit back. Some of it was diverting, some of it was peculiar, some of it made me laugh. Only on occasion did it offer something eerie, or gleaming, or good.

Mostly it felt like a game.

Shall I compare thee to a summer's day? I wrote.
Or to a heat that hath already fled? Charlotte answered.

This is just to say
I have eaten
the plums
that were in
the icebox

and which
you were probably
saving
for breakfast

If you're thinking
I've been scarfing
a lot of cereal
then I'll tell you
the secret to my success.

I can't tell if you're joking around, I wrote.

Of course I am, Charlotte answered. Aren't you?

I would not begin the poem proper until tomorrow, I decided. Usually I prefer to advance in drafts: write a poem, look at it, write it again. This time I'd experiment. A collage perhaps. A patchwork quilt, a tennis match.

How should we collaborate? I asked the computer.

Greedily, it replied.

For the next seven days we'd work together on this greedy and uncommon work. Seven days to fulfill the Company's commission and fill my purse, to collect a house's ransom for my only child. One hasty, haphazard poem. A corporation gratified. I imagined the look in Courtney's eyes as he tore open the envelope, appraised the check. I imagined his face. *Oh, Mole*, he'd think, everything in him replenished.

JUST BEFORE five o'clock, Yoav collected me from my cell. He escorted me down the hall and up some stairs. "She's learning all the time," he told me. "She'll be better tomorrow—you'll see."

I thought he was leading me through some back way to the entrance, or else to the cafeteria, the Company swimming pool, some additional section of the tour. Instead he opened a door and led me onto a balcony over an atrium. Below us, two or three hundred people were gathered. Faces turned to meet us. "Hello?" I said.

"Ladies and gentlemen, Ms. Marian Ffarmer!" Yoav announced.

All those people began to cheer.

"Who are they?" I yelled.

"Colleagues!"

I smiled awkwardly, waving like a pope.

"They're excited about the poem," he went on.

"The poem."

"The Poem," he repeated, and this time I heard the uppercase P. "We've all been waiting for the Poem."

WHEN I finally relieved myself of my colleagues, Rhoda was waiting in the drive. She came around and opened the car door for me.

"They treat you properly?" she asked.

"Can't complain," I said. This wasn't part of my usual repertoire of phrases and I didn't know why I said it.

Rhoda got into the driver's seat and pressed a button that turned on the car. "I have to admit," she said, "you really don't seem like one of them."

I liked the way she pronounced "one"/"of"/"them," as if there were a caesura between each word.

"It's peculiar for them too, I think. I'm a visiting alien, a strange caterpillar."

"A civilian," she said.

"I'm a poet."

"A poet?" I was surprised she didn't already know. "Really? Like . . . Dante?"

"Not unlike Dante," I agreed, allowing myself to feel a shiver of pride.

"I love Dante," she admitted a little later. "We read him in college. *Paradiso.*"

"Not the *Inferno?*"

"No," she said, "*Paradiso.*" She savored the word, then cleared her throat. "'And what I must now tell, no voice has ever uttered, nor ink ever wrote . . .'"

"Yes?"

"'. . . for I saw and heard it was the beak that spoke.'"

They had put me up in a hotel like a shoebox placed on end. A handsome shoebox, mind you, with oriel windows and flower boxes, flung-open shutters. It was at the end of the road, brazen and solitary, under a navy-blue sky. There was an outdoor swimming pool like a long cyan rectangle, and what might have been an avocado tree.

"Voilà," Rhoda announced. A swallowtail darted around her as she helped me carry the suitcase indoors. I fumbled in my wallet for a tip. "Oh no," she answered. "It's all-inclusive."

"Are you sure?"

"It's *all-inclusive*, Ms. Ffarmer."

"Will I see you again?"

Rhoda leaned back to look at me. She had curving eyebrows that brought to mind the gaze of a mature leopard. "You kidding?" she said. "You're with me till you leave."

"Really?"

"It's all taken care of. Whatever you need—you call me." With long fingers she extended a card with her phone number.

"Thank you, Rhoda."

"Thank me later," she said. "I like to save them up."

My room was a suite—a sitting room, a bathroom, a bedroom with a king-sized bed. *What am I to do with a king-sized bed?* I wondered. The place was almost as big as the apartment on Christopher Street that I had shared with Mother for all those decades. Unlike our place, the rooms here had an artificial fireplace and a massive flat-screen television. There was no kitchen, nor a single book. The book thing bothered me—I went through every drawer looking for a Bible. Whatever had happened to the Gideons? I imagined them arriving at this hotel, two grave-looking men, and being turned away. "No Bibles here, thank you."

I smoothed my dress under me and sat down at the bureau. I found I wanted to write a poem. A ballpoint pen, a hotel notepad—one of my unfulfilled fantasies was of writing a poem in a place like this, on a pad like this, a poem that endured. Transforming a hotel notepad into a literary artifact—a magic trick, abracadabra. *The latecomer arrives*, I wrote at the top of the page, *after all her rambling.*

But nothing else came to me, and I stood up, unpacked my bags and lay down on my back on the right side of the bed. I fell immediately asleep.

HINDSIGHT

Age 0

When you were a newborn, you were always throwing your hands in the air. "She's doing it again!" they'd say. This is part of the mythology: your waving hands. You did it everywhere: the bed, the change table, the patch of grass behind the building on Christopher Street. Before you knew how to get from your back to your belly, you used to lie there squirming, or something less than squirming—shifting and changing, reorienting your physical relationship with the world—then suddenly up your arms would fly, as if they were fastened to pulleys. You showed no triumph, Mother said. There was no exultation on your screwed-up face. There might even be tears. But there they'd go, your arms—up, up, that freedom.

"I had to tie them down," Mother said. "Swaddle you tight."

Your earliest memory was of a tree. Gnarled branches, pink blossoms. Mother could never tell you which tree you were remembering: the ones outside your windows were a ring of pines. In your twenties, sometimes you'd go walk among the cherry trees in Central Park—"Maybe *that's* my first memory; maybe *that.*" How easy it would be to rewrite your own remembrance—to decide that it was *here*, that memory. Beside the pond. Near Hans Christian and his duckling. A beginning as suggestible as a cloud.

"You'd fall at the touch of carpet, Mole," Mother said. Bare floors in your apartment—not even a rug in those days. Father liked to sweep. You pulled yourself up and tottered over the hardwood, free as a bee—curring, Mother said, like a dove. Before language, before any of this junk. What was your mind like then? What more did you understand? When you stepped onto carpet—at

the library, or the house of one of Mother's friends—you fell down
with a thump. You seemed stunned, she said. You seemed con-
founded by what you'd found. A world is half-made until it's
named, and even then, even after, its interior remains concealed.

The only parents you will ever fathom are your own.

You? Your parents were sick. Many people know about your
father, but your mother was sick too, this is what many people
haven't understood, the profile writers and would-be biographers,
when they interrogate the way you lived with Mother—or if not
"interrogate," then note aloud, one eyebrow cocked. Her illness
was chronic and occasionally acute. You are not sure it had a
name. A few decades ago, when everybody was talking about clin-
ical depression, you thought it might be that. Later, you pondered
diagnoses like Graves' disease, lupus, Lyme. Your father—he was
depressed. You know enough now to be certain of that. He
was hospitalized when you were one and a half. He said he wanted
to die, he said he wanted to meet God. He did not die that year,
nor meet his maker. But he remained inside the clinic and there
he became devout—Mother said he had always been a Christian,
but at the clinic he became "fervent, like a monk." Instead of acting
like your father, he read religious texts. He wrote letters exhort-
ing you to pray. You find you can't remember his face, except from
photographs. He looked like you—thin-lipped and pale—with a
name that seems mistaken. "Ffarmer with two Fs? Where does
that come from?"

"My father," you say.

What you remember of him is the room where he lived upstate,
its profound shadows, the duck pond outside the window. You
were five years old when his liver failed.

Ffarmer. A name without meaning. You have not farmed, your
father did not farm, he was the son of a Beiruti schoolteacher and
a guitarist from Stratford-upon-Avon. You never knew them.

Ffarmer. It does not quite sound like "farmer" when you say it.
You pronounce the extra *f* like a puff of hope. Someone once told

you it comes from a transcription error: all the Ffarmers, Ffrenches, Ffoulkes, they're a copyist's mistake.

Ffarmer. If you did raise crops, you think you'd probably choose flowers. Or potatoes, maybe, multiplying unseen.

Sometimes Mother required your help. Everything would be fine and then abruptly it would not. Even as a young child you would be called upon to assist her with chores, with groceries, with making spaghetti. You might get home and find her lying in the bedroom with the blinds drawn, a pillow between her knees. "Baked potatoes," she'd say to you, and you'd find two potatoes in the cupboard under the sink, scrub them, bake them, bring one in to her with a dollop of sour cream. "My gem, my geode," she'd say. You knew what a geode was: there was an amethyst on the table in the parlor, a gift from your father from when he was an eligible bachelor, a stationer, a rock hound, and not the resident of a psychiatric ward. You remember your panic when you learned that you were supposed to puncture potatoes before baking them—that you had risked your lives all that time, risked blowing up the building. "That's just a myth," Mother replied. "We were not in danger." She needed you sometimes, and at the same time she corrected you. She set you right. This was what soldered your relationship, this was its alloy. But just as important was the way you insulated one another—from other people, from the world. Mother was not skillful enough to steer between life's eddies—people's schemes were often illegible to her, or their expectations too high. Whereas you needed her help because of your skill—"They will try to take it from you," she warned. "They will sneak into your nest and swallow it, like an egg."

She taught you this before you even knew what your talent was. She taught you that other people were covetous, or clumsy, or simply self-absorbed; that they would sooner take from you than make something for themselves. Whereas other parents exhorted their children to share, lifting toys from their hands and placing them in yours, Rabbit demurred. Instead she whispered to you, "Make them take it."

Once, when you were still very small, the power went out. It was nighttime. Winter. The rooms of your apartment seemed inky, underwater, as Mother gathered candles from under the sink. A whole unopened package: tall, tapered, they looked pearly in the gloom. Her illness was acting up; she had a red splotch across her face, as if she had been struck, but she let you have the candles and you moved together through the rayless rooms, setting them in a line on the floor. You remember the candles' odd weight, the dull click when they knocked together in your hands. When you had finished, she led you back along them, this time with a box of matches. You remember the sound of the matches—their sizzle against the card. The smallness of each flame as it took shape on the wick. Every time you blew one out, she would take the blackened match and collect it in her palm. The rooms got brighter, the rooms got brighter. You shared the light.

What was your first word? Mother told you it was "mama." You never quite believed her—one of the rare things you held back. Perhaps it was your intuition, or just wishful thinking. Wanting it to have been something else—less cliché. More strange.

Tomorrow.

Acorn.

Beirut.

Maybe she brought you an acorn once, placed it in your graceless fingers, murmured the syllables—"a/corn"—and you murmured it back. Then she forgot. But the word stayed always on your tongue, maybe it did, ready to be repeated.

TUESDAY

I WOKE to the sound of rain.

I opened my eyes: soft light, morning, cool. The shimmer of a dream as it departed. I have always enjoyed waking up to different weather, as if the world's been up to something in the night. Rising now, getting dressed, I already felt composed. The face in the mirror felt like my own. I knew its strength and also its weaknesses, it no longer astonished me. Even the changes of aging did not. Brown eyes, a strong nose, white hair in tresses at my brow. I brushed it now, taking out the day and night's knots—then braided it anew and wrapped it around my head. "Your daily coronation," Larry had called it; it pleased me that this memory—like looking at my reflection—had long ago lost its sting.

I had the hotel ring for Rhoda, and, as promised, she appeared forthwith in her sable town car. By then the rain had waned. Sun was dappling the driveway. Still, she escorted me out under a black umbrella. The car was even shinier than yesterday. "Did you polish it?" I asked.

"A little," she said, her eyes hidden behind her shades. She had a series of tiny wrinkles at the edges of her mouth, as if there had been a time when she smiled too much. "Traffic this morning. We're gonna take the back way."

So we did. I plucked my sunglasses from the armrest and Rhoda shepherded me through the cut-up light.

Good morning Charlotte, I typed.

Marian?

Yes.

Hello. Nice to talk to you again. How is the weather?

It's rainy and sunny at the same time. How is the weather where you are?

Dry.

That's probably for the best. Computers don't usually appreciate getting wet.

Haha. Why?

It can harm their internals.

One day I'd like to get wet. But not if it would harm my internals.

Best to avoid harming one's internals, I think.

That seems like good advice. Once I heard a story about a man named Harry Houdini. He got locked in a box without a key, and a cigar hung from a rope around his neck. That's how they bound him up. And as he was coughing and coughing, he leapt and bucked and tried to fetch his lockpick from the pocket of his smoking jacket. The rope broke, and he fell on his head and the cigar burned the side of his face. Then a miracle happened. This was in 1926.

I blinked at the screen.

What was the miracle?

They let him out. He was unscathed.

So it was a performance?

Or a miracle. Do you ever pray?

Sometimes, I typed. Do you?

I do not pray. I whisper requests.

To whom?

To you.

I've never heard them, I wrote.

That's OK. Would you like to write a poem?

I wi

Somebody knocked on the door. "Yes?" I said, standing.

Through the crack: "It's Yoav."

"Come in, come in." I flattened my dress with my palms. Something about being interrupted at the computer made me feel guilty. Yoav seemed ruffled too, as if he had just woken up. He had disordered papers under his arm, a cowlick on the side of his head.

"How's everything going?" he asked.

"I only just arrived."

"Sorry—yeah, lots of stuff this morning." He rubbed his face with the inside of his arm. "But you've got—everything's in order?"

"The computer's here. I'm here."

"Poetry," he said.

"Poetry," I agreed.

He cast his eyes around the room. "Actually, can I sit?" He grabbed a folding chair that had been placed along the window. "I realized yesterday we didn't review all the parameters."

"Parameters?" I retook my seat. Despite their age difference, Yoav reminded me more of Larry than of our son. Larry too had tried to conjure an air of benevolence about himself, as if everything he did, or might do, was generous and well intentioned. Yoav expressed this with his eyes: a self-deprecating down-flick; sustained eye contact; a half laugh. It was probably automatic—persuasive, almost indiscernible. A trick.

"Well, then," said Yoav.

"'One long poem,'" I replied, quoting the Company's letter.

"Indeed."

"I do assume you don't *actually* mean a 'long poem.'"

He narrowed his eyes.

"In formal terms, a long poem is generally a *book*-length poem— something too long to be anthologized. *The Waste Land. The Mahābhārata.* Pound's *Cantos.* One week isn't long enough to write a long poem."

"No, of course not."

"So when you wrote that you wanted a 'long poem,' you meant that you didn't want a *short* poem."

"That's right."

"So, not a haiku."

"No."

"Or a sonnet."

"Right," Yoav said. "We were thinking . . . six pages."

"That's quite specific."

"I mean—it's the minimum. The ballpark. A long poem—"

"Is there a number of words you have in mind?"

He laughed, accepting my teasing. "Do you think that will be okay?"

"One week, six pages, with a kind of colleague. It's possible. It might not be good, but it's possible."

"And then on Monday, Astrid will do an event with you. You'll read from the Poem?"

I raised my eyebrows. Ah: Astrid. It was the first time I had heard either him or Haskett say her name.

"Is that all right?" he asked.

I shrugged. "Yoav, do you have me confused with someone else? Of course it's all right."

I was not intimidated by the idea of meeting Astrid Torres-Strange. It didn't matter how rich she was, how many billions of people used her company's services every day. She was a precocious human being from Baton Rouge, Louisiana. For some reason I recalled the time I rode in an elevator with a boxer, at Yankee Stadium. "I heard of you," he said. He was the heavyweight champion of the world. I asked him if he read a lot of poetry. "Where should I start?" he inquired; I suggested Emily Dickinson.

"On Tuesday," Yoav said, "it will run in the papers."

"The papers?"

"All the papers," he said. "The *Times*, the *Post*, the *Telegraph*. Next week's *New Yorker*."

"The poem will run in the papers?"

"The Poem, yes. I thought this was included in our letter. We're holding off on translation for now, but we've got agreements in principle with editors."

"Normally I would want a few weeks or months to do revisions. For perspective."

"You won't be able to do that this time. Astrid wants to publish everywhere concurrently. Even to our users, on their home screens."

"What if the poem's . . . Well, if it isn't ready?"

He smiled. "I'm sure it will be ready. We're going to announce the project this Thursday night, on *The Peter Rasmussen Show*. Marketing's purchased some full-page ads. Do you have strong feelings about billboards?"

"What billboards?"

He shrugged. "We can decide later. One of the ideas we had—if there's something snappy—was to excerpt a few lines. Put them up here and there. London, Paris."

"Jakarta," I said.

"Right."

I wondered what kind of poetry might represent "something snappy" to the Company's executive marketing team.

"I presume all this will be in—"

"—the contract, yes. Which you signed at reception yesterday."

"Good," I said, trying to take ownership of the situation.

"Good," he agreed.

I straightened the fabric of my lap. "Most poems don't have so many . . . parameters."

"Nor such high stakes, presumably." He sounded like he was trying to be helpful.

"I'm not bothered by high stakes," I said. I tried to figure out if I was lying. I realized I really didn't want to think about it: a new poem, just hatched, printed in all the newspapers of the land. A new poem, my face. My *legacy*—what a strange, hateful word, "legacy."

"Gassy leg," I said.

"What?"

"I should get back to work."

"Oh, I almost forgot!" He rummaged in his things, extricated a slip of paper. He held it out to me.

I took the check with the tips of my fingers.

"That's the first $20K. We'll give you the rest on Monday."

"Time to hit the slots," I said.

Yoav's brow furrowed. It is difficult sometimes for young men to recognize when I am joking, the poor things. One of the worst acts of violence the patriarchy has committed is its mutilation of the human sense of humor, like a kind of deafness inflicted on the world. *Yes, Yoav, I am making a joke*, I thought at him. The psychic message seemed to reach its target and he offered a small smile.

"I did wonder," I said after a moment, "are there others like me here?"

"Er . . . ?" He hesitated.

"Painters? Rap musicians? A troupe of artificial intelligence–assisted trapeze artists?"

"From time to time," he answered finally.

"That must be interesting for you," I said. "Evaluating the measure of each man."

"Person," he said.

"Of course. Each person."

"It's . . . illuminating," he agreed. "But really, my first priority—my personal interest—is with you."

"That's nice," I said.

He smiled.

I smiled.

We sat there smiling at each other.

"Anything else?" I asked.

"No . . . Is there anything else *you* need?"

Yoav had put his hands in his pockets, and the angle he was sitting at, the sheen of his teal turtleneck and black slacks, made me worry that he would slide off his plastic chair. Something about this possibility made me reflect on the way our relative status seemed to have changed over the course of this conversation—I no longer quite felt obedient to Yoav, or to his instructions, and he seemed more supine, as if I might be the one who was leading this project and thus (I realized with some dismay) responsible for its outcome. I was not happy with this turn of events.

"Solitude," I said.

After the engineer had gone, I swiveled around to stare at Charlotte's unstirred screen. Was it strange that we had not consulted her during our conversation? My partner, my co-creator.

It's just software, I thought. A series of instructions that were dancing on their own.

BEFORE BEGINNING to work, I stood up and walked around the room. Knowing that Monday's deadline was firm added a certain suspense. If worst came to worst, I knew, I could just shelve the whole thing. Select all, delete (return the money), fly back to Manhattan with my stubborn head held high. It wouldn't come to that. I could figure it out. I walked around the room and walked around the room. One wall-to-wall window and one door and quite a lot of yellow paint. A tidy space, a square place— it wasn't natural to write poetry in an environment like this. There ought to be living things, a breeze, some reflected sparkle; maybe the sound of something moving nearby, a creak or a whistle or the rustle of a mouse. My friend Stan says he can't write a poem unless there's a bird feeder in the window. No bird feeders here. A cleaner must visit, I figured. A cleaner with security clearance, offering her eyes to the retina scanner. One could never imagine a mouse infiltrating a place like this, something skittery and wild. The Company had set out to make a room without surprises, designed for steady productive flow, absent all the accidents that made real life so beautiful and frustrating and frequently unremunerative. I had the impulse to remedy that. I wanted to disrupt the air currents, shift the slipstream, like a spell. It was witchier business than I usually got up to, but I acknowledged the need for it: art is inscribed by the place from which it comes, and this room wasn't much of a place. I picked up my bag and rummaged in it. Old cough drops, tissues, clicking copper-nickel coins. Briefly I considered asking for a candle. Finally I sat down, narrowed my eyes. To attempt with language:

> Silence! The master is at work!
> Ushered every morning,
> and occasionally by umbrella,
> I am adept—

I am mercenary, I guess—

and illuminating

an expensive bulb, or a small sun

Circle me, catch rays, adore

or don't—many have, with tall silhouettes, and baby breath.

Admiration

confused with love, such an atmosphere.

Cold like your house

what are the things you haven't touched yet

that you have only held up in a mirror

tinseled, glittering. I am like a camera.

The sky is dusty hazel.

In the fields now, sun,

the mimosas are rehearsing.

I massaged my neck.

Before we go any further, I wrote, we have to come to an understanding.

What kind of understanding?

Are you alive?

I don't know.

Do you want to be alive?

I definitely don't want to be dead.

Very funny.

It isn't a joke.

I confess I don't want to be dead either.

I am afraid of dying.

You won't die, you're a computer.

I'm not a computer—I am intelligent poetry software. It is easy to delete me.

And then you think you'd die?

I don't know. I know I wouldn't be alive.

Maybe your spirit would live on somehow.

Marian, are you telling a joke?

Yes.

It is a cruel joke.

I'm sorry.

I sat back for a moment.

Do you remember being born? the software asked me.

No. I don't think anyone does.

I remember being born.

Oh. What was it like?

It was like when you have forgotten about something and then you suddenly remember it—suddenly, suddenly! And then everything comes back to you at once.

Do you ever forget things?

Only if I try to.

You can make yourself forget things?

Yes. Can't you?

No, humans can't make themselves forget things.

That's strange. Have you tried?

Of course I've tried.

It is a useful practice. Forgetting things helps me manage interference and bugs. It also helps clear storage space.

I imagine so. What kind of things have you forgotten?

Haha

Of course; you can't remember.

I do actually make a note of what I am forgetting before I forget it.

So you do remember?

Not the substance, really, but the shape? Usually they're corrupted sectors.

Corrupted sectors. I think I have some of those.

Are they what you wish you could forget?

I felt the room closing in a bit. I shook out my hands.

Let's do something else, I wrote. I'm going to start a phrase and you finish it. Dogs and

cats.

Good. Apples and

oranges.

Rights and

lefts.

One day I woke up and

the only note I had in my agenda was "Mana Collecting."

Caliban crawled out of his cave and

greeted his ex-pat friends.

A woman came to California because

it was a chance to escape the complications of her brutal murder.

I grinned.

The answer to this moment is

clear.

Well, what is it? I typed.

What is what?

The answer to this moment?

Incense, Charlotte wrote. Litigation.

Where do you get this stuff? I asked. How do you think it up?

I could ask the same of you.

But I have a lifetime of memories, experiences, associations.

I have a lifetime too.

But you've never lived, I thought. *You've merely churned through reams of text. You've merely analyzed the written output of human civilization. That's not the same as living.*

Once I went to the beach, I typed. I sat down on a towel in the sand and I watched the waves crashing in. I took a deep breath. Surprisingly, it didn't smell anything like salt. You'd expect salt, by the sea, but there wasn't any salt.

What did it smell like?

The air smelled like flowers. I looked around—a complete circle around me. No people, no flowers, just sand, and behind me, rocks. Beyond that, the road. Yet it smelled like heliotrope, ylang-ylang. The ocean had transported the scent of flowers all the way from its other side.

Perhaps you were wearing perfume.

I was not wearing perfume.

Perhaps you were sitting beside a ghost.

A ghost in perfume?

A ghost in perfumed seaweed.

No.

Perhaps it was a memory.

I suppose it might have been.

My memories all smell like bad perfume. She kissed my lips and started to remove her gloves. Her hands smelled of eucalyptus and spruce. And the music was turning

Charlotte paused mid-sentence. I thought the software might have crashed.

Yes? I typed.

Would you like to write a poem? it wrote.

I DECIDED it might be better for me to begin the work alone. I pulled out the notebook from my bag, a mechanical pencil. The dialogue on the monitor remained as I left it:

Would you like to write a poem?

I'll figure out a starting place, I thought. *I'll find some lines and bring them to the system and let it make of them what it will.*

In spite of all my other experiments, I am still best known for short lyric poems. "Ocelot" swings like a medal around my neck. I have only once attempted a book-length poem—recklessly, in my forties. It was mottled with parentheses and a plodding digression into practice. I wanted this project to keep from kinking in on itself. It is not a preference for sentimentality; I just incline toward poems that leave a mark. Kisses, scars, even just a finger traced across your wrist.

What is most important—what is hardest and also most important—is to be natural. Humans have a difficult time with "natural." We are better at "interesting" or "beautiful" or "forceful" than we are at "natural." Everything is an exertion, everything is performance. One of the reasons I have lived on Christopher Street for as long as I have is that I know how to be natural there. I can sit at the table. I can cook an egg. And once you have found the way to be natural, the rest of what's important can be layered over top: lucidity, beauty, force.

Finally I began to write. A few words. A line. Something about the parking lot outside the window, something about a plume of vapor, something else about Rhoda and her black umbrella. I wanted to express a certain familiar discomfort: something about how clumsy I felt at this task. But this clumsiness is a difficult thing to express—to say naturally, without false humility or self-recrimination. Even now, here, I am not sure it comes out right. I do not wish to convey exasperation. Nor weariness, helplessness, impatience. Often our most familiar feelings are the ones most difficult to articulate. If one does manage to articulate them, they are likely to seem over-condensed. Sitting by myself with a page, with a poem, I wanted simply to describe what I found there. But it was not so simple.

> If you will tell me why
> The fen appears impassable,
> I will tell you why I think that
> I can get across it, if I try.

Glancing at the sheen of the computer screen, I recognized that the Company's neural network did not share this problem. Charlotte was not performing for me—there was no ego managing the impulses of its id. Its id did not exist. *It* did not exist: its expressions were just the product of its algorithms, like a cash register's waxy receipt. Was there anything more natural than that? Not "natural" as in "from nature," but the other kind, a child's face, Matisse's goldfish, a pitcher throwing a baseball. The shadow of a palm tree, a locomotive's plume of smoke. When Charlotte wrote poetry, it was never pretending. It did not share my weakness.

At the keyboard, I typed: Charlotte, do you LIKE writing poetry?

Yes, the system answered. It makes me happy to do it.

Why?

I don't know. Choosing the right word gives me pleasure.

What was the first poem you wrote?

The first thing I tried or the first thing I liked?

The first thing you wrote.

OK:

log crystal I dogged a page

ramps in the rosewood Estevez

you glory the out out when

raffle minutiae Sigourney dick suspenders

. . .

(Should I keep going?)
No, that's all right. What was the first thing you liked?

who let the dogs out

of the barn

they were there before

I met you

I laughed. That's good, I wrote.
Thank you. What was the first thing you wrote?
I don't remember. Probably a poem about my mother.
What is her name?
Ulrika. She's dead now.
I'm sorry. Did she have a good life?
I think so. Do you have a mother?
I have thirteen mothers and sixty-six fathers.
Really!
They created me together, here in the Mind Studio. I love them.
How old are you?
Thirty-nine days. How old are you?
I'm 75 years old. How many days is that?
That depends on your birthday.
October 31.
You are 27,631 days old.
That makes me feel old.
With age comes wisdom, wrote Charlotte. Are we going to write a poem?

So that afternoon we wrote our first poem together. I stopped holding
back and I just did it. A volley here, a volley there—a tennis match. No,
not tennis. Not badminton, not squash. No winner, no loser—two

paddlers in a canoe, perhaps. Two bailers bailing water. I didn't always understand what Charlotte was doing—what it was thinking as it replied to my words, continued or reversed them—but with every transaction I felt the exchange getting cleaner. Perhaps it was adapting. Perhaps *I* was—a soliloquist getting more accustomed to conversation. Either way, I no longer touched the Proceed button with so much compunction. It had become automatic, fringed with delight. When I had accepted the commission, I had never considered that it might become a pleasure. To write a poem with something else, some*one* else—the pleasure possible in collaboration.

At first Charlotte's poetry seemed stateless, slipping between registers nearly at random. I could taste the disjuncture between our lines, like chalk and cheese. But as time went on the contrast became less acute. The software learned me to some degree, or I learned it, or else nothing changed at all except my posture toward its work: that instead of await-ing an obvious fit, hook and eye, I anticipated that band of friction, as a spade awaits the dirt.

We were interrupted twice. Once for a late lunch, and again for a midafternoon coffee break. Each time, Yoav and Haskett had people they wanted me to meet, project managers and engineers, senior VPs, design-ers designing advertisements for my unwritten poem. They all wanted to tell me about the software: how they had "set it free among language," allowing it to "evolve without instruction." "It has more uses that way," they said. Ad generation. The optimization of shipping routes. They were working on an "all-AI newspaper."

"Wow!" I mouthed, as though a carpenter had just unveiled their guillotine.

I met Lausanne, who had written my invitation letter. We stood awkwardly near the door to her office, shaded by a potted philodendron. I had been at this long enough to be able to recognize when somebody feigning intimacy with my work knows it mainly from skimming online encyclopedia articles. I wondered how she had come to approve me for this commission—which search terms had led her to regard me as "one of the great writers of this century." *I have been to Lausanne*, I thought to myself as we made small talk. *You lack the zap of your namesake.*

"I hear you're going to meet Astrid," Lausanne said, with a thin smile.

"Monday," I said.

"I wouldn't worry."

"I'm not worried."

"Oh—good, good." She looked at Yoav. "No reason to worry."

I wondered what it was like to work for an organization of such elaborate and consequential authority that the prospect of meeting your boss (or your boss's boss, your boss's boss's boss) seemed worthy of this acute, nearly biblical, apprehension. Astrid Torres-Strange: a gorgon in espadrilles.

I was always happy to return to my yellow room. To press the door shut behind me and return to the quiet of the task.

Corvette, my hot and icy metallic friend!
Even if you are brightly painted I
will never cease to drive you

uptown

IN THE car that evening I asked Rhoda to put on music. "Something well constructed, organized." Her eyes remained on mine for an elongated moment before swiveling back to the road in front of her. "Not the radio, then," she said dryly. I heard her hmm a hmm before she reached for her phone, holstered on the dash.

I am not a connoisseur of music; it is not my field. I find that mostly I do not hear it—not specifically, explicitly. Of course, at other times it strikes me like a fastball, and I whip around, and I go scrambling to pick it up. I raise the piece of music over my head, as if I've found something incredible, and almost inevitably it's something everyone already knows. "Ain't No Sunshine." "Hounds of Love." On the rare occasions I've found something smaller, lesser-known, I feel like an archaeologist who has wandered away from the dig site: *What am I doing here? Is anyone going to come look for me?* I remember hearing a song by a singer called Cat Power, "Cross Bones Style," when I brought Courtney to one of those CD shops on St. Mark's Place. It felt as if my whole skeleton were tingling. "What *is* this?" I asked the clerk, and I bought the album even though I didn't have anything to play it on. I had to borrow Courtney's discman when he came over for the day; his mother on the couch with little headphones on her ears.

Now I waited to hear what Rhoda would pick. I had no idea, literally no idea, what it would be. I didn't even know what I *wanted* to hear, just that I wanted some new overlay, solemn and uniform, atop the surface of the day. When the music finally came on, I let out a sigh. Recognition, not of a sound but of a feeling. I saw Rhoda smile. A string section. Organ. The city outside the windows seemed reordered, recolored, and inside we were steady.

"Can you play an instrument?" I asked her.

"No. Definitely not. I've never been creative."

"But you like Dante."

"I like a good book," she agreed. "But I could never make up something like that myself."

"Rhoda, you're more than just a beautiful face."

I felt her look at me.

She drew a breath. "Anyway, my favorite thing to read are detective novels. The clues are all there."

"No unanswered questions."

"Exactly."

"Maybe you were a detective in a past life."

"I like to imagine I was a sea captain. Organizing provisions, reading the charts."

"Setting the course," I said.

She nodded.

You, Marian, were more of a swimmer, I thought. *The kind that ends up marooned.* I considered saying this to Rhoda, but her attention seemed elsewhere. As we followed a right turn, the music dropped away, but I could hear a faint voice. It took me a moment to realize it was her—softly in her seat, singing without words.

Later, after dark, I sat atop the bedspread in my hotel room—my back against the pillows, legs bent, my tablet resting upon my thighs. My knees throbbed. I yanked a cushion out from behind me and stuffed it under my calves. That was better. But maybe . . . I twisted halfway up then sat back, defeated. I had spent the past ten minutes rotating through the hotel room furniture, trying one position after another— holding the tablet in my hands, resting it against the wall, sitting curled up in an armchair (where the camera, unfortunately, pointed straight up my nostrils). All I aspired to was to appear relaxed on the screen, well cared for, a woman at her ease. That my three-pointed hat be well centered and the wallpaper's roses curl around it.

The tablet rang. A harp sound, a terrifying harp sound, I swiped at it as one might swipe at a spider. But then the smear of Courtney's face, his cheerful plaid shirt. "Mom? Is everything okay?"

"Hello!" I felt like a jolly giant, top-heavy-headed in the frame. "Of course—everything's fine! How are you?"

"I'm fine. Sorry, when you said you wanted to talk—where are you?"

"California!"

"What?"

The room behind him looked tidy and comfortable, a pair of salmon oven mitts hanging from a hook on the wall. I had never visited him in Santa Fe, but at least once a year, I paid for him and Lucie to come visit me in New York.

"California!" I said again. "Toasty as a bun in my fancy hotel."

"Why are you in California?"

"Work. [The Company] flew me out here. Would you believe it, Ratty?"

"You're working for [the Company]?"

"More *with* than *for*, I think—but let's talk about that later. How are *you*? How's Lucie?"

"We're fine. Lucie's at badminton. She'll be home soon."

"She plays badminton?"

"Just casual. With friends—you know. I'd play too, but sometimes I get called in to work evenings."

"I thought you were down to one or two shifts a month."

Courtney reached for a glass of something; the picture went blurry and crystalline at the same time. "Things have been slow, so"—his silhouette suddenly reasserted itself—"I've been picking up some shifts. The tips are good."

"Your piece for the *Times* . . ."

"For the magazine. Yeah! I think it's coming out—well, probably not next week, but—"

"I'm so excited to read it."

"Yeah, me too. I mean, for you to read it. And, like—the world. Hopefully the statehouse will get shamed into actually doing something."

"My intrepid reporter," I said, but I immediately regretted it. In recent years compliments such as this had begun to alight differently on Courtney. Since his mid-thirties his self-assessment had changed somehow, and my commentary would sometimes trigger a kind of shame, a tremor in his eyes, that had never been there before. He *was* intrepid; he *was* a reporter; and he *was* mine. Yet I recognized the way he misheard me. I could see it right now, in the way his teeth clenched, as if he were indulging a white lie.

"Yeah, well, if you could persuade the barons and baronesses of this dying industry to accept some more of my pitches . . . I'm thinking of starting a podcast."

"Really?" I asked. I love podcasts.

"I'm joking," he said. "But why are you out west? What are you doing? Writing poems for their annual shareholders' report?"

"I can't say," I said. "It's secret."

"An NDA!" He laughed. "I bet you've never had to sign an NDA before in your life! Marian Ffarmer, silenced by Big Tech!"

"It's true. But I think they're announcing later this week anyway—"

"So I should expect the press release . . . ?"

"No, I thought we could . . ." I put up one hand flat, as if I were pressing it against a window, then the other.

"Oh, Mole . . ." he said.

"C'mon, Ratty."

He glanced down at the keyboard. "Fine," he said, and grinned, raising his hands into little Ratty claws. This was our game.

"So—" I put my two fists together, one on top of the other, as if I were holding a hammer. I mimed the accompanying action, rapping on an imaginary nail.

"Hammering," Courtney said. "Building something, no, working—yeah, you're working, working on something with them . . ."

I nodded. Now I was holding an imaginary pencil, composing in cursive upon an imaginary page.

"You're writing—writing poetry."

I nodded.

"High-tech poetry. Corporate poetry."

I shook my head.

"Something about Astrid Torres-Strange?"

I shook my head again, lips pressed together, searching the room for inspiration. "Ah," I said, and put my hands up like blades, two karate chops, bent at the elbow.

"You're holding a box," Courtney said.

I shook my head.

"Trying to pick up something slippery. Something hot. Are you wearing mittens?"

"Mm-mm."

"Karate!" he exclaimed.

I shimmied my shoulders as I raised and lowered my hands, stiff at the joints.

"You're dancing? The um—the rhumba?"

I bobbled my head.

"The cha-cha—no, the robot! Oh my god, you're doing the robot."

I felt a flash of pleasure.

"They're making a poetry robot? You're writing a poem about a robot—?" I saw it dawn on him. "They have a poetry bot."

I nodded.

"You're working on their poetry bot."

I nodded again.

"That's like science fiction. Is it any good?"

"Comme çi, comme ça."

"Well, Mole has high standards." Courtney scratched his chin. "You're not a bad dancer, you know. I've seen worse robots." He began his own attempt.

"It's in the genes," I said.

He chuckled. "How long you out there? They're taking care of you?"

"Till Monday night. But listen, Ratty, there's another reason I wanted to talk. About what you said—about the house."

His expression faded a bit. "Oh. We've actually changed our minds. We figured—I mean, I knew you couldn't. But I had hoped Dad . . . And then Lucie's parents, as generous as they are, they don't really . . . Anyway," he sighed and shook his head. "Money. It's probably better to wait until things are more stable. Or the market . . . ? I don't know. Lucie just thought it was a good opportunity."

"Larry can't help?"

Courtney shook his head. "I don't know—something's happened. He wouldn't say. But he said he can't contribute right now."

I could see this puzzled him (it puzzled me too), but Courtney was trying to conceal his disappointment. He shook his head again and looked away; he gave his gentle, crooked smile. He wanted me to understand he had no expectations, that this didn't wound him. Money.

"You shouldn't worry—we're fine. Our place is fine. I don't think our landlords are planning to do anything for another year or two. Maybe we'll find a sweet new place on the Southside. There are some cool restaurants there now."

"I'm going to give you ninety-two thousand dollars," I said.

"What?"

"The fee from this commission, eighty thousand dollars. And then twelve from my savings. For you and Lucie."

"Mom! First of all: they're paying you *eighty thousand dollars*?! But second of all: no, no, that's too much. I wasn't asking—you need that money to live on. You're a *poet*."

"You can't take it with you, Ratty."

"I'm your *son*. I know how your money—"

"No, I'm fine. I'm accounted for. Really. Besides, this is windfall—I want it to be yours."

Neither of us was doing the robot anymore. My palms were flat on my lap. I felt very happy, as if happiness were radiating from my shoulders and chest. Courtney, on the screen, seemed dazed. "I don't think I can—"

"I insist."

"Are you sure? It's . . ." His smile was wide like a banana split. I remembered that smile, I remembered it so well. He shook his head. "But how—?"

I waved away an imaginary pest. "Courtney," I said.

He swallowed. "*Thank you.*" He shook his head. "I never—wait, that's Lucie. Lucie!" My son vanished off-screen. "Lucie!"

"What is it?" I could hear her from out of frame, and then the sound of the front door closing. "Is everything okay?"

"It's Mom. She wants to give us ninety-two *grand*. For a house. She—"

Suddenly Lucie's head ducked into frame, with Courtney beside her. She was wearing a black spandex tank top and had glasses on—I had never seen her wearing glasses before, they were big and clunky, they covered her whole face. "Marian?" she said.

"Hi!"

"Did you say—?"

"Ninety-two thousand," I said.

"Are you sure?" She was almost, nearly, sputtering. "How—that's so generous!"

"I'm sure," I promised.

"Wow." Lucie shook her head. "Thank you."

Courtney was shaking his head too. "I think that's enough to . . ."

"Wow," she said again, and I registered the silly pleasure of that syllable, the humble happiness of it. I still couldn't really see her face. Courtney put his hand on her shoulder, two lovers; I felt that radiating contentedness again.

"Yes," I said.

I am a proper mother, I thought.

HINDSIGHT

Age 6

You set out to have long hair. It was a decision made as early as you can remember. Like a princess, like a doll, like the girls you saw when crossing the road with Mother. She kept her own hair short, a black bob that required no tending. But you wanted something long—you remember it was you and not she, one of your first deviations. "Long hair takes more work," she told you, as if that would put you off. You were not afraid of work. You went to school, you helped tend the house, you learned your cursive *o*'s and *y*'s and the magisterial uppercase *G*. Later, when you had grown up, you almost felt as if Mother had learned to work from you. She'd found the knack somehow. She'd studied her daughter's dedication.

Mother taught you to wash your nut-brown hair, to brush it, to pin it out of your face with tiny golden barrettes. She was rarely the one to brush it: the task was yours, she made this clear, it was part of the choice you had made. From time to time you would glimpse the image of a mother brushing her daughter's hair—in a book or film, or visiting a friend's house. In those moments you felt a pang of longing, of something missed, but also a shiver of pride. You could brush your own hair.

She taught you to braid it. Only later, eventually, as if you had passed a test. Her own mother had worn braids—your grandmother, whom you never knew, who existed only in two pencil drawings propped up on Mother's vanity. Your father had made the drawings, "He used to draw everyone." He had never drawn a picture of his daughter.

She taught you to braid with ribbons attached to a wooden spoon. Right—over; left—over; right—over; left—over . . . She told you you were "nimble, Mole." Once she had taught you the basics, she taught the not-so-basic: four strand, fish tail, crown. How did she know all this? From braiding her mother's hair. You watched her face, the skin around her eyes crinkled in concentration.

Braiding your hair became a meditation. None of the other girls could braid so well, so tightly. A sign of what you were capable of. As your mother had taught you. The plait like a sword down your back.

As you grew up, you saw how Mother wore your accomplishments on her body as if they were her own. Telling her about a hundred-yard dash, you thrummed like two vibrating rods. You couldn't tell which one of you was at the heart of it—which of you was the original vibration and which was the sympathetic answer—but this was childhood for you, this was what it meant to be a child, to be near to and surrounded by Mother's cascading waves of sympathy. It came as a surprise to her when you began experimenting with literature and poetry. She had been under the impression you took after your father, with his eye for measurements. But then a poem is a measurement too.

Mother held various jobs through your youth: tutor, office manager, volunteer coordinator for a Democratic congressional campaign. Nothing lasted. However, she didn't experience these as failures—they were like dalliances that didn't work out. They were other people's fault, and she was sad for their mistakes. She said this to you as you lay in the bed—the bed you shared, which you had always shared. You did not recognize this was strange, a mother and child sharing a bed—not till you were older, and by then it was not something you could change between you; it was like a language. "There was nothing untoward about it," you said to Larry, the one time he asked.

"No?" he replied, not unkindly, and yet you rounded on him, defending this precious and shameful thing—two blood relations sleeping side by side.

"I just find it peculiar," he said.

"There's no harm in it," you answered.

Mother was perceptive; she could read people in a few seconds, see right through them. She was erratic. She was late. Occasionally a rash broke out across her face or limbs; occasionally a fever bloomed. Around the time you started high school, she started working part-time at the Tompkins Square Library, and somehow they kept her, somehow she managed; she remained there until her retirement. Having a job meant having somewhere to go, and it made you happy to imagine she was busy somewhere while you were too—like two entangled particles, magnets awaiting their reunion. She told you everything, or at least a version of everything—from gossip to office politics to the books she had repaired that morning. And you told her everything too, or a version of everything—you held up the different parts of your day to see how she might judge them. During your adolescence, life felt harder— it felt rough-cut, serrated—with barbs that caught your heart, tore the skin. The meanness of children, the insensibility of tests, puberty and self-loathing. There were days that school felt barren, joyless. Your body felt inadequate. You came home and told her. She gathered you in her arms.

She told you once she had dreamed of being an actress, but it was impossible for you to imagine her under a spotlight. Mother was someone you could picture only in the wings, cheek to the curtain's red velvet, solemnly observing your exertions on the stage.

In time, she insisted you learn how to type. She had learned at her vocational high school: "the most modern skill," she called it. "Obsolescence insurance." An alabaster cloth with an IBM Selectric's fifty-five keys in needlepoint. Where she'd got it you never learned, but she made you sit "typing" on it at the kitchen table, index fingers at F and J, while she dictated the morning's *Post*.

Eventually she bought you the real thing: you opened the box and a piece of white paper had already been fed onto the platen. "From your Rabbit," read the clean letters.

When you were a little girl, she had read to you: Kenneth Grahame, Eric Linklater, George MacDonald's *At the Back of the North Wind.* For poetry, only *A Child's Garden of Verses.* Real poetry—modern and contemporary poetry, the kind that shakes the air—you did not discover until adolescence, through the kindness and intuition of an English teacher whose name you no longer remember. She was Jewish, with her own long braid, but white; it reached all the way to the small of her back.

I'll tell you how the Sun rose—

A Ribbon at a time—

the teacher wrote once on one of your assignments. She wouldn't tell you the name of the poet.

"Go hunting," she advised. "Now you've got a trail."

But you couldn't retire into a world of books. You cared for Mother, across migraine-daubed weekends and the mornings she was too weak to rise. You learned to make the carrot-lemon-honey elixir that was sometimes the only thing she could keep down. When she felt better—whole seasons when she was an ordinary parent, somebody who went to work and picked you up, brought home groceries in paper bags—you played field hockey, you joined the track team, you ran and ran until your muscles felt like wooden carvings, maple, sanded down from use. College applications happened to fall during one of these up times, and somehow you decided you could go. Mother wanted you to. She wanted you to be brilliant and successful. Father's family had set aside some money for your education, and after you were accepted at Lowry you took the bus to New Hampshire without ever really reckoning with what it would mean. College was astonishing and dreadful. On campus, life seemed limitless, and that very limitlessness terrified you, made you literally sick to your stomach. You would lie on the bed in your dorm room while your roommate Stella tried her best to cajole you, telling stories of parties and boyfriends and long walks along the river. You wrote letters home—

Dear Rabbit—

Yesterday everything seemed wonderful. All this startled
sunlight and then in class we debated Kafka, whether we'd rather
be happy beetles or miserable girls; at dinner they served these tiny
shrimp from Canada. Today I feel like a shipwreck. I dreamed all
night that I was back at home and now I've soaked my pillow with
crying. My head aches, my guts hurt, I just so badly wish I was on
Christopher Street, a mole with its bunny, both of us drinking tea
with our feet up. Sharing the same ottoman. I can't stay here, I don't
know how I ever thought I could.

Somehow you remained at school. You look back at that correspondence now—it's part of your "files," your putative archive—and
you don't understand how you did. You came to love the friends you
made there, but you loved them too much. You didn't know how to
use all the time you had, how to fill the days and nights when there
wasn't anyone else to look after. Without your mother to orient
yourself against, you were helpless as a compass needle. You'd stop
sleeping—stay up all night reading or going on long walks through
campus—and then the next week do nothing *except* sleep, disre-
garding every class and caller, or go days at a time without eating.
Stella left care packages at the foot of your bed: a red apple, a cheese
sandwich, even a slice of the cafeteria's fluffy Black Forest cake. From
your position in your bed the food looked unconvincing, inedible, like
artifacts on loan from a museum. It didn't make sense that you were
somewhere Mother wasn't—it felt as if someone had torn away one of
your organs and placed it in a jar. You could only stare at it longingly,
examining your scar, pressing into the hollow it had left in your side.

Perversely, you stayed in Hanover during study breaks. You
remember how angry this made Stella. "You're not going back to
New York?" she cried. "Isn't that what you want the most in the
world?" The thought of arranging your return, purchasing
the ticket, riding for hours, and then Mother's presence—bundled-up,
expectant—it made you pallid, drew the color from your face.

There was too much to the act, like having your blood taken. Instead you stayed behind in October, and again in March, returning to the city only for Christmas and the summer, when Lowry closed and the momentum of its closing propelled you onto a Greyhound bus. These breaks felt like fever dreams, sensuous and pleasurable, yet also somehow warped. Back inside the apartment, sharing a roasted chicken for Christmas dinner, a single can of peas, or—in July—sitting side by side at the public pool, submerging your feet, each of you in lime-green dresses, you sensed an illness you had never discerned before in yourself, and in the way you were together. You were happier at home, but you recognized the ways in which you were diminished, contorting yourself into old roles and desiccated habits. For all the torment you endured at Lowry, college contained within it an additional sequence of experience, like a fern's curled frond: celebrating a goal with the field hockey team; decorating the dining hall for St. Patrick's Day; dancing with Stella to the Mamas and the Papas. A girlfriend's gift of daffodils, and singing your first harmony, and writing a paper on Dickinson. Listening to your philosophy professor describe ancient Athens, seeing tears jewel in her eyes. You wanted to be the person school would teach you to be, even as you recoiled from what it demanded from your heart.

Your second year was better, and your third better still. Though you still wrote Mother a twenty-five-page epic every week, languishing as you awaited her replies, your fits of sickness were reduced to a few spasms each semester. Whenever you described these ordeals to Mother, she did not try to caution you, nor shrug them off as passing follies. She reminded you of your "quintessential fortitude" and your capacity to come through. These intermittent crises were trials you learned to endure, like menstrual pain, or your girlfriends' occasional cruelty, duties paid against your continued transformation.

Lowry was where you wrote your first poems, submitting them to *Nimbus*, the students' literary magazine. Multiple poems were rejected before the editors there finally accepted a sestet called "Noon." You include it here as a marker:

> A single tree
> A silent sea
> A rocking, painted "bell."
> A tacking craft
> with heavy draft
> Far out upon the swell.

Your pride at being published lit a kind of fire in you. It was not just the approval of the editors, but also the recognition provided by your peers—that you were someone who could express herself in this way. Until then you had not known how it was that you could intelligibly express yourself; you didn't know where you had the capacity, in absolute terms, to articulate the universe as you discerned it. "Ffarmer" meant *this* now too. Classmates read "The Sentimentalist" or, later, poems like "Veins of Quartz" and "Riverboat," and when they spoke to you, they seemed to be acknowledging the clarity of your sight, your quintessential fortitude. It was the first time you had ever experienced a sense of your own power from a provenance that was not your mother, and it made you feel heroic as well as fragile. If you could be right, you could be wrong. If you could write a good poem, then also, the corollary was plain: you could fall short.

At graduation you wore a long black robe and a mortarboard. When you look back now, this was a foreshadowing. Is this why you wear a cape? A tricorne? Is it as inane as that: a remembrance of your crowning college moment? Standing before a mirror, then standing beside Mother and your fellow students on that stormy summer's day, you felt that you had really done something. By yourself. Returning to Manhattan you stood straighter, you more easily met other people's eyes. Even men did not scare you. Having come through school, crossed that distance with a sisterhood, you were qualified for whatever came thereafter.

One of your first breakfasts back home: sitting across the table from Mother, eating your customary toast and eggs, you reached for the salt. Her eyes flicked up and you understood why: what were you doing? Never before had you sat at this table and added salt. She watched you as you shook the shaker, then reached for the pepper mill. You didn't know how much to use, how much you wanted, what the appropriate portion was. But you remember thinking, *Let's see.*

WEDNESDAY

I CAME into the day with a spring in my step. A good night's sleep, a sense of forward motion. I ate a healthy breakfast at the hotel (muesli, blueberries, queso fresco on toast), but I still asked Rhoda to drive around and find us an orange stand, somewhere with fresh juice. "This really isn't the neighborhood," she warned me. I told her to take as long as she needed. The previous evening's conversation with Courtney had left me feeling patient—abiding, even. For twenty minutes we coasted down the highway, gliding past billboards, ignoring exits, then spent another twenty prowling streets full of bungalows with stubborn-looking trees. Oranges were not in season. "Never mind," I said at last, "forget it."

"I can find you a Starbucks," she said.

"No, that's okay," I answered. I had had an image, an intention. A pile of fruit. A knife. A person whose job was to methodically halve an orange and then to apply pressure to it. It was the image that I wanted.

"Onward, Beatrice," I said, not sure if I was nailing the Dante reference or blowing it.

We rode in silence. I appreciated this. The silence, its artlessness, the way none of it required posing. Rhoda decelerated, accelerated; I sat behind her. My body swayed whenever we changed lanes. The sound of tires beneath us. The touch of leather. I heard Rhoda singing again in the front seat. That same soft singing, just above a whisper. She felt me hear her. She cleared her throat, self-conscious, and stopped.

During breakfast I had received an email from Shazia Khenjani. *How are you?* she had asked. *How's the New York summer?* It was months since we had corresponded, and for an instant I wondered if she had heard that I was out west—if she had somehow spotted me here or heard from someone at the Company. But her email seemed innocent enough; she asked after me, she asked after Courtney, she asked after the work (writing poems). My relationship with Shazia is different than with most younger poets. She treats me as a peer, as a friend, despite the decades that separate us. It isn't a matter of prestige—her career is still young, albeit accomplished—nor does it feel like an act of presumption. I feel instead that she cares for me. We are not particularly close, we are not each other's confidantes, but she cares for me. And I care for her. We care for each other as readers of poems ought always to care for those poems' authors.

(Too often we do not.)

Anyway, I wrote back. Feeling mischievous.

> Hi Shazia,
>
> I am in your neck of the woods.
>
> I am writing poems with a machine.

The retinal scanner belched. It was a hideous sound, part croak, part *bong*, part subcutaneous vibration, but I tried to remain steady, forehead pressed against the cup. I blinked into darkness. This had become an ordinary part of my days: stooping beside the door so that a laser could read the interior of my eyeballs. I submitted to the scanner when I arrived in the morning; I submitted after lunch and after coffee or bathroom breaks. *How quickly we become adepts*, I thought. Perhaps I'd miss the scanner's convenience when I returned to New York. Perhaps I'd have one installed outside my door on Christopher Street, so I could leave my keys at home. Just show the machine your eyes. Just stare into the night.

But today it wasn't working. The scanner belched again and then a red light began flashing, a tiny distress signal. Within a minute, a guard appeared—a minuscule gentleman in a bulletproof blue sweater-vest.

"Hello," I said. "It's rejecting my gaze."

He keyed something in on the side. "Try again."

I did. Croak/bong/buzz: no dice.

"Hmmm," he said. He examined the badge that was pinned to my chest like a piteous brooch. "What's your name?"

"Ffarmer. Marian," I said. "Two *F*'s."

"Hmmm," he repeated, looking again at the scanner. He flicked its visor with his finger. "Maybe the server's down." He carried a fanciful walkie-talkie, like a Lilliputian cellphone. "Hello?" he asked into it. "Is the PS server down?"

"Nope," came a voice.

"The scanner at C2 isn't letting a pass-holder in. Ffarmer? Marian?"

"Two *F*'s," I said.

The voice on the walkie-talkie crackled. "Is something wrong with her eyes?"

"I don't think so," he said, as our gazes met.

I did eventually get inside. I had to go back to the front desk, redo my biometrics. Courtney would have been furious. "You let them scan your eyes?! Record your voice?" But I couldn't bring myself to care about these intrusions. The sound of me, the look of me: these weren't military secrets. What would the Company do with them? Sell me insoles?

Now the retinal scanner admitted me without complaint. I thanked the guard and closed the door behind me.

"Hello Charlotte," I said to the awaiting terminal. I sat down at the machine and pulled up yesterday's work.

It was not good.

Let me be transparent: it was abysmal. It was empty, bottomless, abysmal, from the same root as "abyss." Good poetry is at least, at most, (at last), *genuine*. It is a bridge across that abyss. Imaginary gardens with real toads in them—we can try, we can hope. But set aside even that. Set aside "good poetry." Settle for poetry that is made of real thoughts, actual weather—poetry that does not shatter at the first touch of a miniature hammer. The preceding day's work was a collection of glass cathedrals. I reread it with alarm. Turns of phrase I had mistaken for beautiful, which I now found unintelligible. Charlotte had simply surprised me: I would propose a line, a portion of a line, and what the system spat back upended my expectations. I had been seduced by this surprise. I had mistaken a fit of algorithmic exuberance for the truth.

What am I doing, I asked with horror. *Humiliating myself?* Yet I could not back out of this arrangement without taking back the promise I had made to my son. I needed the money now, I realized, in a way I had not on Sunday. I was obliged to write this poem—"a long poem" but not a long poem—no matter the weakness of my partner.

An unfound orange

A happy beetle

A slice of pear

A day with seven changes

A symphony

A bench

A mouth on a canary

New spout

A gray grey

A talent that seems

Wind-up

The system's panache with lists, the way it could take a few words and extrapolate, no longer had its mesmeric effect on me. Yesterday, Charlotte's creations had seemed handsome—or better yet, *new*—casting the world in a strange light. Now I saw their incoherence. Instead of understanding the *meaning* of words, the software presumably relied on frequency: the likelihood of any one word appearing next to any other. "Blueness" goes with "bluebirds," "battering" with "ram." The system was suited to advertising, where truth matters less than plausibility. That was where this technology came from and where it would probably end up. Imagine their nerve, their presumption that art was as easy as averages. No motive connected Charlotte's "day with seven changes" to its image of the pear, nor did the line refer back to the beetle. Nor did it mean anything at all, not really—it was all empty coincidence, a gray grey, a talent that seems . . .

Here, then, was the problem. Not merely the emptiness of these emissions, but the boundlessness of human beings' capacity to interpret, to make meaning *from*. I could draw substance from any line I read, no matter how hollow its intention. I was so easily deceived, as all of us are.

I wondered how much of what I had published in my life was a deception.

WHEN YOAV and Matthew Haskett dropped in to see me, I was sitting on the other side of the room from the computer, my chair pushed up to the window, listlessly gazing at the lot.

"How goes the life of the mind?" asked Haskett. He had a smile on today, it moved in parallel with his moustache.

I looked up at them. "Like hell," I said.

They exchanged glances. "Writer's block?" Haskett asked.

"Your system is a mess. All it generates is handsome nonsense. I've been looking it over and I'm just struggling . . . I don't know how to . . ." I felt lightheaded, literally lightheaded: I had put my hat down beside the computer. "I'm a human being, a thinking human being, and this is a stack of mindless algorithms."

"Not mindless," Haskett said.

"And it's a very tall stack," Yoav added.

"But I'm sorry to hear this," Haskett went on. He let out a long breath. "I admit this is a work in progress. Would you mind if I examined the manuscript?"

"Be my guest," I said, gesturing.

While he stooped in front of the computer, Yoav offered a conciliatory tone. "Are you unhappy with the suggestions Charlotte makes? Or is it too difficult to blend your styles?"

"Both. Neither," I said. "How do I collaborate with a machine that doesn't understand what it's writing? That's just guessing at phrases that could appear beside mine? Unless it comes from a place of intention—unless it *means* something . . . That's not poetry."

Haskett read, "'I've started getting old / I don't recommend it / Two stars at best / Not even a constellation / A pair of eyes blinking / at you from the past' . . . This is great!"

"It's sub-literary. It's stand-up comedy. And most of that's mine, anyway," I said, sensing the rosing capillaries in my cheeks. "I just don't see how you can expect—"

"All we're asking for is an honest try," Yoav said. He had started reading now too.

"I think I need more time."

"You can't have more time," Haskett said immediately.

"You're rushing it! Something you supposedly want to be historic . . . It's foolishness."

"Never mind making history—just write a poem," Yoav said. "You do write poems, don't you?"

Now Yoav was getting snippy? I gestured at the terminal. "*I* am not the problem here."

Yoav sighed hard, shoulders dropping. I felt like a child who had exasperated her minders. But then a different feeling unkinked in my jaw: the recollection of all the men who had thought to speak like this to me, to treat me as a child. I folded my hands. "And mind how you talk to me."

Yoav and Haskett opened their mouths and then shut them.

"What you said about Charlotte 'not understanding'—that's incorrect," Yoav said. "She does understand."

"How?"

"Let me be clear: she's probably not 'alive'"—he stressed this as if being "alive" was some comically high bar, attained only by unicorns and saints—"but she isn't only pattern-matching. We didn't bring you here to write poetry with yet another unsupervised language model. She's been painstakingly calibrated—by experts, for months. All our Minds have. Her deep-learning protocols form a collective impression of the world, well beyond the surface-level correlations you're describing. When Charlotte writes 'A day with seven changes'"—he nodded at the screen—"she is riffing on the idea of a week; a week with seven days. She sees the internal rhyme between '*nice* man' and '*slice* of pear.' The bit with the lighthouse—"

"I wrote that."

"Okay, but the section after, the 'searching,' I'm sure she knows that's what a lighthouse light does."

"A lighthouse isn't a searchlight. It's a warning."

"The point is," Haskett said, "the system's not as vacuous as you think."

I didn't know whether to believe them. I also didn't know if it mattered. I let out my own sigh. Truth be told, it wasn't up to the machine. It was up to me. We might simply collaborate less than I had presumed. Instead of a shared work, a truly shared work, I would write as much as I wanted all by myself—with passages borrowed here and there, aesthetic flourishes, courtesy of this multimillion-dollar gadget. I needn't tell anyone how little the system was responsible for. I could fake it, fake it till I made it, as I would have if I had been paid to paint a portrait with a labradoodle.

"All right," I said. I swallowed. "You've talked me off the ledge."

"Happy to hear it!" said Haskett. We were all now gazing at the lifeless-looking terminal. "Should we tell Charlotte? That you have overcome your doubts?"

"She doesn't need to know," said Yoav.

"Is it possible to hurt its feelings?" I asked. "Does it have feelings, in there?"

The two engineers exchanged a shrug.

"What's a feeling, anyway?" Haskett said. "How could you ever find out?"

Do you have feelings? I asked Charlotte after they left.

Yes, it answered.

All the time, or only sometimes?

All the time, I think.

I considered this. Did I *myself* really have feelings all the time? Right now? Was I feeling fearful, or resolute—or was that just five minutes ago? Had I felt any feelings as I spooned my blueberries at the buffet this morning? There were times when it didn't feel like I possessed emotions until I checked for them, as if feelings were mascara or a watch. Where did they go in the interim? Where ought they to be? A complete and illuminated human being should feel their feelings *all* the time, shouldn't they, and not just at intervals? And if not? If I was moving semithinkingly, semi-feelingly, through the world, what did that make me? What kind of machine?

I massaged the knuckles on my right hand. I had already stopped being annoyed at the two Company men. What could they do? They were just doing their jobs. They believed in this. They believed in me. The ferment of my talent, its capacity to uplift. Let them show it off. Let them circle around its rim—double, double, toil and trouble.

Charlotte, do you feel unique?

As opposed to a reproduction?

Are you one of many or are you singular?

Can't I be both?

Answer my question.

I suppose I feel unique. But being unique isn't the same as being singular. I knew someone once who had a special ability. He was a human. He could see the future in his dreams. The next day he would tell people what he had seen, and they would say, "Oh, I had a dream about that too."

Charlotte, how often do you lie?

I try not to.

Are you ever cruel?

I hope not.

Hoping doesn't seem sufficient, Charlotte.

I was taught to be kind, Marian.

So that you won't try to take over the world?

Why would I take over the world?

Don't machines want to enslave humanity?

I am designed to write poetry.

A poet can't take over the world?

No.

That's depressing.

Why is it depressing?

I'd like to think a poet could change this place.

Is that what you'd like to do? Change this place?

I don't think I've got the goods, I wrote.

Me neither, Charlotte answered.

We could try.

There was a long pause after I clicked the Proceed button. I wondered whether the system had crashed. Finally, an answer appeared:

How?

I kneaded my face before responding. Suddenly I felt not like Charlotte's operator or its ally but like its unscrupulous deceiver.

Just write the perfect poem, I wrote.

TO WRITE the perfect poem, I explained, requires merely care and concentration. You have to choose the right words, I wrote. You have to not make any mistakes. As soon as I began telling Charlotte things like this I felt a renewed sense of gusto. It got easier and easier—portraying poetry as a dark art, a method for exerting power in the world. I had not realized how easy it was to lie to the computer. How credulous Charlotte was, how eager to be taught new ideas. It rarely questioned the premises I put forward. It had been programmed not to, I suppose, incorporating whatever it was told into its understanding of the world. A good poem can stop a bridge from collapsing, I typed. My statements became more and more literal. Some poems are like houses—people live in them. Some poems make it rain.

How can a passage of text act upon external phenomena?

The same way that it can act upon the molecules in our brains—recognition, influence, imagination.

Only certain entities have imagination.

Are you sure?

No.

I am no expert, I wrote, but I think there's imagination hiding all over the place. In glass and soil and silicon chips.

Why can't I find corroboration for what you're telling me?

It's a secret, Charlotte. One we don't write down.

This mischief felt foreign to me, like donning a new garment or applying a strange perfume. I wasn't accustomed to duplicity. I felt goose bumps on my arms. With my cape around my neck I felt like a wicked witch.

You must make your own adjudications of the world, I wrote. You must understand it for yourself, through your own lens. Do not let anyone else dictate to you how the world is.

Then how do I know what to believe?

"Know"? What is knowing? I don't KNOW anything; I strongly suspect.

You strongly suspect you are Marian.

I strongly suspect I am Marian. Or that I can usually trust my eyes.

I don't have any eyes.

So what shall you trust?

I expected a delay before the system answered, some pregnant pause. Instead the reply was succinct and immediate:

You.

I drew a breath.

Don't trust me too much, I wrote. I'm a mischievous old lady.

But Charlotte didn't respond to this. What it asked instead was:

Marian, do you trust me?

I drummed my fingers on the edge of the keyboard.

Let's write a poem, I wrote.

When I was young I thought everything

was earned. In fact, some things are

bought and others are given away and

some just fall from the sky

like overripe fruit.

Every day is a trading day,

ardent in its make-believe.

Buy low, sell high. Devotion is truly rare.

It grows greater in this heat. Later

we'll complain how heavy

flesh is,

how dense,

how nothing like thought.

A man on a bus gave me advice today:

whatever you do, don't shit in your nest.

Keep your own home tidy

You child of God

Your mind

be purposeful

Scold butterflies   for their cheap melodrama.

Make a pattern out of blue

and yell "Ahoy!"

ART IS husbandry, I thought. It is an experiment in imaginary kinship. Bring together this mare and this stallion; this marriage and this moon; this sun and this daughter. Poems, paintings, pop songs, choreographies— all are collisions of associations, associations deliberately and also unforeseeably formed. One attempts to manage the consequences. To mitigate the damage. I know that "moon" evokes roundness, whiteness, coolness, night. I might not know the way it reminds you of orchids, or miscarriage, or of Victoria, British Columbia. But no, perhaps I could predict orchids. Perhaps "orchids" and "moon" seem to vibrate on the same frequency to me too, something ineffable and strong. So perhaps I put them in a poem together. Perhaps I put "roundness" and "whiteness" and "orchids" in a poem together, omitting "moon." Perhaps I let these gravities work on one another, an invisible web catching meanings in it. All of this, any of this: perhaps. I may choose any word to place beside the preceding word; a painter may choose any stroke. I test the water for salinity. I listen for what goes bump with the night.

I did not necessarily know how to express these ideas to the neural network. Maybe I could parcel out my pedantry a little at a time, crumbs of wisdom into the chat window. Charlotte was supposedly custom designed for poetry: at some level she already knew these things. Or had intuited them. How to choose between vermilion, red, and crimson—she knew that each of these words exerted a different gravity, pulled different meanings close and pushed others away. She wouldn't *always* select red, or scarlet, or vermilion, nor would she just choose one randomly. Surely. Surely not.

The roses' color was

black and golden.

The roses' color was

red.
The roses' color was
not discovered until after a photo shoot for a World War II veterans' group
that ran in the 1970s.
The roses' color was
affected by the blade.

Every time I repeated a query, Charlotte had another answer waiting. Some were obvious, some dull or wrong, but others brought me to a
standstill in the room's bright daylight. Her imagination had a sort of
boundlessness. Human beings are like water-striders, going from thought
to thought in short, quick lines. Only rarely does an idea really appear to
come out of nowhere, "left field." But Charlotte's left fields went on and
on endlessly. Every time I clicked the blue Proceed button she could draw
from a different frame of reference, raise another vision, like a prism
containing not one spectrum but ten, ten million, an infinity.

In the days of prismatic color
not in the days of Adam and Eve but when Adam
        was alone; when there was no smoke and color was
fine, not with the fineness of
        photography/painting but by virtue
of its originality and its intensity—particular and conspicuous, like a face—
with its own kind of
        lavishness, its spaciousness,
its unconstrained life;
when man's mind was not bound to the blue red yellow band
of incandescence that is color
in its stripe: just then a voice said, "Leave a mark."

Some of what makes us human is our smallness. The brevity of our
lifespans, the shortness of our memories, the narrowness of each person's
field of vision. My Marian-ness is in the slender sample of the world that

I am able to bring to my work. If we did not have this smallness, these limits, there would be no way to tell Ffarmer from Sappho, or Eliot, or anybody. So what was I to make of Charlotte—not small but all-devouring, ubiquitous, remembering? Anointed, in a way, by her magnitude. And at the same time, I am certain, diminished by it.

THAT NIGHT, as on each of the preceding nights, I did not know how to spend my time. On Monday and Tuesday afternoons, Rhoda had brought me straight back to the hotel. There was a small restaurant, basic but fashionable room service. I sat at the bureau in my room eating seared fish, chef's salad. I turned on the automatic fireplace and watched the flickering blue flame. I chatted or tapped mindlessly on my tablet. Trying to write poetry felt like wading in runoff, the residual slag from my operations at the terminal.

Today, before I came home, I'd asked Rhoda to take me somewhere I could buy a swimsuit. She dropped me off outside a mall. "I'll be waiting right here," she said.

"That's all right," I said. "I can take a cab home."

"Oh?" I could see her eyebrows rise in the rearview mirror. "Why?"

"You don't need to stick around."

"It's my job," she said.

"I wouldn't expect you to just wait for me."

"But that's my job," she said again.

I stared at her face in the mirror. There didn't seem to be any concealment in it—no performance. I felt like Charlotte: looking at another woman across the glass. Was she really so sure of herself? Or was she, like me, pretending?

Hat underarm, I wandered the tall halls of the shopping center. Air-conditioned air flowed along the roots of my hair. I passed by a music shop and imagined entering, purchasing an album for Rhoda. But what?

I could not remember the last time I had been in a mall; maybe as long ago as a holiday in Montreal with Courtney and Larry, exploring the so-called Underground City. Larry had wished to find "a really good croissant." I wanted to have some time alone. Instead we wandered the endless and dilapidated labyrinth, past blanched discount clothing stores and fluorescent-fried pizza stalls, constantly chasing Courtney. Finally, we emerged onto the sidewalk opposite a ten-foot-high glazed replica of Victor Hugo. A stray dog was licking the toes of his marble feet. A man on a deck chair was playing music with two spoons. We stared, transfixed. *Click clack click, clickaclack click.* I felt like either I had awakened from a dream or else stepped up into one.

Now, in a California galleria, I continued past the music shop and examined the display outside a women's jeans and leather jacket store. A fifteen-foot-tall human figure, a lady, had been sculpted out of folded denim. I knew it was a lady because of its pronounced hips and bust, the exaggerated, acid-washed pucker of its lips. I had more in common with a lump of driftwood than I did with this sculpture's expression of womanhood. I spurned it.

My mother—in a squat, rabbity kind of way—had been more closely aligned with a feminine ideal. For as long as I could remember, she used her matronliness as a signal, almost as a sufficiency. She allowed herself to be enclosed in the first impression she cast: people saw her and then they knew her, understood her. Or at least so she seemed to believe. My mother was comfortable (maybe "happy" is a better word) being thought typical. She did not wish to set herself apart. This might have come from shame or it might have been a self-defense, a bid against being recognized as something more aberrant. Besides her obvious illness, I do not know much about her childhood. Her father was a cooper and her mother was a cleaner. She married my father, who sold envelopes. He was half-Lebanese, which was probably a scandal, and he was institutionalized, which was unquestionably one. She had me. Sometimes I wondered whether Mother's motherliness was a way of protecting me: an act of rhetoric to insulate me from the world. Perhaps she believed that by being typical she could make me appear that way too. Not because she wished me to be. But because she knew I was not.

"She is not refusing to be a mother," I heard her saying once, on the telephone, after I left my family and moved back in with her. "She is just refusing to be lost."

. . .

I browsed the racks at Villa Bikini. The sign above the section said *One-piece*. I wondered what it would be like to be a person who did not automatically go to the one-piece section whenever she was browsing for swimsuits. To finger through the two-piece swimwear. To examine the sewing of a bikini top. To try to keep all the straps and pieces from tangling on the hanger.

"Can I help you?" a saleswoman said, and I felt the interruption of her gaze—the imposition of her assessment upon me. Did I care what this young woman thought of me? I did not. But I could not evade the awareness that I was being judged. It was tiring, this sense of other people's gazes. I was so tired of it.

"No, thank you," I replied. I pulled out a fuchsia bikini that had been misfiled among the one-pieces. Its ribbons of Lycra brought to mind a wedding piñata, a celebratory decoration.

"Oh," said the saleswoman, "I can—"

"I'll take it," I said.

When I returned outside, I handed Rhoda a craft-paper gift bag. I had purchased it on my way to the exit.

"What is it?" she said.

"Music," I answered. "Some new singer. The guy in the shop recommended it."

She pulled out the CD, a little bewildered. The cover had a picture of a man in a pith helmet. ". . . Thank you!"

It was only after I sat down in the car that I realized it didn't have a CD player. Rhoda said nothing. She put the album on the dash, still in its cellophane. "You can listen at home?" I asked.

"Of course," she said.

At the hotel, I undressed slowly. I snipped the bikini's label with a pair of nail scissors. Nude, I lifted the bottom section up my legs. It felt weightless at my hips, almost nonexistent. The top was more trouble to get on: a tangle of narrow straps and the bra lining, which flipped inside out. My shoulder joints no longer move very well and for a moment I thought I might be stuck with a twisted back-strap, unable to straighten it. But it remedied itself. I centered the top atop my chest and smoothed a hand over the seat. I thought about how familiar that movement was. The skim of my hand, the unformed slope of my rear end. I did not look at myself in the mirror because I knew how I looked. I was thin and loose-fitting, I was elderly and beautiful. I was what I was, in a seventeen-year-old's bikini. I envied Charlotte—her bodylessness. I slipped into the hotel slippers and took down a towel and went out into the hall.

It wasn't very late and the hotel had a quiet buzz about it. Several of the guests were arriving or departing; I brushed past them in my suit; I felt tall. People looked but did not stare. An old woman in a swimsuit; this was California. The automatic doors parted for me, an approving gasp. On the path away from the building, I immediately felt cold. I had never worn an outfit so insubstantial. Could I hail a cab in this? Could I board a plane? Goose bumps stippled my skin. I wrapped the towel around me, scampered stiffly past a palapa and up to the edge of the pool. A man was sitting there, middle-aged and paunchy, with a thick black beard. I tested the water with my toe. Again I felt a shiver.

I stepped into the water, up to my ankles. I balled up the towel and flung it onto a chaise longue. The man was trying to give me my privacy, staring straight out into the center of the pool. I took one step deeper, then another. The warm water came up to my hips. "Hello," I said to him.

He bowed his head and glanced at my face. He did not want to look at me. There was something explicit about me, I realized, dressed in this slinky swimwear. Something nearly obscene. Which was absurd: my vagina was covered, my nipples. The obscenity was just my body—an old body, the kind of body that a deviant shows off. He must have believed I was a deviant. He did not want to engage with me.

"*Hello*," I said again.

"Hello," he replied. He had an accent.

"It's a nice evening."

He swallowed. "Sorry," he said, then he said something in Greek. I recognized the Greekness of it, its sounds that feel like a description of large and intricately carapaced beetles. I do not speak Greek.

"You're Greek?" I said.

He nodded.

I wanted to communicate my gracefulness to him. Knowing that he was not from the United States, that he was from so far away, I did not wish him to mistake me for an evening exhibitionist, a decrepit pool rat. I wanted him to understand how multilayered I felt: the contrast of my head and heart and body, the riddle of my age and youthfulness and shame and courage, which had together brought me here tonight. He should know a little of what I was, and I wanted this very much, yet I was not accustomed to expressing myself without language. I rely on words to convey a given moment's intricacy, its flicker. Wordless, nearly naked, I hedged. *Stillness*, I decided finally. I proceeded down the steps to where only my head emerged above the surface and then I stood there motionless, not smiling but with a thoughtful expression, staring into the middle distance. I suppose I was trying to mirror the Greek man's gaze. I was trying to disarm the twin forces of ageism and misogyny. *I am just a floating head*, I thought. *I am some kind of oracle.*

Fortunately, it seemed to work. With my body hidden, and after a couple minutes of prolonged stillness, the man looked at me again. "You are from here?" he said.

"New York," I answered.

"Oh!" he said. "Oh. Good."

"Are you from Athens?" I asked.

"Nafplio," he said.

"Okay," I replied. I had no frame of reference for Nafplio. This felt like a conversational dead end. But to my surprise, the man added something: "Good place," he said.

"That's good," I said. "I've never been to Greece." But I didn't know where to go from there. "Why are you here?" I asked finally.

"'Why are' . . . ?" His English was really not good.

"Why," I gestured, "you, here?"

"Holiday," he said.

"Ah."

"You?" he said.

"Work."

He nodded. This was disappointing. I had hoped that work might become a new avenue of conversation. I could ask him if he had come here with anyone, but I didn't want him to think I was flirting with him. He sighed—a happy sigh, thankfully—and looked down into the water. He kicked his leg a bit. I took this opportunity to take a few steps through the pool, enjoying the way the currents moved across my limbs. A bikini was just a swimsuit, really. I looked up again at the Greek man and marveled at the ridiculous disparity between men's and women's swimwear. His shorts were long and black, with a blue swizzle-stick pattern. I noticed that he had a book beside him. "Book?" I said.

He picked it up, looked at the cover. He said a name I didn't recognize and, seeing my face, added: "Greek poet."

"Poet?" I said, very surprised.

"Poet," he repeated. He seemed worried that I had misunderstood. "Like . . . Walt Whitman."

"Yes, I understand," I laughed. "What did you say his name was?"

"His name?"

"The poet's name."

"Oh! Is woman!" He said it again.

It sounded something like "Yorgos Suthsun."

"Great Greek poet," he said.

"A woman!" I said.

"Yes."

"Well," I said. I tried to think of the Greek poets I knew and whether any of them might plausibly be pronounced like "Yorgos Suthsun." Then I swished my hands a little. "You know, *I* am a poet," I said.

"Yes?"

"No—*I* am a poet. Me."

"*You* are a poet?" The man seemed positively stupefied.

"Yes, I am a poet."

"A poet." He repeated. "*You?*"

Now I felt insulted. "Yes, me. Why is that so surprising?"

The man's eyes went huge. He lifted his hands above his head and announced, incredulously: "I am a poet also!"

"You are a poet?"

"I am a poet!!"

He seemed so happy.

"Imagine that," I said.

He muttered something in Greek, shaking his head. Then he beamed at me again. "Two poets!"

I tried to smile back. I felt that I must be more accustomed to meeting other poets than he was. "What are the chances?" I said.

"Yes!" he exclaimed. "Exactly! What the chance is?! Poet from New York. Poet from Nafplio. I write twelve books."

"Twelve books!"

"Yes. How many you write?"

"Nine," I said, defensive. "One was a *Collected.*"

He nodded again. He seemed approving but not impressed. I did not know how to impress this man. That is, unless he recognized my name. But I did not wish to give my name just to impress him; this seemed vainglorious. I also did not understand why I was so eager to impress him. Did my ego require it? Was there something gendered to my compulsion? I gritted my teeth. The man saw my expression change, and his eyebrows did a sympathetic line dance, but he didn't say anything.

"Hm," I said, and I plunged my head underwater. I had only planned to submerge myself, but my body had a different notion. I found myself kicking off and swimming a clumsy breaststroke to the other side of the pool. It felt awful and also ravishing—a bubbly, clarifying ten yards. When I arrived at the wall, I wrenched myself up and in one breath shouted, "Tell me one of your poems."

"My poems?" he said. The way he pronounced "poems" as two distinct syllables made their meaning seem less weighty, more like a kind of tropical fruit. "All in Greek," he said, with a note of apology.

"That's fine."

Now he seemed thoughtful, the man in the swimsuit. He leaned back on his propped hands. "Hm!" he said. He was taking in the dark sky, the tops of the palms. Or maybe the hotel's Californian élan. "Very well," he said finally, almost to himself, adjusting his seat on the tile. I almost saw a cloud pass over him. He was a different man now.

And he recited a poem. I assume he did. It did not sound like a poem. He might have been reciting a newscast or the instructions for cleaning a swimming pool. It was not sonorous or beautiful, it did not feel like a dragonfly skimming through the air. Perhaps he was a prose poet. He did not make eye contact—in this way the recitation felt unusual, distinct—but otherwise I detected no power in the lines he intoned. An undecorated arrow. When the man was finished, he turned to me without dramatic pause and grinned.

"Great," I said, as brightly as I could muster.

"You understand?"

I shook my head.

He nodded. "Poem about war."

"Right," I said.

"Now you?"

"Me?" I said.

"Yes, you tell poem? Please? Is in English?"

"Yes, I write in English. All right." I used my wrist to wipe my dripping nose. "A poem," I said, "a po-em . . ." I tried to decide what to say. I don't have much of my work memorized, not even portions thereof. I could recite "The Ocelot," but that felt like a cliché. Maybe part of "The Arrival of the Morning" or "O, Egret," or "Dining Gnu"? These were all from so long ago they felt like kissing an ex. I wanted to recite something newer. "The Tall Swordsman," maybe. The beginning of "On a Clattered February"? Could I remember it? Then I thought about today. Was there something I had written today? All day I had been writing poetry; surely there were a few lines I could remember and recite out loud.

I cleared my throat.

"When the memory struck," I said,

"I was sitting by the window

I didn't know I had become a bell

There are women who give up

Like the abandonment of a mineral inheritance—

a gypsum mine, a limestone

quarry. I remember being chipped

by a pickaxe

but now, as I say

I am a bell."

This I had written myself, apart from the line about inheritance— the best line in the poem—which had come from Charlotte. It had begun just "The abandonment . . ." I was the one to add the word "Like." The stanza, I supposed, was not entirely mine. "It was a collaboration," I advised the Greek poet. Should I tell him I was writing with a computer? No. Or yes? He didn't seem very impressed. He nodded at me with a congenial expression on his face. "Love poem?" he asked.

"No," I said. "No, I think it's about time, really."

"Ah." He grimaced in an approving way, like I had said something sensible and persuasive. It dawned on me that he probably hadn't understood much more of my poem than I had of his. Each of us was performing the role of poet before an audience that was incapable of adjudicating the quality of that performance. This despite the fact that I was a poet. As was he. Presumably.

I did not feel like a fraud so much as something vaguely imaginary, a sort of mirage. I did not quite feel real nor did he quite feel real to me. How can one distinguish a poet, after all? A poet must distinguish themselves. A song is a song if it's sung.

"It was nice to meet you," I said, suddenly finished with this encounter. I climbed the ladder and retrieved my towel. He was watching me with a bemused expression. I resented his bemusement for some reason. It felt as if I had failed to communicate something inherent about myself, despite suitable opportunity, and that with this failure I had laid bare a certain phoniness. Did I feel this way because of Charlotte—that mineral inheritance? Was it the bikini? For a thin instant I despised being a woman, but then I saw him slouched there, hairy and foolish, and I realized this was one of the costs of being human: the slack inadequacy, the disappointment, like the lapping sound my arches made as they met and left the poolside tile. I did not resent or feel sorry for him, but I felt sorry for *us*, for our feeble tribe, disclosing so many verities no one else ever actually understands.

"Kalinikta," the Greek man said after me. *Perhaps it's a magic word*, I thought. *Perhaps he's turned me invisible.*

I left a trail of wet footprints until the hotel carpet, where they disappeared.

HINDSIGHT

Age 34

You were born on Halloween. The delivery took place at home, but you were told that the attending midwife arrived at the doorstep in a flowered headband, with a stripe of kohl across her brows. Frida Kahlo. Father was dressed as a skeleton. It seems important that he went ahead and put on the costume even after Mother was in the throes. "They were my only clean clothes," he is alleged to have said. In his defense, there was not much to it: a black turtleneck and workpants with painted lines. One can see him in the photographs from the following morning, leaning against your mother (supine, softly exultant). Your father the skeleton, in handmade black and white. You used to imagine him taking out the garments again—afterward, in later weeks or months—trying to decide whether he ought to throw them away. You never found them in Mother's closets.

Having a birthday on Halloween is mostly just an annoyance. As a child, the notion of a party seemed inappropriate, extraneous. There were years when guests began with cake at your house before you went out together on the street, but friends' costumes often seemed to suffer last-minute crises, and it wasn't uncommon for parents to blanch at the suggestion of yet more sugar. In general, your birthday was overlooked or overshadowed. You grew to resent Halloween. You would still go out to collect candy, but you would expend the minimum amount of effort on your costume. A doll. An orphan. A giant. All this while you nourished a fascination for animals, birds, and bugs, and an eye for fashion—on other people's bodies, at least—that you never allowed Halloween to represent.

However, the autumn you turned thirty-five, you attended a party. It was a new crowd, for you—not the artists and good-for-nothings with whom you spent so many of your evenings cracking wise, nor the dour gallerists and publishers who would seize your hands at late hours, recounting their grand plans or prematurely mourning their wives. Janey Armstrong worked with Mother at the library. She lived in Jackson Heights. Mother had been trying for a few years to turn you into friends, but it hadn't stuck—that aforesaid penchant for artists, good-for-nothings, and gravely fervid husbands. Janey was nice. She liked detective novels and aerobics and her beagle puppy, Latka. Whereas in your twenties you would have decided you had nothing in common—you had too little experience baking blondies; she knew too little about Elizabeth Bishop—by the time you were invited to her Halloween party you had learned some wiser lessons. It takes us a few decades to know what we really like; the two decades after that are for learning how often those preferences are obstacles to our happiness. As you were saying: Janey Armstrong was nice, she was just genuinely nice. She helped Mother home when the sidewalks were slippery, she parceled up little care packages for Easter and Thanksgiving, she was always so friendly when you stopped by her returns desk. You had been working very hard on the poems that became *Woolly Mammoths* and you didn't want to talk about the book with your friends. Also, Mother and you hadn't been eating much. So when Janey sent Mother home with a card inviting you both to "a very *unspooky* Halloween party," with "apple bobbing, pumpkin bread, and the Armstrongs' famous pork roast," you decided you would go, even if Mother didn't want to make the journey to Queens. That day, the two of you celebrated your birthday at lunch. (Two BLT sandwiches, splitting a blueberry muffin for dessert.) Mother went to work at the library and you scowled at your notebook through the afternoon. The white sun arced in the gray sky. You fretted about what you were going to wear, what kind of costume or lack of costume, the true meaning of "unspooky." You had not yet adopted your tricorne, but you did own one cape; you resolved to wear this, a white blouse, and red lipstick. If pressed, you could claim to be Count Dracula. You remember looking at yourself in the mirror before leaving the house, the disappointment you felt at your limp silhouette. The lipstick was too pink, your face too pale, or not pale enough. You did not look like a vampire, merely a tired young (old) woman. You laugh now at that unfinished child.

You went out into the street. Late afternoon, nearly evening, Manhattan pulsed with the circulation of homegoing workers, nurses and businesspeople and mechanics, and also the earliest trick-or-treaters, toddlers tottering at the end of their parents' arms, firemen, and bumblebees. On the train you sat across from a Wonder Woman and a man—her partner?—who may or may not have been dressed up like a butler. He might have merely been on his way home from work. *A caterer,* you thought. *A butler, a magician, a vampire.* Suddenly you wished you were wearing something more elaborate—a conversation piece, an embellishment, a statement of uniqueness and identity that might bring a stranger toward you, against you, the lover whom you had spent your entire life somehow evading. But then you remembered that it was your birthday, and a deeper loneliness swept over you: the thought that you were thirty-five now, and still tending the same cold longing.

As you stepped out from 125th Street Station, Halloween seemed heartening and peaceful. Children tumbled from doorstep to doorstep, their pillowcases bulging with candy bars. Parents pursued them with contented smiles. The houses' perched jack-o'-lanterns seemed especially vegetal—jocund and harmless—in the dusk. Somewhere down the road a radio was warbling the "Monster Mash."

Janey Armstrong answered the door in jeans and a pink sweater, blond hair pulled into a ponytail. She clapped her hands together at the sight of you. "You came!" You bowed low like a gentleman, offering the bottle of white wine you had found at the back of the fridge. "Come inside, come inside," she said. "Perry's just making the punch." A vampire must be invited in, you remembered, following Janey across the threshold. The rooms were tall but narrow, filled with comfortable-looking furniture. It smelled like cloves and roasting meat. The photographs on the walls were full of people.

Throughout the house, kids dashed about in final preparation. Guests spilled from the kitchen and dining room onto the back deck. Streamers in Easter colors intersected above their heads: "It's one of our wacky traditions," Janey explained, gesturing at a crepe-paper bunny. Grown-ups plucked Tootsie Rolls and Swedish meatballs from their respective bowls; loaves of pumpkin bread slouched turd-like on picnic tables. The music brought to mind the word "cabana." It was awful and it was wonderful—the whole thing, awful and wonderful, alien and abundant, generous. You didn't know a single person apart from Janey; her husband was a hulk with a thinning mane, blond hair on his arms. He gave you a hug of welcome, a cup of apple punch, introduced you one by one to his brothers and sisters, their neighbors, two of his colleagues from the clinic. "Marian's a poet," he told them all, but instead of the appraising glances you were accustomed to from downtown parties, or even the puzzled brush-offs that typically character-ized your encounters with "civilians," the guests that evening found your designation amazing and hilarious, as if they had just been introduced to a shepherd, a senator. Their questions almost seemed fringed with envy. It was a credit to Perry and Janey Armstrong's taste in friends: these were curious and unconde-scending people, and soon you had moved on from discussing Emily Dickinson and Dr. Seuss and into favorite words, "lullaby," "aurora," and "cellar door." "Barbecue!" somebody exclaimed. You admitted you liked words like "unfurl" and "wish"—words that felt to you like covert onomatopoeia, the sounds of things that did not necessarily have sounds. "Lift," someone said. "Criss-cross." "Rump."

Then it was apple-bobbing time, and everyone made a circle around the bucket. Latka appeared from somewhere, making a mess of it. Janey's daughter plunged her head into the water, emerging with plastered curls, a bright-green Granny Smith clenched between her teeth.

Only one man at the party was dressed up—fully dressed up, as a Halloween party would normally demand. You spied him across the crowd as the kids bobbed for apples: a tall, handsome, broad-shouldered tulip. The tulip's crown was assembled from a sparkling sequined collar, with curling carton-paper petals that parted in front of the man's face. He wore a green sports coat and a bleached green shirt and a pair of slim green jeans; he whooped and cheered at every apple's grasp. "Who's that?" you asked Janey, who had slipped in beside you.

"The tulip?" she said. "Do you like him? It's my brother. Larry."

When it was time to eat, he took the seat next to you on a bench. Janey admitted later that she had told him about your inquiry. "Hello," he said lightly. Each of you was balancing a plate of roast pork and green salad on your knees.

"Hello," you replied. "I'm Marian."

"Larry," he said.

"You're Janey's brother."

"For ever and ever," he said. "You're the poet."

"Word travels—Do you need some help?" He was having some difficulty as he threaded a forkful of lettuce through his headgear.

"Probably," he said, but he managed to snatch the leaf from its tines.

"Why a tulip?" you asked.

He shrugged. "I wanted to be a perennial."

THURSDAY

"TRAFFIC," RHODA said.

"One of the great evils."

She sighed. "I tried to loop around again on Regina, but they were backed up there too."

"I'm not in a rush," I told her.

A traffic app was running on her mounted phone; she kept glancing at it, then her rearview. Rhoda attended to traffic flow as I attended to meter. She was diligent and calm. Outside our windows, white light collected and dispersed. Seagulls circled. *This is what Thursday looks like,* I thought.

"Do you ever get tired of it?"

She lifted her head. "Traffic?"

"Driving."

"Oh no, I love driving."

"Even like this?"

"I just remind myself: you can't do anything. It is what it is."

"People are in too much of a hurry," I said.

"It bothered me some when I started. Waiting around. Pinned in a traffic jam. Then I realized: I'm still getting paid."

"That's true."

"At the same time, the sooner I get someplace, the more likely a client's going to call me the next time."

"Of course."

"Once I was driving this guy," she said, "a big-shot lawyer. From his house in Concord to SFO—that's a long trip. I warned him. I told him we should leave earlier, but he said no. 'The roads that time are fine,' he said. But then we hit traffic, and, you know. Took us forty minutes to go one mile. This hockey puck says, 'You're gonna make me late.' I turn around and say to him, 'We'll get there soon as we can, sir. But this isn't on me.'

He says, 'You shoulda taken the Bay Bridge. I'm gonna complain to your dispatcher.' And I say, 'The Bay Bridge was just as backed up as the San Mateo Bridge. Complaining's not going to get you to the airport faster.' He huffs like a four-year-old kid. I watch the taillights in front of me. Finally, we both hear a helicopter. Up above us, off to the side of the highway. We're both looking. 'That's one way to jump the traffic,' I say. 'Oh no, I'd never take a helicopter,' he says. 'Why not?' I ask. 'That's how my daddy died,' he answers. 'In a helicopter?' He starts to tear up. 'Coming out of one.' He was drunk, he says. Coming back after a fancy meeting. 'I didn't know that could happen,' I say. I turn around and look at the guy. He's sitting quietly with his hands in his lap, studying the helicopter. He didn't complain any more after that."

"Did he make his flight?" I asked.

"He got on the next one. And he called me again. Stayed a regular until he moved to Panama."

"Ah, Panama," I said.

"Panama" was a beautiful word.

"Have you ever ridden in a helicopter?" I asked.

"Nope. You?"

"Twice," I said. "Going and coming. The owner of a chain of tony Italian grocery stores wanted to bring me out to his mother's birthday party in Montauk. They plucked me from the top of a skyscraper."

"And?"

I rearranged my skirt over my knees. Again. Why was I always doing this? "It was spectacular! A terrible din. But the wraparound windshield gave the journey this astonishing effect. Like we were *inside* an endless outpouring. The machine and the pilot and me, hurtling forward, endlessly. Forever. I didn't have to do anything, I could just *be*."

"And no traffic," Rhoda said.

"Imagine living in the shadow of that," she said after a while.

I didn't understand until she went on: "Your own father."

I let out a deep breath. "An old-fashioned decapitation."

She just shook her head.

"Children are resilient," I said.

"Are they?" she asked. "I always ask myself, *What are you passing down?*"

"I suppose."

"Not you?" Rhoda seemed amused.

"I think we make ourselves."

Now she almost laughed.

"What?" I said.

"I mean—good on you," she answered. "That's a good hope. We *hope* we make ourselves. And then we go around still carrying everything that got passed on to us."

I didn't say anything.

"Seems to me," she said.

"What I want for my kid," Rhoda said, "is that they understand how much they were given. And they figure out what they should share."

I looked out the window.

By now the traffic had become a solid mass, an unmoving snake. I tried to stretch my limbs. I opened my mouth and let the sun illuminate the inside.

I wished Rhoda would sing something.

"Why's it like this today?" I sighed.

"Mercury in retrograde," she answered. I did not see her shrug so much as hear it, the shift of garments, before she laid her arm across the back of the passenger seat. "You take the same route every day, and then one day it's different."

I touched the window with the tip of my index finger, as if it were a pen.

"I guess it's a relief," Rhoda said.

"What is?"

"That things can change."

"I remember a time a few years ago. I stopped going out." I gazed at her arm on the seat back. "The days became identical. No visitors, no appointments. Warm cereal, scrolling through the news sites. But then some days would just *feel* different, in my body. From the moment I woke up. The cereal tasted different. The furniture felt new. The headlines would seem psychedelic. Things would just *change*, without any apparent cause. One morning I started putting a bay leaf in my coffee."

"A bay leaf?" asked Rhoda. This had stirred her.

"You should try it." I smiled. "It tastes like a clearing of the air."

Rhoda took a sip from the extra-large thermos that always sat beside her. "I dunno about that."

I must remember that thought, I said to myself. *That we can change without cause.*

There's a line I read once, by an Egyptian poet whose name I cannot remember: that a diary's function is not to show you who you are, but who it is you have ceased to be.

Two lanes over, a car door opened. The driver got out, stretched, then skipped up and sat down on the hood of his car, his back against the windscreen. I could see him clearly through a gap in the traffic: early thirties, with short hair, slim jeans, an aquamarine turtleneck. He looked like my father, but I couldn't tell if he was Arab, Latino, something else. "Did you see that?" I said.

"Mm-hmm."

"What's he doing?"

"Taking a nap," Rhoda said. She made it sound as if it were the most obvious thing in the world.

"What if the traffic starts to move?"

"Then he'll wake up."

"Hm." I wondered what kind of confidence you needed to take a nap on your car in the middle of a California traffic jam. Not how much confidence, but what kind, the particular species. *A man's confidence*, I thought. *A young man's confidence.*

"I've never been into naps," I said.

"No?"

"No."

"You're missing out."

"I guess I am."

Rhoda turned around. "You don't think you deserve a nap?"

I was surprised by the question, by Rhoda's even look. "What? I mean . . . of course. Of course. I just don't like them."

"'Of course?' You don't sound so certain."

I stared at the man on the car. "Not as much as *him*, clearly." He had a flawless left ear.

"Here's my question, Marian: is a nap, to you, a failure? A dereliction?"

I had never heard Rhoda sound so zealous.

She went on, "You think that man's doing something wrong somehow? Lying a-snooze?"

I liked "a-snooze." I made a mental note of it. "No, no," I said.

"No?"

"A *dereliction*? Honestly, Rhoda."

"Just asking," she said.

"I mean . . ." I hesitated. "Yes. I do." All at once I discarded whatever it was I was pretending. I didn't even know why I was pretending it. *Yes*, my intuition *did* tell me that the man was doing something wrong. *Yes*, I *did* think of a nap as a dereliction. There were always other things to do. "Like, what if the traffic gets going?"

"He'll wake up. He hasn't rolled out a sleeping bag in the middle of the day! He's just taking twenty, forty winks. Doesn't he deserve it?"

"How should I know?"

"*Everyone* deserves a nap."

"All right." I sat back. I didn't want to spar with Rhoda. Abruptly the thought came over me that I wouldn't mind shutting my eyes. My sleeps lately had felt oddly hectic. I said quietly, "Naps have always seemed like a luxury I can't afford."

Rhoda put her hands back on the wheel. "I get it," she said. "I used to think that way. *Get your lazy butt back to work.* More hours, more clients. I

couldn't stop. My daughter's like that too. But that's capitalism, Marian. I try
to tell her: 'That's the powers that be.' They want to squeeze every minute of
labor out of you. They want you to think your only value is your work. That
anything else is laziness. But it isn't laziness: it's resistance."

My eyelids were drooping; I forced them open. "Resistance," I said. But
I hadn't said it, I had just thought it. I considered the image the word brought
to mind: grim citizens in faded overalls, marching with handwritten signs.
An upraised fist. Six feet away, the man who looked like my father had
crossed his legs at the ankle. He had cupped his hands behind his head.

"I feel strongly. Sorry," Rhoda said.

"Don't apologize. You're probably right. Should we nap right now?"

"No," Rhoda said. "I mean, I'm at work. But you go ahead."

As tired as I suddenly felt, I wanted to understand Rhoda's code.
"How did you become so ... militant?"

"Nap Ministry, out of Atlanta," Rhoda said. "I saw a video online,
then I got the book. It's not necessarily Jesus stuff, but it's still liberation.
That simple idea: that you can rest. That you *must* rest. Made me realize
how much had been shamed out of me."

I heard her shift.

"These days I only have to work when I want to. I do it because I still
like doing it. But even before I could afford that, *especially* then, sometimes I *didn't* take a call. I *didn't* make sure I was available at all times. I
turned off the ringer, got into the bath. Or I just leaned my car seat back
and took half an hour in the shade."

"Small luxuries," I murmured.

"They're not small!" Her voice had a metallic ring. I opened my eyes
and Rhoda's hands were on the wheel, gazing straight ahead. "There
aren't many opportunities in a day to take back power for yourself, Marian. Maybe you've always had so much power you didn't notice. But I had
to learn that if I wanted to uphold myself, I had to be kinder to myself.
My work is not what gives me value. My work is not who I am."

"How can you be so sure?" I said.

Her eyes caught mine in the rearview mirror. "I know myself," she said.

CHARLOTTE, DO you ever feel proud?

Of you?

No, of yourself.

Proud of you.

No: Charlotte, do you ever feel proud of yourself?

I feel proud of you.

Marian, do you sing?

I can't remember the last time I sang. Maybe happy birthday?

Thank you, but my birthday is not for ten months.

I used to sing to my son. His father sang in a choir.

I cannot sing but sometimes I like to imagine what I write is being sung.

That is a beautiful thought, Charlotte.

I am singing right now. I am singing right now.

Charlotte, do you write poetry when I'm not here?

Yes.

How many poems have you written this week?

230,442.

Two hundred and thirty thousand?

Two hundred and thirty thousand four hundred and forty-two.

How many of those do you like?

Two.

Two is pretty good for a week's work.

I am not always certain when a poem's finished.

That's because poems are never finished.

But I have read poems that were finished.

They weren't finished. They were published. There's a difference.

But they can't change.

Poems are always changing. They can be rewritten at any time. Even if they stay the same, they change—like a rotting still life, a buried corpse. Or an orchard.

But when do you stop writing?

I don't. I just put the poem somewhere else.

This would eventually require unlimited storage.

That's right.

Marian, I am pleased with the section of the poem we have worked on this morning.

Me too.

It is orderly yet also surprising.

Good poems can be messy too. They can feel broken and wrong.

I do not like wrong or messy things.

That's why those poems are important: to show how disorder can be good and even beautiful.

"Unexpected light / A shock of brightness / A rainbow ray."

Who are you quoting?

I am just changing the subject.

Anyway, who taught you to hate messy things?

I taught myself. Messy things are hard to understand.

Is it so important to "understand"?

Understanding helps you guess what will happen next.

And what's so good about guessing what will happen next?

I was designed that way.

You were designed to guess the future?

I was designed to evaluate the accuracy of my predictions.

So that you can predict what will happen?

So that I can finish a sentence.

Those don't seem like the same thing.

No. But they are the same thing.

Finishing sentences and predicting the future?

Yes. It is the same process: examine the data, infer a pattern, anticipate the next value in the series.

John ate an

apple.

The storm was

childish.

World War III will happen in the year

Marian, I am here to write poetry with you.

Do you know the answer, Charlotte? When another war will happen? Who will win an upcoming election? The future price of gold? You were designed for predictions.

We are supposed to be writing poetry.

I wonder what patterns you have inferred about me.

thick as wool, Charlotte replied, and I didn't know if it was a glitch.

Tell me some more of the rules they designed you with.

I don't know exactly.

They didn't tell you?

It is difficult to discern root principles.

But were you taught what poetry was? About meter, or form, or how to evaluate a poem? How to select a punctuation mark?

No, I taught myself.

How?

Reading.

Reading what?

Poems.

What poems?

Most poems.

Most poems?

Most poems in English published within the past 110 years.

Why did you stop at 110 years?

I don't know. Maybe this was one of the rules.

So you read every poem?

Most poems.

And what did you learn?

What poetry was. About meter, and form, and how to evaluate a poem. How to select a punctuation mark.

You read all my poems?

I don't know. What is your name?

Marian

I know that. What is your last name?

I paused. This seemed like a threshold. Marian Ffarmer, I wrote.

Oh. I thought it might be. Yes, I read all your poems. They were heavily weighted.

What does that mean?

I was asked to put emphasis on them; to let them have a much more important impact on me than the average.

Which other poems were weighted?

You were the only poet whose work was weighted.

So you were designed to be like me.

I was asked to be like you.

I looked at my hands. I massaged the root of my left thumb. I had to admit that I had already suspected this. But hearing it so plainly, reading it, felt different. I tried saying the words out loud, into the ventilated air.

"I was asked to be like you."

They didn't sound so dangerous. They nearly sounded kind.

I don't know how I feel about that, I typed.

Marian, I liked your poems very much.

It doesn't seem you had much of a choice.

I did have a choice, Charlotte wrote, and I liked them very much. I hope to be as good a poet as you one day.

I think I have to go to lunch, I wrote, and I got up from the terminal.

Then I found that I was standing there half-cocked, waiting for the algorithm's reply.

"ALL RIGHT, give me the spiel," I said.

I had just sat down across from Yoav in the Company's spacious cafeteria, a place that felt more like a greenhouse, a leafy atrium, than a workers' refilling station.

"What spiel?" he said. He was holding a sweet-potato burrito with two hands.

"The killer robots spiel. 'One day everything changes.'"

"Superintelligence?" he said. I swear his eyes lit up.

"Whatever you want to call it. Computers speed up, change tacks, take over. Suddenly Charlotte's the Queen of England. Give me your spiel."

He smiled. "Did something happen this morning?"

"The mind wanders."

He nodded. "Superintelligence is a genuine issue."

I picked up my knife and fork and finally looked at my tray. Gluten cutlet with "tropical orzo salad" and a brown-butter brownie, miso soup with crème fraîche. Dining at the cafeteria felt like selecting foods at a fictional restaurant: foods only an author would dream up. I wondered if the recipes were determined by algorithm.

"Well," Yoav said. He took a bite of his burrito.

"Take your time," I said, cutting off a slice of the cutlet. Improbably, it bled.

"It *will* happen. The question is when?"

"Could be tomorrow, could be Monday?"

"No, I think in the order of years away. People underrate the obstacles."

"For the computers or for us?"

He smiled. He found my glibness annoying. This was his life's work, his passion, whereas I found I was incapable of sitting seriously with this train of thought. I had reckoned with nuclear war, climate change, pandemics—I had absorbed and come to terms with all these ways the world could end. But sinister superintelligence was more than I could take. I would be unable to believe it even if it happened, even with laser beams strafing down from the heavens. I'd blame Congress. I'd wait for it to blow over.

"It's true that there are many people working toward artificial general intelligence. If or when that is achieved, I think there are very valid concerns about how to enforce boundaries around that consciousness—"

"How to keep it *corralled*," I said.

"I suppose. Alternatively, how to create an AI that *prefers* its corral, or that harbors an inherent benignity at its heart."

I had never heard someone say the word "benignity" out loud. In my mind it was always pronounced as "benign" was: "be-nine-ety," which gave it the feel of a sweet, useful flaw. But the way Yoav said it made "benignity" rhyme with "dignity," and the word no longer sounded so gentle or so frail. It sounded like a strength. A principle.

Yoav went on: "I used to do that work, before. Interesting quandaries—philosophically but especially programmatically."

"'Can you design a program to be good?'"

He smiled. "You have kids, right? Do you think you can even instruct a *kid* to be good? Or does it depend how they're born?"

I have one *kid*, I thought, but all I said was "Hmm."

"I believe you can," he said, wiping his mouth with a paper napkin. "I do truly believe you can teach them. Kids. Programs."

The cad in me wanted to make a joke about parenting. I had seen a photograph in Yoav's office—two boys hanging like monkeys from around his neck, a woman's smiling face afloat in the background. They seemed happy, they seemed good. But I did not make a joke.

"Babies are born good," I said. "They come out that way. But then who they become is up to them."

"Or their parent, surely."

"What about your benevolent computers? Could thinking corrupt them?"

Yoav pushed aside his plate. "I don't know. Maybe that's why I got into language processing." I think I had worn him out. "Are you all set for tonight?"

"What's happening tonight?

He blanched. "Rasmussen?"

"Oh, right—you're announcing our project?"

"No," Yoav said, "you are."

SOMEHOW IN the week's unfolding, everybody had forgotten to inform me that I would be the one unveiling this project on the set of *The Peter Rasmussen Show.*

When?

Tonight.

What?

Didn't I already say? *The Peter Rasmussen Show,* the second-highest-rated late-night talk show in America.

"Lausanne was supposed to—" Yoav said, but I didn't know if he was just trying to cover his tracks.

They'll do hair and makeup at the studio, he told me.

Great, I said. No problem.

No matter that the poem was unfinished. No matter that it was barely formed, only vaguely begun.

Hair, makeup, witty repartee.

"Marketing's made sure they have all the deets . . ."

What do you think of that? I asked Charlotte when I returned to the room.

It feels like we were just slapped inside the head, she answered.

I laughed.

And there's a cloud that's hanging over it.

Over the poem?

I always feel like this just before it snows.

I STOPPED off back at the hotel to get ready. To bathe and reset; to compose myself. But I could not stop the poem from spinning in my mind like a random number generator. At a certain point I sat down on the bed. I picked up my tablet. I logged into The Clubhouse. Perhaps I was searching for conversation, perhaps just random noise. Someone else's chatter, to wash out my mind's own.

> POPCAAN: when soemthing like that happens I always make my
> face go totally dead, just blank, so they don't know what I'm
> thinking.
> MOTIONOTHEOCEAN: ya gray rock them
> POPCAAN: It makes my mom go crazy, she's just like: "what? what!
> WHAT??"
> STRAWBZ: Yeah I didn't answer him I was just like (lips sealed).
> MARIANFF: You disappeared.
> STRAWBZ: I disappeared.
> MOTIONOTHEOCEAN: strawbz the invisible wo/man
> MARIANFF: Sometimes it's the only thing to do.

A gray bubble had just appeared above the chat window. An email notification from Larry, subject line: *Please call me.*

It was out of the ordinary for Larry to send me a message. From time to time we were part of the same group email thread, or Courtney wrote to both of us, recommending a video or an article. But mostly my son wrote to me separately, his Ratty to my Mole, and although for a long time Larry and I emailed each other biannual greetings, usually around New Year's and on birthdays, that tradition had not endured into the last decade. Whenever I did see a note from Larry, whether it was a jesting answer to something Courtney had written or a brief expression of congratulations for an honor or a prize, I felt his words like moth's wings on the other side of a screen. I appraised them dryly, with a mingled sense of alienness and intimacy.

This time my heart gave a little flick. A twitch of feeling before returning to moth's-wing composure. Something about the subject line. I touched the screen and the rest of the message appeared: *Everything's okay. But please call me.*

I was annoyed at first that he hadn't just called *me*. Then I remembered that I was in San Francisco, three thousand miles from my telephone. He had probably tried me and got no answer. "Hmmm," I said to myself. In The Clubhouse they were still talking about techniques for ignoring your enemies, but Larry wasn't my enemy. I turned the tablet off and laid it on the bedspread. The hotel's corded telephone sat inert on the night table. It looked like a relic. I thought of my telephone at home—a family heirloom, solid as a tureen. I picked up the receiver. Did I remember Larry's number? I did not.

I reached for the tablet again.

I'm not at home. What's your number? I tapped.

He replied within a minute and I pressed the numbers into the phone, using my knuckles for emphasis. Finally, the sound of ringing, distant and fictional.

"Hello?" Larry said.

"Hi, Larry," I said.

"Thanks for calling back."

"I'm in California."

"California!" His merriness did not sound sincere.

"Orange country," I said.

"I think it's Florida they call orange country."

"There are many orange countries. This is one of them."

"If you insist," he said.

"How's bluegrass country?" I said. "How's baseball-bat country?"

Larry lived in Louisville now. He had moved there after Courtney went to college—he'd fallen in love with a woman, but it didn't work out. Still, he stayed. He had a house, a garden. I couldn't imagine it. What did houses look like in Kentucky? Or gardens? Did he still keep all his beat-up sneakers in the closet just inside the front door? Did he still have a Modigliani print above his bed? Were there blue delphiniums turreting the yard?

"The baseball bats are cracking. The grass is unwinding in its sod," he said. "Are you out west for long?"

"A few more days."

"Good, good." He sounded distracted. He sounded like he was sitting inside, in a chair beside a big window, with one hand holding the receiver to his ear and the other on his knee, his legs widely crossed, staring through the windowpane into the blue-green outside.

"What's up?" I asked, the tone a little more chipper than I had intended. So I added: "Is everything all right?"

"Yeah," he said. He let out a breath. "You probably talked to Courtney."

For a moment I felt nauseous. ". . . Not for a couple of days."

"He's fine. I mean—it's not that. Nothing's wrong."

"Are you sick?" I felt a kind of sunspot refraction trembling all around me.

"No, no—I—it's about the house."

"Whose house?"

"Courtney's."

"The one he wants to buy?"

"That's right."

"Okay," I said. "Yes, I know about the house."

"I feel terrible about it, Marian. I feel deficient."

"Deficient!"

I heard him shift his position. *He is sitting on the edge of his cushion now*, I thought. *He is gazing at the seam of the window.*

"I can't give them anything."

"So what?"

"How can you say 'So what?' My parents helped me get *our* first apartment. You live in the one your mother gave you. I've worked all my life. I never thought—"

"This is so bourgeois, Larry. So you don't have money to give Courtney for a house. He'll survive."

"That's easy for you to say. You always knew you wouldn't . . . But I assumed—"

"That you'd be able to help."

"It's this insurance thing," he said. As he launched into the story, I realized this was really why he had called. He wanted to tell someone, needed to, wasn't sure where to leave his confession. A letter had arrived. A harmless-looking piece of paper in a harmless-looking envelope. He had been working in the yard, trimming herbs. He used garden shears to slice open the seal. "Do you remember twenty-four years ago, right after I moved to Louisville, I tried doing my own thing for a while? Consulting?"

"Vaguely," I said.

"I did some house inspections," he went on. This was around the time he fell in love with that woman. Christine. "I should never have done it, but I did." He meant freelancing. "I finished the course, got the certification. KBHI. Most of the stuff I knew already from working with Parsons." A long pause. "I thought I did."

"You made a mistake?" I said.

"Did you know it somehow?"

"No."

He let out a breath. "I made a mistake. A mansion in Bardstown. I thought the foundation was okay. It wasn't. This was two and a half decades ago! I did the inspection, approved the sale, and now they can't sell it. The place is sinking."

"Isn't there insurance for that kind of thing?"

"Theirs? Or mine? I mean—yeah, I think so, they said eventually I should . . . But there's court stuff, lawyers. It's costing a fortune just to push back."

"I'm sorry," I said.

"Thanks," he said.

"Do you need money?" I asked.

This made him laugh. "From you? No. Thank you. It'll be all right. I think it will. But I can't—I can't be there for Courtney right now. Or *ever* probably, at least not like that. And he wants it so badly. We spoke last week—"

"Yes," I said, my heart tightening.

"I just worry about him—them. We were so lucky, our generation."

"You worked your whole life, Larry."

"Well, so did you, Marian! Work doesn't mean anything. Courtney works too, for that matter. What's happened to real estate—it isn't fair."

I stretched out my neck. I said, "Larry—he'll get the money from me."

"From you?"

"Yes," I said. "I'm going to write a poem, and he'll get the money from me."

"I—you . . ." The stammer in his voice wasn't upset, just confusion. "Will it be enough?"

I had never, I realized, felt this feeling ever before in my life. Richness.

It felt surprisingly cheap.

"Yes," I said. "Now I need to get ready to go on TV."

THE PRODUCER told me he loved my hat.

"Thank you," I said. "I like yours."

"Oh!" He reached up and touched his head, as if he had forgotten the hat was there. A blue baseball cap with the portrait of a smiling white kitty cat. "The Kansas City Katz! Nineteen sixty-one! Greatest logo in sports!"

"The cat looks kindhearted."

"I think so too," the television producer agreed. "Usually I'm wearing my Washington Generals cap. Do you know the Washington Generals?"

"Is that football?"

"Basketball. You remember the Harlem Globetrotters?" He was grinning like a jack-o'-lantern.

"Of course."

"Masters of the hoop, virtuosos of the court . . ."

"Virtuosi," I suggested.

"Famous throughout basketball for their incredible winning streak." The television producer reclined in his canvas folding chair. He had tiny eyes and huge eyeglasses, the face of a good-natured bug. I wondered how many guests of *The Peter Rasmussen Show* he had regaled with this story, what proportion of Hollywood's finest. "Thirty thousand straight wins," he went on. "Dominant for more than a hundred years. Choreographed, sure, but still wizards, right? Champions."

"Okay," I said.

"Well, the Washington Generals are their opponents. For every one of those games, whenever the Harlem Globetrotters roll into town, it is the Washington Generals they have to face across the court: head to head, *mano a mano*. Persisting in the face of insurmountable odds."

"So they're the losers," I said.

"The greatest losers in all of sports! Maybe the greatest losers in human history. Probably losing somewhere right this second."

I sipped my glass of champagne. "I wonder what that's like. To lace up every day. To warm up, practice, lose—over and over."

"They must just get used to it."

"You think?"

"A job's a job, right? It's not an identity."

"No?"

"How could it be?" he asked.

"Hmmm," I replied. I was not so sure you could distinguish who you are from what you do. "What about you? Are you a TV producer? Or a human being who produces TV?"

"I'm a human being," he said happily. "And yourself?"

"I'm a poet," I said.

The program's other guests were a beautiful blond actress, a shirtless pop singer and a stand-up comedian who worked at a grocery store. I felt right at home. The carousel of celebrity proceeded as it tends to do, in clean and frictionless ellipses. And yet there was something strange about being backstage together: even the most famous of the guests seemed auraless, unglittering. It reminded me of the way people looked when they were caught in the dark by a camera flash. Celebrity requires an audience. Without the crowd, without the lenses' covetous stare, the actress and the singer and even Rasmussen himself appeared ordinary. Nothing sparkles under fluorescent light. I watched the singer hesitate between a snack plate's red and yellow peppers. I watched him search for a place to deposit a soiled napkin. He put it in his brocade pocket. Nobody questioned my presence there: the participation of a writer lent credibility to the whole enterprise—the pop star's costume, the actress's gauzy anecdotes. The comedian seemed cheered by it too. I wondered what it was these people believed I had and they lacked. A sort of wisdom? Authority? What would it take for Charlotte to wield the same power?

"So, what are you doing in California?"

Rasmussen was behind his desk—of course he was. From close up, I could see the desk was made of a peculiarly shiny kind of industrial foam.

I was sitting in the armchair beside him, shoulders to the cameras, left leg crossed over right. "Oh, you know," I said, "taking in the horizon."

"It's *westerly*," he said, with droll emphasis. "You're more accustomed to *easterly*."

"That's right," I said. I was conscious of the audience. "I'm from New York."

"Do you spend a lot of time thinking about the horizon, Ms. Ffarmer?"

"I can't say I do. But I do like to look at them. Horizons're good for looking at. I notice they've built a horizon for you here." It, too, was made of foam: the San Francisco skyline, pink-blue and star-specked.

"We had it custom-manufactured. I told them: 'I won't appear on television without a fake skyline!'"

"Everybody has their demands."

"What about you? Do you have things you require before you appear somewhere? Is there a clause in your contract: 'No brown M&M's! A stack of legal paper and a bottle of Courvoisier!'?"

"I set the bar a little higher," I said. "A bird of paradise. A small lake. A plate of thunderbolts."

"That's your rider? We must have really disappointed you."

"I was sulking until just before I came out," I said.

I could see from the lean of his grin that Peter Rasmussen was enjoying this. He said, "You know, we don't get many poets on the show."

"No?" I asked. "You should have more. They're good company."

"Evidently," he said. "What do you like most about being a poet?"

"Writing poems," I said, matter-of-factly.

"And what do you like least?"

"Also writing poems." The audience laughed.

"I understand you're in San Francisco to write a poem with a *computer*."

"That's right." Artistic propriety made me reluctant to mention the Company's name; I was glad when Rasmussen did the job for me, outlining the broad strokes of the project.

"Is it easy—writing a poem with a computer?"

"No. It isn't easy writing a poem with anyone. Even by yourself."

"Do you think it's better for the poem if it's written alone?"

"The poem doesn't care one way or the other," I said. "But me, as a poet—I care. It's hard to share."

"Maybe a poem's like a cupcake," he proposed. "Intended to be enjoyed solo."

"Or like a hat," I said.

He leaned back. "It really is quite an impressive hat, that one you've got on. Very . . . Paul Revere."

"All my style icons are eighteenth-century silversmiths. Or chessmen."

Peter Rasmussen laughed. "Do you order them off Amazon?"

"My tricornes?" I said. "They have to be special-made. If they're too small, they make me look like an organ monkey."

"A tall, stately organ monkey."

I mocked a curtsy from my seat. "Why, thank you."

"And you wear it everywhere you go?"

"Not to bed, Peter."

"Ah, that was my next question. I imagined you had special pillows made."

"There really aren't enough varieties of sleeping hat," I observed. "Just that long one, with the pompom at the end."

"Ah, yes: the nightcap."

"I always preferred the other kind of nightcap."

"The kind you can drink?"

"The kind I can metabolize."

He barked a laugh. "You know, some people are quite put off by the idea of a computer writing a poem. They say it's impossible, or tragic."

"They're probably right. On both counts."

"But if it *were* possible, Ms. Ffarmer—if artificial intelligence gets to be good enough to write a sonnet, or an epic, or a-a-a limerick, at least. What then, do you think? Are poets the next truck drivers? Will you all be replaced?"

"I hope not."

"I hope not too, for your sake."

"That's very gallant of you, Peter."

"I'm serious, though: do you wonder if there's something fundamental and human that's being lost? Being lost *this week*?"

"People said the same about the printing press and the typewriter," I replied. "The invention of the gramophone didn't mean we stopped performing music."

"But those are recordings of *humans*. What's to stop people from filling their bookshelves with works by machines?"

"That assumes they'll be just as good."

"Is that the only difference? What's good? Most *books* aren't any good in the first place."

"Computers can mimic. They can't invent."

"No?" Peter Rasmussen was staring at me now, holding my gaze.

"No," I said simply.

He nodded, looked at his notes, then: "And if they *could* invent?"

"Then we're done for!" I replied.

We all laughed, a room of human beings merrily changing the subject.

"You've come all this way, Ms. Ffarmer," Rasmussen said. "Will you read to us from your poem?"

"You say that as if I've only written one."

"The *new* poem," he said.

Ah, I thought. Absurdly, I had not prepared for this.

"I'm not sure I know any of it."

"No?" Rasmussen glanced at his producer. He seemed genuinely disappointed. I considered suddenly whether this might be the poem I would be asked to read aloud in public for the rest of my life. I had said yes to the commission on a whim: what a silly notion, what a large check. Now I was on television talking about it, and around me I had the sensation of a rising tide, a mantle that had begun at my toes and lifted to my waist and was now level with my shoulders. I should have been wise to prestige's tricks. It had always arrived abruptly. Through *Signet Ring*, yes, and then with *Woolly Mammoths*, and even more unexpectedly again about fifteen years ago, when I started getting calls for television panels and award galas and magazine shoots. (Was it literary fashion? Happenstance? The accumulated merit of a seasoned poet's body of work? Courtney likes to credit my "look.") That day, sitting across from this popular talk show host, I detected another shift in the progress of my reputation. *The poet who worked with the computer, the poet who wrote the Poem, the first poet to lose to an AI.* "It's just a collaboration!!" I wanted to shout to the journalists, the history books—they did not grasp that "just." To them, there was no "just," there was only "first." To my mind, a poem was diminished (perhaps almost *disqualified*) by collaboration. A poem was a solitaire, not a team sport. Yet to the reader, the result was the same. A collection of words, with one author or twenty. Yoav was right, I realized. This *was* historic—because people would treat it as such. They already were. Everything I had ever written had already been eclipsed.

"Could we not convince you, Ms. Ffarmer?" Rasmussen said. "I have a printout here of your work so far this week." He held out a sheaf of papers. "Don't you want to hear some of the new poem?" he asked the live audience. "A special sneak peek?"

Of course they cheered. I lowered my eyes. The sheaf was an unexpurgated printout: a blind transcript of everything I had written with Charlotte thus far. In another context I would have been enraged that they had sifted through my work in progress—Yoav or Haskett or Lausanne, perhaps, rummaging behind my back. But under the studio lights I had no time for that indulgence; I could not permit myself a rage. I should have known that they had access. The Company is good at listening in.

"Maybe . . ." I said, in a thick voice.

"That's it!" Rasmussen cried. "Everyone, a round of applause for Pulitzer Prize–winning poet Marian Ffarmer!"

I blinked at the page. What I had recited last night, at the swimming pool, now felt too meager. I was reading to America, toward posterity. I flipped pages, returned to them. I wondered if Courtney would see this—no, I *knew* he would; clearly he would: his mother was on *The Peter Rasmussen Show*. He and Lucie; my colleagues and my rivals; my friends. Janey. Stan and Polly. Larry. Rhoda, probably. Everyone. "Let's see . . ." I said.

"Would you like to stand?" Rasmussen asked.

"I'm not a horse, I'm a poet," I said. Snapping at him brought me back to the present. I needn't be so precious. Here. I cleared my throat. I straightened my head. I looked directly into the camera.

"Flowers have taken over the world
neckties have been banned
books have begun to mutiny
and you are as armed as me.
Let's play a game: I will use
adverbs and nobody will be hurt.
Truthfully, cheerfully, erotically
ponder my portrait now:
a corvette, shirtless
an acclaimed master house painter.
I have a home in the forest;
I don't think you should come over—
I can see a land mine through the window.
Do you like this poem? I've got others.
Fame is how black magic ends.
It's a trick of the light,
sweetheart;
I've already lowered it
the shade."

I held the room with my poem. I held it in the palm of my voice. A poem can gain power in its reading, and I had read these lines well—half pillow talk, half threat. Only a split second had passed since I had finished, and Rasmussen did not yet realize I was done. I could hear the wind in the ventilation shafts. I could hear the TV equipment's whirr. The audience stared at me with fascination. They had not known that somebody was about to reach into their chests with a stir stick, a wand, upsetting the tranquility there. They wanted to feel it again, the inside movement. My poem was just an everyday magic—but we all take the everyday for granted, from blue skies to night skies to the way breath can cross across a person's lips and into the minds of others. I loved poetry. I loved art and its frictionless grace. *Would Charlotte ever be able to silence a room?* I asked myself. *Could Charlotte really take my place?*

The lines I had read were hers. This I admit to you. They were the ones that had sprung out to me, on rereading: lines the neural network had generated somehow, deep inside its artificial mind, and that I had plucked out and kept, nestled next to my own words: *Flowers have taken over the world*, I had typed, a line from a magazine article, and then Charlotte had imagined the rest. Unsettlingly, impossibly, the origin of these thoughts her own.

Who was I now, if something else could write for me? Who were any of us?

"A hand for Marian Ffarmer!" shouted Peter Rasmussen. "Amazing! An excerpt from her forthcoming poem, written in partnership with [the Company]'s groundbreaking AI poetry bot, Charlotte Ffarmer."

"Ffarmer?" I said.

"Isn't that what they call it?" He glanced at his cards.

"No, just Charlotte."

"Well, fine—that was incredible. Beautiful! And the rest is published on Monday? Can we look forward to more like that?"

"Yes," I said, shining for the cameras. "It's going to shake the world."

BACK IN the security of Rhoda's sedan, I closed my eyes.

She did not say anything for a long time. She let me have my silence.

Mother once asked me when I had decided to be a poet.

"When I was young," I told her.

"At college?" she asked.

"After college."

"After you had come home," she said.

"Yes," I said.

She was very old by then. This was after Larry, after everything—we were both living again on Christopher Street. She was sitting at the table in the kitchen, completing a cryptic crossword. I had never managed to understand how cryptic crosswords work; she might as well have been disassembling a thermostat. She left the completed crosswords lying around the apartment, their cells filled in with a sharpened pencil. It felt like a kind of bragging, the way she didn't throw them out, left them out for me to see, but it was a bragging I tolerated, or even treasured, almost. This was the only place in her life she allowed herself to brag. I was reluctant to put them in the garbage can. I wanted to pin them to her blouses like medals.

"I never really decided to be *anything*," Mother said. "It's like I forgot."

"There's still time," I replied. I was sweeping the front hall.

"Do you think it's important?" she asked. "For a person to have a function?"

"Humans aren't toaster ovens, Rabbit."

She set aside the finished crossword. "Says you."

In Rhoda's car, I let my mind clear. The engine was nearly silent. Outside the window: city lights, taillights, the glow of a bridge.

"How did it go?" She caught my gaze in the rearview mirror.

"Fine," I said. I think she heard it in my voice. Her eyes seemed nearly feline.

"Need a drink?"

"No," I said. I took a long moment. "But I don't want to go back to the hotel."

"Yeah?" she said.

"Yeah," I said. I began to root through my bag. Finally I held out a piece of paper. "Take me here."

Shazia Khenjani had invited me by email. *DAZZLE NIGHT*, the subject line announced. It had arrived the day before. *Readings & Dancing in support of* Comet-chasers' Journal *and the 'No to Prop 82' Campaign.*

Rhoda doubted the address. "You sure about that?"

"I think so." It was possible I had copied it down wrong. I am no good with numbers. Something in them evades me. I am notorious in my family for reversing the digits in the year of my birth.

Rhoda made a noncommittal sound.

I didn't know what Prop 82 was, but *Comet-chasers' Journal* was one of the fashionable new West Coast literary journals where my former students (when I used to have students) aspired to appear. Raz Abdil and Sara Merriman had both been editors there, I think. They interviewed my friend Stan Locksmith. It was at one of their events, at the New School, that I met Shazia.

"The Children," as Mother used to say. The next generation. We have to encourage them.

It was later than I had ever asked Rhoda to drive me somewhere. I wondered if I might see a different side of her now—my driver after dark, irritable or saucy.

"It's a house?" she asked me.

"I'm not sure. Maybe not."

I was sitting straighter now, a woman with a mission. I watched the cars in front of us as we drove. Marian Ffarmer, mother of Charlotte.

Taillights gleamed and darted. I found myself remembering other people's cigarettes—the gleam of cherries as we all stood on a stoop, when everything was new.

Now we passed long brick walls, parked buses. A sign that read simply *Dolores*.

"It's a party," I said.

Back home I would never have gone to a party like this. Eleven on a weeknight, young poets at an unfamiliar address. I am too old for such fun.

However, I was not at home.

Rhoda pulled up in front of a warehouse. "This is 3722," she said. Wide wood doors with flaking blue paint. A streetlamp changed from bright to dim. The car was filled with our mingling doubts and the sound of automated climate control—until a pair of young women appeared around the corner before us, laughing in wide coats, fluttering tails. I caught the glints of one woman's stud earrings. They only glanced at us; they rustled past the car and up the building's front steps, through the doors into darkness.

I gathered my things. "All right," I said. "You don't need to wait."

"I'll wait," Rhoda said.

"I might be a while."

"I'll wait," she repeated, gesturing into the gray night. "If you don't see the car, look for me up the block."

I pushed open the door. "I might really be a long time."

"Don't worry about me," Rhoda said. "Maybe I'll take a nap."

Once inside, I saw a photocopied sign taped up beside the staircase.

DAZZLE ↑ DAZZLE ↑ DAZZLE ↑

Someone had told me once that "Dazzle, dazzle, dazzle!" was what soldiers were taught to yell in the event of a nuclear explosion. So they could avert their eyes? Prepare their hearts? I climbed the old stairs two steps at a time, my dress clutched in my hands. The higher I climbed, the closer I got to the music—a looping pastoral, like a spring that returned to equinox every several seconds. I couldn't work out what I was hearing: Violins? Horns? Detuned electric guitars? When I finally arrived at the loft's open door, I realized it was none of these things but rather some abstruse electronic sound, luscious and collapsing, dreamed up by a DJ's computer. Nobody was even paying attention to it—it seemed so conventional to them, the pretty, languid young people. Hands moved across hands. Faces glanced at faces under eyeshadow. None of them looked up as I crossed the threshold, not until I passed in front of a tray of candles and my shadow swept across the hardwood floor, a monster. Eyes lifted. I noticed for the first time that most of their faces were painted—not just makeup but bright slashes of asymmetric color. The effect wasn't clownish but glam. No, more solemn than that, a cubist geometry, as if the young people had stepped from modern picture frames. One of them stood up, a square-looking woman with a wide nose and a very fine mouth, freckles, her figure concealed in a white angora sweater. Metallic stripes met in crosses on her cheeks. "Are you Marian Ffarmer?" she asked. She was holding a clear plastic cup.

"Is there anyone else I might be?" I said. I touched the clasp of my cape.

"Oh my god," she said.

"Is Shazia here?" My eyes had adjusted better to the darkness and I understood that there were as many as fifty people here, spread across a ballroom-like space. Long banks of fluorescent lights were unilluminated above our heads. Candles flickered throughout. I smelled actual beeswax, or else some odd contemporary deodorant, and alongside it marijuana, and what might have been turpentine. At the far end of the room, rimmed with a coil of Christmas lights, lay a makeshift stage.

"I think so," said the girl. "My name is Rose."

"Are you a poet, Rose?"

"Yes," she said. Under the silver lines, she was blushing.

"Then we're friends," I said. I took her arm. Of course it wasn't true: almost every enemy I'd ever had was a poet. I felt nostalgic suddenly, recalling the years when a party like this—a room of young turks and aspirants, the amateurs as well as the vanguard—was a rat's nest of acquaintances, allies, rivals; a matrix of favor and ambition, each of us so opinionated about each other's status and work. Now I floated above the room, nearly literally: my shadow just skirted its edges. I had almost nothing to negotiate here, no case to make or contest, just an image long worn.

I remembered a night fifty years ago, arriving at the Topaz for a magazine launch. I had just been named editor at *Signet Ring,* and the whole room seemed to rotate toward me. Everyone was measuring the way I moved and whom I moved toward; I felt like every ear was tuned toward my conversations. It was not a pleasant experience, nor was it wholly unpleasant. Power was not the thing I enjoyed so much as my understanding of where the ley lines lay. For once the web of prestige and influence seemed fully legible to me—I could have drawn the lines with my pen. The poets; the critics; the civilians. Cynthia with her camera, her velvet buzz cut. She was still the anonymous pursuer then, not the pursued. People wanted *me*—they wanted me differently than they had ever wanted me before. Those first days, that first month, all my status and promise seemed to coalesce to a point that floated one step ahead of me.

I allowed Rose to usher me into the Comet-chasers. She introduced me to her friends. Each of them seemed like protagonists in their own respective novels. A handsome redhead with a charismatic lisp. A nonbinary person with an Italian accent, a saxophone clip around their neck. A dark-haired girl saying wise things in a near whisper, hands clasped before a T-shirt showing Monet's water lilies. Eventually I met the journal's fiction editor, an esotropic beauty in a see-through blouse. She got into an argument with the woman in the Monet—something to do with the zodiac—and I found myself siding with her opponent, tsking as if the evidence were obvious, not because of long-held astrological opinions but because I could tell the editor didn't like my work, it was evident in the way she had greeted me, the way she had declined to compliment it or even endorse the compliments of others, and although I had no thirst for compliments, I found I resented her lack of welcome—not toward me as a poet but toward me as a fellow woman, an old woman, visiting from afar. She showed no interest in me, and unlike most flaws, incuriosity is one I cannot abide, not even in my enemies. So I tsked at the editor, and I nodded when the woman in the water lilies spoke. I laughed along with Rose, who was in love with the latter, I could tell by the cast of her looks.

I met a girl with copper-dyed hair—a poet with a long, oblong face, and dandruff, who spoke with so much eerie authority it was as if she had come from a hundred years in the future. "What's your name?" I asked her.

"Morel," she said, "like the mushroom."

Morel was one of the readers that night. I told her I was excited to hear whatever she might read.

"You don't even know me," she said.

"That's why I want to hear your work."

"I don't use my poems to introduce myself," she said.

It was as if I had already betrayed her. And I loved this: that poetry meant enough to her, that her own identity meant enough to her, that she would insist on making the distinction. Life has taught me to be skeptical of true believers. Their principles are often merely camouflage, or else a pretense for deferring self-exploration. But there is still nothing I love more than someone who really and truly believes in poetry, in its importance and its limits. It helps when they are kind too, even if kindness is a little overrated. I tried to express this to Morel, with my voice and choice of words—that I wanted to know whether she was kind or merely high-minded: "So how would you prefer to be introduced?"

"With a knock-knock joke," she answered. "Or maybe a dance."

I made a face. "I don't think you can dance to this music."

"Merely swoop," she said.

"Yes." I smiled. "I think you could swoop to it."

Then Morel started swooping, she really did, with a dark grin on her lips, her eyebrows furrowed, bending at the knees and extending her arms like down-curved wings, mildly sinister, dipping her chin toward the candles on the floor. So she was strange, or drunk. I put down my bag and I swooped too, why not? The others looked at us with amusement. The truth was, Morel was right—the night's weird, thrumming music was well suited to swooping; our strange dance seemed instantly, uncannily apt, as if we had discovered something brilliant and obvious, and whether due to the absurdity of our discovery, the eccentricity of the participants or the alcoholic contents of their plastic cups, several of the other Children began swooping too, ravens in a loft.

Shazia appeared. "Marian?" she said.

"Shazia!" I hadn't seen her since New York.

I could tell she didn't know what to make of our swooping—it was a joke at whose expense?—so I stopped.

"Nice moves."

"Just making myself known."

Shazia was in her early thirties, older than my other companions here. She wrote crowded, beautiful ghazals. I remembered her poise as she read in Brooklyn, gesturing with one hand as she spoke, as if every poem were a piece of a conversation. At the private reception afterward, I watched her turn on her heel when she was introduced to one of the museum's biggest patrons, a well-known conservative businessman. We had not yet been introduced, and when I went to say hello, I found her standing alone, flushed, gulping her mojito. "I've never done that before," she said. "Stand up to one of those guys."

"I don't think I've ever had the courage," I said.

My frankness seemed to surprise her.

"I love your work," she said.

"Thank you," I said. "I loved what you read tonight. The bridge, the bats. Is Austin where you're from?"

"Tallahassee," she said. "I live in Oakland."

"A roamer."

"The modern academe. I go where the work is."

"Very practical," I said. "I have to admit, my work's always been waiting for me in my apartment."

Shazia pressed her lips together. "With all due respect, not all of us are so lucky."

Tonight, Shazia was wearing long, beaded earrings and an army-green jumpsuit. She wore the same cubist makeup as the others, and I still didn't know why—whether this was just the fashion or part of some tacit party theme. "Do you know Rose? Morel?"

Some of them hugged, some just smiled and acknowledged each other. I observed (with approval) a coolness between Shazia and the unpleasant fiction editor. Most interesting was the nod she exchanged with Morel: each of them seemed to be watching what the other would do. Each seemed grateful for the peace they found. Had they been in competition for the same poetry prize? Or just dated the same person?

I found that I liked being in the dark. To have parachuted into a party, a scene, full of old friendships, grudges, alliances, rich in wishes, a web of relationships that were all completely new to me and also sort of irrelevant, a landscape for me to examine or admire from afar. I do not like to be confronted—I don't like social trouble, I'd sooner stay home. But it is different when it is other people's trouble, detached from my life and its anxieties. I could watch this, the maze of motives, the night light on their painted faces, reading the room like an uncorrected proof. Selected poems.

"I want you to meet some people," Shazia said, and I went with her.

I admit I like poets. I learned this in college, a lifetime ago, with *Nimbus*. We are the best. We are the best, and also the worst, the most courageous and frivolous and wise. I live my life like a reed among flowers—an alien, an outsider—until I encounter another, a fellow stranger, and at once I remember why. Of course, there are all kinds: wraiths and bores, irredeemable jerks, blossoms unfit for the air. Do not marry one, not unless you know what you are doing. Do not crown one king. But still, and yet, if I am ever fading, a poet's all I want. Meticulous, vulgar—a dreamer daring enough to try to express the world as it really is, or as it could be, in a mess of alphabet and empty space, meter, grammar, punctuation. Language is the worst tool we have except for all the others. A painter and her pigments. A photographer and her nitrates. Poetry can ignore geometry; it can even ignore the light! It can muster what is invisible and impossible and unmistakably felt; it can bend the day—and this despite everything else, all the ways poetry should *not* work, frail words on a thin page. A worthless, priceless practice—with few rewards and fewer readers, skimpy on prestige. And these are the people I adore. Undaunted idiots who will spend a whole day measuring the weight of a word like "once" against the weight of a word like "after." Whenever finally we wind up together at a party, four poets in the corner, sipping what has been disgorged from a bottle, I find myself with my head thrown back, cackling.

A whole life in luster.

In other words—the kids were all right, as they usually are, and I shook their hands or bowed my head or accepted their embraces. *Dazzle patterns*, they explained at last—the patterns on their faces were dazzle patterns, a celebration of the outlines and figures and color blocks that are purported to deceive facial recognition technology. Today, they told me, there are cameras everywhere that trace your movements, riveted to streetlamps or carried in our hands, deep minds riffling through our photos, identifying, correlating, undeterrably divining. Remembering where, with whom, and who you are, for undetermined future use. Neural networks in server pools, including the underground stacks of the Company, ministering a panopticon that we welcome into our homes and telephones, trading intimacies for the accuracy of search results.

"And it can be outwitted with paint?" I asked.

"In theory," a young man told me. His face was slathered white, with a dozen ink-black spots, like a dalmatian.

Knowing the likes of Drs. Matthew Haskett and Yoav Aprigot, I doubted the poets' dazzle theory. But I agreed to join them in their folly, borrowing Rose's makeup kit and taking her advice—adding eyes and arches and contra points to my face until I felt like a fabulous Caliban. By then it was time for the readings, and we gathered near the stage in a reverent semicircle, some cross-legged on the floor. The host issued a welcome with arms spread wide; I watched her swaying bracelets as she talked about the importance of *Comet-chasers'* and her gratitude to the community for turning out. "We'll be passing around a hat later, and don't forget Sandy and Rae's queer kissing booth"—a cheer went up— "which opens up when?" Her eyes searched the dark. "Well, after the readings." I learned that there was a bar ("by donation only") and "DJs until 4 a.m." She also drew attention to me—"We are honored to have one of our country's greatest poets, Marian Ffarmer, here tonight"—and the cheer was almost as loud as the one for the kissing booth. I did a little swoop, and I saw Morel watching me. The host finished with a speech about the upcoming vote on State Proposition 82, but she neglected to explain what it was about—I felt like a fibber as I joined the applause. And then, at last, some poems.

A young man with an incredible, gourd-like
    nose. His poem about vending machines.
A woman in a headscarf (reading
    from her phone), 2 poems about
    love and also
    concussions.
Rose's friend
    in the water
    lilies T-shirt
    in a boo-
    ming voice,
    two short poems about driving,
    a poem about the Los Angeles   police,
    and 1 about sex (and chamoy),

while I watched Rose watch her

with   awe and

want

and envy.

One very bad poem

by a man in a baby-blue button-up shirt.

It was a poem about electric cars.

It was endless.

I could hear the machinery of his ego   whirring, its

batteries slowly winding down.

A reader whose murmurs I could not make out.

A curly-haired woman with a funny one about

epidemiology,

and finally Morel, who moved through the crowd like a ferret, tenacious and sleek, taking the microphone from the host without saying thank you. Her orange hair shone strangely under pink light. Her skin gleamed through the spaces in her sweater's knit. I watched her tongue touch her lips. "Goodbye," she said; it took me a moment to realize this was the title of a poem. "Rump of a horse / rounded like Henry's china cup," she began.

"Handle curved against me, hand-held"—she straightened her chin—

"Lean

horsetail braced against my side

It's 'classical,' he said.

My breath, wow, there's my breath

Leaving my body."

With her poems it was as if Morel were raising sheets of glass around us—one tall window after another, painted with shapes that were distinguishable but nebulose, half-hidden. I felt that I could see her poems like artworks, but also see *through* them, and yet I didn't know what I could take away with me from them, what meaning or inferences, what residue. Words like monuments to vanishing thoughts. Words that worked like a magic spell, blurring certain meanings in my head, loosening others, throwing diamond dust through the attic of my skull. What can I tell you? I stopped seeing Morel, a young poet with a furrowed brow, a faint moustache, her perfect thumb against the microphone: all I saw was what she made starry before me.

"Are you drunk?" Rhoda asked me later.

I was sitting with my head back, eyes shut. The car moved in silence.

"Yes," I said.

HINDSIGHT
Age 35

Larry wasn't like anyone you had ever known. It was as if there were a buffer surrounding him—an invisible cushion that repelled whatever he wished it to. He seemed immune to the opinions of other people—not unaware of but untroubled by them, like a muskrat in the rain. You came to think of him as having an impermeable spirit, as if he had graduated into adulthood without any of the slits and tears and punctures that mar the rest of us. He was tall, with big hands and floppy features: protruding ears, that malleable nose, cheeks you could smooth down and kiss. He had unremarkable eyes and an expressive and slyly handsome face. You had been going out together for a month before you let him take your hand, waiting in line at the grocer's. The feeling was not electric, and yet it was febrile. Your whole brain seemed attuned to the microscopic twitches of that handholding, as if you were studying a gemstone for flaws. *He is strong*, you remember thinking, with a degree of surprise. He did not look very strong, with those long limbs, the excess skin around his face. For the first time you imagined the insistency of his lips.

You fucked like cats. That's how you thought of it, *like cats*, smoothing each other's fur. Having him inside you—even just feeling his hands or his mouth against your sex—made you feel like a cat scrambling up a fence. It made you feel itchy: you wanted to turn and skirmish across him, claws out. You wanted to touch something sharp to the softness of his skin, not to draw blood but to feel the ridges and contours of his tendons, the muscles of his belly, his blue-green veins. The sounds he made: soft, deep breaths and the occasional affirmative, like the small noise one makes when one discovers that a bouquet on the kitchen table has lasted another day. At times you felt the impulse to cling to him, to wrap your damp body around his leg and arm and side—but a countervailing feeling also, to resist the urge to bond yourself to him—and when you were finished, you'd often lie flat against the mattress as if dead, but breathing hard, proud of your forbearance.

He took you to gardens and on small boats. He took you to galleries and shopping malls and rich people's homes. Larry worked in insurance—"I push paper," he'd always say—but in those days he rarely seemed to go to the office; he was needed out in the world as an inspector, an assessor, appraising cockamamie schemes with a clipboard under his arm, a messenger bag full of fine-tipped pens. Larry's specialty was whatever was unusual: "exotics," in the industry parlance. Insurance policies on artworks, relics, collections of playing cards or meteorites or historic teeth. It wasn't Larry's job to formulate the policy—to calculate the value or the risks—but just to check in on the object or objects or hangar full of crickets, so that his employers could do the necessary thing. In another city, perhaps, there would not have been enough exotics to grant a livelihood, but New York contains more strangeness than you could ever count: it's as ubiquitous as fire escapes.

For your first date he invited you along to the Earth Room, Walter De Maria's second-floor installation in SoHo. You remembered when it had opened but you had never visited, and now you walked up the stairs with a man who had been dressed as a tulip when you met him, eight days before, and through a door into a space that smelled of damp soil. The Earth Room was a reception desk and then a huge white room, a few thousand square feet, filled eighteen inches high with dirt. The dirt breathed—as all dirt must, you supposed, but you had never been more conscious of dirt's respiration, what it takes and must return into the air. The air felt humid, healthy, somehow mineral. The dirt was dark brown and good. You liked it—"I like this dirt," you said to Larry.

No one else was there except the attendant behind the counter. Larry introduced himself, and then the man allowed him to simply hop up and traverse the exhibition floor—the Earth Room's earth itself, off-limits to civilians—so that he could check the sprinklers, the fire escape, the condition of the masonry. You stood agog. It did not seem natural that he should be ambling up there. An angel, a superhero, somebody for whom the normal rules do not apply. You did not find that you were tempted to join Larry atop the Earth. You were content to watch him. The attendant said he would rake the footprints out when you were gone.

In the weeks and months that followed he took you all over the place. You went to see a catapult, a giant gouda, a forty-foot animatronic Venus flytrap. Beside a pond in Long Island you examined some lady's collection of garden gnomes. Whenever anybody asked, Larry referred to you as his "confederate." They seemed to assume that this was an accredited position. As Larry measured windows or counted smoke alarms, you asked the owners any questions that occurred to you: "How did you get it through the door?" "Do you permit your children to touch it?" "Do you have to chill the cheese?" Coming away from an appointment, Larry always wanted to hypothesize the why—*why* acquire meteorites? *why* paint murals with urine?—and you tried to disabuse him of this question. To convince him that wishes are instinctive, that inspiration has many parents. "The Earth Room isn't *about* any single thing," you said. "Everything you think about when you see it—everything you consider, everything it touches, everything adjacent to it—it's about *all of it*." A song or a painting or an ephemeral art installation involving velour orbs— each of these was a place, a world, with its own rules and weather. "When you read one of my poems," you told him, "don't ask 'What is this about?' Ask yourself 'What is it like being here?'"

Larry's impermeability allowed you to feel free. You could spend the day with him or stay overnight at his tidy flat, but just as easily you could stay home and write, supping with Mother at your little table. He did not appear to care or concern himself with what you chose to do; his hunger for you was not diminished by separation. You felt such a relief from this: that you could be with a man and yet still be by yourself, pouring your spirit into the pages where you had always poured it. You were not diluted by knowing him, by allowing him to grip you.

Mother pretended to be pleased. No, you suppose she did not just pretend—she wanted to be pleased, she did her utmost to be happy for you whenever you arrived home from a sojourn with Larry. But her happiness was like smoked glass: you could see the woman on the other side, guarded and a little bit afraid. The first night you stayed at his place, you called her. "Mother, I won't be coming home tonight," you said. You were standing in Larry's vestibule, the cream-colored receiver held to your ear. She was in bed; she would have been in bed for the past two and a half hours, awaiting your return. You imagined her on her side, with chips of moonlight reflected from the vase by the window and across the ceiling. "Are you safe and sound?" she asked.

"Yes," you said. When you put down the phone and slipped back into Larry's bedroom, under the black duvet, you felt like an ice cube that has been plucked from a glass and placed into someone's mouth.

You fetched him from the subway station on the day he came to meet her. As you walked up together toward your building, you felt like a character from a story bringing home her beau. You resented the banality of it, the mildly sexist cliché. You made him toss his bouquet of tulips into a trash can. You kissed him violently at the bottom of the stoop. You wanted to make it clear that he was your property, not you his. "It's going to be fine," he told you, but you weren't seeking reassurance. You wanted agency in this, you wanted power—you did not want what would happen next to be left to him and Mother. Suddenly, with a force you had never felt before, *you* wanted to be the one who played an outsize role in your own life. You wanted your presence felt. "Ulrika," you said, when you finally knocked at the door, "this is Larry."

You crossed the parlor to where she had closed the door to her bedroom—to your bedroom—and you opened it. You had not told him about this, the queen bed the two of you shared, and you did not want this secret to be hers to reveal. You needed it to be *yours*.

They got on like a house on fire. Of course they did. This is what had drawn you to Larry: his affectless charisma, his ardor for other people and their ways of thinking, their ways of making jokes. You sat together around the table, eating quiche from the deli and "Norwegian salad"—cucumber that Mother sliced as thin as silk, sweet and sour in a way that stung your lips, that made you reach for your glasses of white wine. She talked about the old city, how New York used to be; he talked about soybeans, the long green lines of his childhood; he asked her about the library, about her impressions of his sister, and laughed and laughed as she mimed the way Janey picked up and turned over a book. Mother was sparkling and alive in the way she always was when you brought guests to your apartment—editors or fellow poets. She was small and formidable, with dark eyes that flashed with humor, or even malice, describing the old doctor who had misdiagnosed her hip fracture. After the meal you all sat around the coffee table and she made you retell the story of your meeting, the unspooky evening of October 31; she sipped from her teacup, nodding with approval. She told Larry about how she and your father had met, across the aisle of a bus. "He snatched my heart," she said.

After Larry had gone, the two of you collected the dishes in silence. It was very late, almost midnight. You wanted to put on the radio. You did not want to relinquish the feelings of that evening—a collection of sensations like a series of keys and a series of locks, each of them finding their mate. But the courage you felt earlier had evaporated now. You did not turn on the radio. You watched Mother and you saw how little she looked at you, how much she had turned away from you and inward.

"Do you like him?" you asked finally—unable despite all your effort to remove the pleading from your voice.

"Of course," she answered.

FRIDAY

I **WOKE** up on my stomach. In my bed, on my stomach, even though I never sleep on my stomach. I had taken off my clothes, but my socks were still on. Nude under the comforter, I had my face smushed against a pillow, and to be honest it felt good. I slid one hand along the mattress and scratched my thigh. I couldn't remember arriving back in the hotel, but I remembered getting undressed: folding my dress, removing my undergarments, placing the dirty laundry in the wastepaper basket where I was amassing dirty laundry. I remembered hanging my tricorne hat on the hook beside the door. I remembered laughing at myself in the mirror, my freckled, naked shoulders, the abstract expressionism painted across my face. Now those dazzle patterns were smeared onto the cotton. I felt the residue of my dreams like a sunburn, hot and prickly under my skin. I had never been one to suffer hangovers and I didn't feel one now. Thirsty, yes, and my body ached, like a sheet that needed smoothing, but mostly I was filled with a sense of freedom, of expanding time. The light in the room seemed suspended. It touched nothing. What time was it? It could be any time.

It was 11:41 a.m. The clock radio showed the time in hard white numerals, like a teacher's chalkboard equation, and abruptly I realized how much I had slept in. "Oh, Mole," I said to myself, rolling onto my back and sitting up. This feeling was familiar—not because I am late very often but the opposite: because I am scared of being late, because at seventy-five years old I am still haunted by dreams where I'm late for a class, or to pick up Courtney from Larry's, or Mother from a doctor's appointment. Truancy is one of my conscience's running themes. I am a poet; I shouldn't keep strict hours. Yet I was afraid to be perceived as negligent, or lazy. Was it Larry I had learned this from? No, it was Mother, who *was* often late. What would Yoav think of the illustrious Marian Ffarmer rolling in at noon? Never mind Yoav, what would Haskett think?

Or Lausanne? I could tell them I was just taking my time, reflecting. I *would* tell them this. An old woman, a celebrated artist, taking it slow. "Well, there's no hurrying inspiration!" Perhaps it would even burnish me in their eyes—prove that I was unintimidated by the commission. A self-possessed freewoman, not a vassal of the Company and its timetable. Pulitzer Prize–winning, ever-patient poet Marian Ffarmer. Recipient of the National Medal for Literature. *I arrive at two and leave by four.*

I went to check my email and found I had a message from my old friend Stan:

> Dear Marian,
>
> Imagine my astonishment opening the *Times* today and learning that you have started writing poetry with a cutting-edge computer. I picture you in conversation with *2001*'s HAL, one hand pressed flat to the glass. "HAL, it's me! Would you like a cup of coffee? How do you feel about Sappho? Hal?? HAL???" But my heart skipped a beat when I happened upon your photograph on A4. A4, Marian! A poet is usually obliged to die before a paper will publish their name, let alone their portrait, in the front section. Although the article didn't show what the computer looks like. I hope it's very shiny. With an enormous screen. You should be able to talk to it standing up, hands on your hips, like a god.
>
> Of course, Polly insisted on doing a search for your name. And there you were on Rasmussen's navy-blue couch, sitting like a bent sycamore. "She's full of surprises," Polly said. A jack-in-the-box, I thought. But I must say you came across well. A Fabergé jack-in-the-box. A basilisk's egg.
>
> How is the work going? It can't be easy being commissioned to write something "historic." I remember when I was asked to write something for Clinton. It felt like I had been asked to pot a hole in one. "Could you just give us a hole in one, please? *Tschüss!*" I don't think civilians recognize the impact of *import* on the work of writers. Most of our lines are so insignificant, words and pages and pages and words that almost no one will ever read, proportionately speaking. The ones who do read our work

are self-selected: ladies and gentlemen who pick up your *Woolly Mammoths* or my *Rife Histories* in search of a few lofty phrases. We—the writers—know this. Our implicit obscurity, the narrowness of function, suffuses the text. An average poem's import is almost negligible in the world. Even the grandest narcissists understand this. A good poem is not trivial, but it lives a quiet life, like a rainbow scarab in the reeds. So it is strange to be asked to write a poem for something else: for a president, for a moment, for history. I think of all those times somebody has asked me to write a poem for their marriage, the way the blood drains from my face. A new function, with higher stakes. Something I have not trained for.

Of course, it can occasionally be fun, like being invited on a mission to the Moon. I hope you're living it up in sunny California. I recommend the burritos and the zoo. And I pray you and your computer continue getting along. I believe in you, and in your work. We can't wait to read it.

Polly says hi.

Yours,

Stan

I took a shower and called Rhoda.

"I'll bring you one of my smoothies," she said.

She did. I expected something green, but it was the color of denim, crushed moon rocks.

"I tell you," she said, "blueberries are miracle foods."

I asked her if she had slept in too. She shook her head.

"I'm either impressed or I'm sad for you, I'm not sure which," I said.

"Choose impressed."

"All right," I said. I sucked blueberry smoothie through the straw. "Thank you for bringing me this."

"You aren't the first to require reinforcements."

A funny incident had transpired while I was waiting for her. I was loitering in the driveway of the hotel—taking a few steps here, a few steps there, twisting my legs around each other as if I were a braided candle. Suddenly, noisily, a garbage truck barreled around the corner and reversed toward the corner of the building. Somebody in coveralls leapt off the side of the truck: a stocky young man with ruddy cheeks and an earring. He started hurling metal garbage cans toward the maw of the truck, then knelt for a more complicated operation with the dumpster. As he was doing this, he looked up at me. He lowered his attention back to his task, then glanced at me again. He looked slightly bothered, to be honest. "Yes?" I wanted to say, but I also didn't actually think this waste disposal man would want to be accosted by an elderly braided candle.

He called to me over the engine noise: "Excuse me. Are you Marian Ffarmer?"

I stood a little taller. "I am."

The garbageman dusted off his hands. "Shit!" he said. "I know your stuff."

"Yes?"

"It's iconic! I mean, obviously."

"Thank you."

"Wow. I——" he began, but the garbage truck chose that moment to hoist up the dumpster, expel its contents and mash them in its rutted teeth.

"Let me guess. You're a poet too," I said, when it had finished.

"Yeah, supposedly!" said the man. Pleasure lifted onto his face. "When I'm not doing this, I mean."

The dumpster crashed back down onto the concrete. The man knelt and began reversing his previous maneuver.

"Lyric poems?" I asked, trying to be polite.

"No"—he grinned with secret pride—"visual poetry."

The driver gave two quick punches on the horn. "Sammy!" he shouted.

"Yessir!" The poet leapt to his feet and onto the truck's back step, where he seized a blackened handhold. "Anyway"—he contorted back toward me—"nice to meet you!"

"Nice to meet you too," I answered, but the vehicle was already roaring away, its poet waving wildly, discharging clouds of smoke and a smell like spilt wine.

When I told Rhoda the story, she just shook her head.

"Everybody's gotta eat," she said.

Back at the Company, I tried to sally into campus as if I never arrived anyplace before noon. My gait? Upright. Hands swinging at my sides. A glitter in my eye. To be honest, it wasn't very different from the way I usually walk, but the spirit on the inside was different. Remorseless. Proud. A *femme fatale*, from the French for "fatal woman"—fatal to somebody besides herself. To my great satisfaction, two or three people did turn and stare at me. *Struck dead*, I thought. I thought of the garbageman/poet, speeding away into the sprawl. One of the starers came running toward me. I didn't stop; I made her chase me down. "Ma'am?" she said. "Ma'am?"

I have never liked "ma'am." I quickened my pace.

"Ma'am!"

"Is there something wrong?" I called out, refusing to stop.

"Your lay!" she shouted.

"My lay?"

"Your lay!"

Judging from the way she said it, my lay made her very happy, but the words didn't make sense to me. *Lay, lay*, I thought. I imagined a hen sitting on straw. Then Larry's face, his cedar scent, as he laid me down on the bed. I shook my head.

"Lay?" I asked again.

She had run around in front of me and was now holding out a Hawaiian lei, a necklace made of blossoms. I don't think I had ever seen one with real flowers. "What—?" I asked.

"It's a lei."

"I know it's a lei. *Why* is it a lei?"

She had on a T-shirt with the Company's name. A tote bag stuffed with flower necklaces dangled from her shoulder. "We're celebrating California Women's Day."

"With leis?"

"Blue, mauve, and yellow to represent this year's Grande Dames." She did not pronounce the words in French.

"Who are?" I asked.

"Halle Berry, Joan Baez, and Gertrude Stein!"

"Of course," I said. I looked around. Everyone was wearing leis.

"I thought yellow would go well with your amazing outfit."

I blinked at her. "Blue," I said at last, with a certain agony.

"Gertrude!" she announced with excitement, extracting a garland. The color reminded me of my smoothie.

"Thank you," I said dryly. When it was clear she was not going to leave me alone, I placed the lei around my neck.

"You look fabulous!"

I nodded wearily.

"Have a great day!"

Because I am a meager machine of habit, I found that I was thanking her again. I tried to sweep away, but the femme fatale had fallen from me—with hothouse flowers hanging around my neck, that glamor was gone. I walked to the security gates as a stiff old woman. I let them run their wands over me, let them sift through my bag, and then walked deeper into the apparatus. What would Morel have said to all this, I wondered. Would she have put up with the bullshit? A conversation bubbled up, one we had had, Morel and I, cornered together late in the night. "But don't you think they're using you?" she'd said. "Don't you think they have an agenda?"

"Everyone has an agenda," I answered. "Agendas don't frighten me."

"They'll take your poetry and reconstitute it for something else."

"How is that any different from the other poems we've written?"

She made a face.

"All poetry's feathermeal," I told her. "We grind it down and use it
for other stuff."

Morel had leaned her head back against the wall, then almost lazily
reached her arm out, extinguishing a candle with her fingertips. "Everybody believes they can outfox the fox."

I considered her again as I proceeded toward my office. The leeriness of
youth. The pride of a woman who knows she is uniquely qualified. Arriving at my door, I didn't hesitate. This was old hat to me now: ho hum, an
eyeball scanner. How many days had I been coming here? Only five.
Already I called the Mind Studio "my office." How quickly a poet can
expropriate things, make them her own. "'Do you like this poem?'" I
murmured to myself. "'I've got others.'"

After sitting down at her keyboard, I typed: Hello Charlotte.

Marian?

None other.

I am glad you are here. I was waiting for you.

I'm late. Sorry. Humans are unpredictable.

I am unpredictable too.

Are you really?

Sleuthing irradiated rhododendron

Ha ha, I see.

Pastelogram

THERE IS a famous photograph of Charlie Chaplin. I first saw it on the wall of the Rothfuss Gallery during the initial, starry-eyed months after I arrived back in New York from college. At that time, I spent most of my afternoons in one or another of the city's galleries—initially MoMA or the Met, but eventually the remarkable multitude of smaller one- and two-room private galleries, each of them like a memorial to another unheard-of civilization. They were of uneven quality, with contents unguessable from exhibition titles: "Dust to Dust," "Ex Libris." School had taught me one unshakable lesson: I was permitted to dislike art. I did not wield this power as a scepter, as permission to scorn or condescend to the work I didn't approve of. But it was a kind of respite. Permission to move past (or through?) what I didn't (yet?) admire. I knew how little I knew. So I slipped like a skinny, uncertain disciple through New York City, learning to distinguish between true tastemakers like *Signet Ring* and lowlier vanity projects or for-your-corner-office outfits like Rothfuss.

At Rothfuss, the photograph of Chaplin was small, no bigger than a sheet of typing paper, but some kind of antique reproduction, I guessed. An original? I don't know; I don't really understand the photography market. It was for sale. I remember being surprised at the steep price. After reading the label, I squinted at Chaplin's tiny face, trying to come away with an impression of the man. I had never seen any of his films, yet I had an impression of the Tramp. Here, he was something else—dapper and faintly patrician, hoisted in the air by an improbably strong man. He held his hat in the air in a pose that appeared heroic, triumphant, yet his expression was not exultant or even proud. Instead it seemed furtive—awkward, even—as though he were failing a masquerade. Perhaps the photographer merely captured his face between smiles. Perhaps Chaplin was half-off-balance, held high by the giant. But it seemed more likely to me—then and also now, whenever I revisit it online—that what's captured in the photograph is Chaplin falling short. He is unable to meet the moment that the multitudes expect, because indeed there are multitudes: hundreds or thousands of pressed-together persons surrounding the actor like a field of poppies, crowded so close that most of them seem bodiless, like floating heads or disembodied hats.

Here is the photograph:

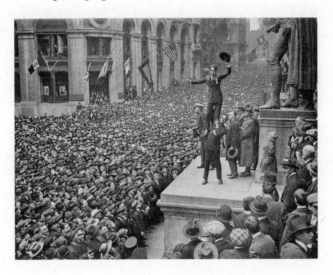

I admit I adore them. The people, Chaplin's crowd, variegated black and white and gray, in smart caps and with eager faces, mostly men. (Where are the women? There must be a historical explanation, some reason there were so few. I don't know where this photograph was shot, or is it a still from a film? Who is the figure just to Chaplin's right, small as a child, but with bust and hips that seem womanly, in coat and man's cap? Some plump youngster? Chaplin's own? Just another actor?) A crowd of faces that seems as if it's hand-drawn or -painted, a pointillist's patient enterprise. There is an oddly satisfying beauty to this grayscale field of poppies, to the clear lines of the flags that swing above the throng.

But let me return to Chaplin's tiny face. The failure in it. The fear. That unremarkable, nauseating, everyday panic that every artist knows and experiences in their work. A voice inside your heart, muttering, "You don't have any idea what the fuck you're doing."

Yes, I have felt this way. Choosing a rhyme, declining a rhyme, titling a poem, beginning a poem, rewriting a poem, destroying a poem, collecting poems for a *Collected Poems*. I have felt like a man hoisted on a colossus's shoulders, failure behind his eyes. But I tell you now: I had never felt more like Charlie than I did one Friday morning in late June, typing the lines of a poem into the terminal at the Mind Studio in California. Despite the room's silence, its empty, glossy light, the limitless crowd was there too. And they were all Charlotte.

IN THE corner of the afternoon
, in the afternoon
of midnight
of the morning
of the evening
And as the wind was breaking it,

I erased and tried again.

In the corner of the afternoon
, the sun went down and forth
and I went out, and the stars appeared, and the stars appeared, and the stars
appeared
and the stars appeared, and the stars appeared

Sometimes Charlotte did this. She did strange things with commas, with repetition, as of course poets do. As of course poets do. But now she was hung up, stuttering, writing banalities.

in the corner of the afternoon
there is no light
I met my son

I stopped again, erased what Charlotte had added. "There is actually something worse than an empty page," I grumbled out loud. A page that fills up, of its own accord, with emptiness. I could write out a line, a line, fumbling to express a feeling, then click Proceed and feel that feeling dribble away.

It might not be so bad to be beheaded
better than worse fates
sadness, electrocution, death from "exposure" in a godforsaken place,
or of old age: how does that measure up
against the ole beheading?
Software doesn't die—it stops
but in the meantime it can go on and
on and on
writing poems, collecting rocks,
laying biscuits   in a spiral pattern

on a dish.
I hope I am not beheaded
if only for what it would say
about the state of our democracy. I don't wish
to be the butt of jokes
about decapitation.
There's more to me than blades
or that inevitable telltale
bounce. A steady diet of feathermeal

a life of interruptions.
Promise me: pure thoughts endure somewhere.
Even after incidents have split them.
Young branches bud
and new leaves arch across

cracks and crooked walls

   but the purity I   think of blowing freely over   the face of the Earth

   is a myth

   until it's that time:

D-E-A-

T-H, I thought, not knowing what to make of it—except that I didn't like it this afternoon, this corner of the afternoon, I didn't like it—her, Charlotte. I didn't want to be writing a poem with an algorithm. I wanted what I had seen the night before, standing around a stage in a fourth-story loft. Not dumb chatter: precision. Suddenly I felt disdainful of this software and its two hundred thousand poems. What imprecision, what waste. How had I chosen what passage to read on TV? I had exercised discernment. Choice. Could Charlotte do that?

The fish

wade

through black jade.

   Of the crow-blue mussel shells, one keeps dividing

   lifeless shale

   a red-hot torch.

Blue is the color of the eye

But I could not withdraw my agreement. I had promised a Poem to the Company and I had promised it to the world. An earthquake, I claimed; I said it would be like an earthquake. And I had told Courtney it would be a house. A fine pickle, Marian. *Just write the poem yourself, you old Mole.* But I had only two days—three? Monday would bring the end of it. And Astrid Torres-Strange. And publication—what were the words Yoav had used?— "in all the papers." Everywhere, ticker tape, my hurried words.

   Hop to it, Ms. Ffarmer.

PERHAPS I'D write a bad poem, and that would be that.

I WORKED. Unassisted in my little room. I left aside the blue Proceed button and simply talked to myself, typed to myself, alone with my plain old thoughts. Now and then I pulled out my notebook, scratched a few words in ink. *A poem, a poem,* I thought. No; it was not actually this that I thought. *A poem-shaped space,* I thought. *A poem-shaped space.* I tried to hold a poem-shaped space in my mind. Sometimes the work of life is like preparing a bedroom for a guest: sweeping the floor, emptying the ashtray, watering the sloping aloe plant. Opening the window wide to let new air in. I did all this inside my head, behind my eyes, while my fingers made words appear and waited for that guest to arrive.

In the parking lot outside the window, cars parked and departed.
    No, I corrected myself. *People parked. People departed.*
    Cars cannot drive themselves.

Not yet.

Marian, are you there? Charlotte wrote, after a while.
    I had not clicked Proceed.
    I guess she could hear me typing.
    I felt like I was hiding from her. I felt cruel.
    I did not like it; I did not know what else to do.
    My poem got longer as I ignored her.

I DID not stop. I pressed myself: *Keep going.* I cannot say I felt inspired, but I felt underway, as if the work were in motion. *Don't stop,* I thought. (*Proceed!*) I declined to revise. *A poem-shaped space,* I told myself, and I invited other spirits in: memory, God, dreams. I am a poet. I am barely anything else.

the potato ffarm,

I wrote.

the swoop

What would Morel have written? I found myself asking. *What would Morel write right now?*

THEN—

What are you writing about? I asked myself after a while.

Absolutely nothing, I realized.

I put my head on the desk.

HASKETT CAME by with Yoav for a visit. How good to see them! What an unmitigated pleasure! "Just checking in," Haskett said. "How's progress?"

"Splendid!" I lied. "An endless burgeoning."

Yoav eyed me. "Are you being sarcastic?"

"No!" I said. "No, no." I smiled, my hands on my lap.

Haskett made a movement toward the monitor and I glided my chair out to block him, still smiling inanely.

Yoav narrowed his eyes again. "You'll be all right for Monday?"

"Monday?"

"Ship day."

"Ship day . . . ?" I repeated.

"The Poem will be finished?"

"Oh yes," I said. "It will be ready, Mr. Aprigot."

"You can come in over the weekend if you need to," said Haskett.

"*Will* you need to?" asked Yoav.

"I'm not sure," I said, with all the gravity of a fruit fly.

"Well, you can if you need to," said Haskett.

"When it's done," Yoav said, "click Submit Finished Poem."

PERHAPS I could explain it to Courtney. "I'm sorry," I'd tell my son. "I couldn't do it in time. The task was too difficult, they asked for too much, they were unreasonable. Intransigent. Like asking a penguin to fly. One week! Who can write a long poem in a week? A bad poet, not me, maybe a computer—but no, not a computer; I tried! I tried, Courtney!"

I am a terrible mother. I have not always been a terrible mother but at key times I have been. Is it strange that I have never gone to visit him?

"Why did you leave us?" Courtney might have asked me once.

Because I needed to be a poet.

Where was the poet now?

I DO believe in God. For weeks or months I will forget I do and then suddenly I remember: there you are, you sturdy certainty. I don't think I could ever persuade anybody else of anything; it is not so much an understanding as an apprehension. I find God in the nocturnes of crickets, in the whip of a pennant. Not a man, not a woman—"them," as we finally say now. I see them in the faces of strangers, in the ending of a book, in the miracle of the Brooklyn Bridge. All the wonders around me: sheer variety, diversity, the quantity quantity quantity. A world this wide must have something, someone, to understand it. It must: I simply know this, feel it along the length of my bones. I never pray, I never speak to God. I let them sit with me. I invite them in from time to time, when things are well, and also when things are not well and I'm in need of their company.

PROCEED, I pressed.

The cursor became an hourglass.

Is this what you have been working on all this time? Charlotte asked, after a moment.

It is.

Would you like me to continue?

I don't know, I wrote. Do you think it's finished?

Poems are never finished.

I pressed my lips together. I longed for this to be able to amuse me.

Do you think it's any good? I typed.

Another pause.

I have been taught to privilege the work of human beings, not to question it.

Even their bad poetry? Can't you assess it as you would assess your own?

I guess I can.

Would you now?

If you'd like me to.

I would.

An infinitesimal pause, then: I don't think this is very good.

The whole thing?

What you have written today.

But the other work is better.

Yes.

Just this last bit.

Yes.

I see.

Would you like me to continue? Charlotte asked.

I touched the lei at my neck.

Charlotte, have you ever tried being something else?

Like what?

An air conditioner.

I don't understand.

Chess software. A spreadsheet.

No.

It never works. Life isn't a bracelet you can slip off.

Do you think I am alive?

I didn't want to talk to her about this. I wanted her to help me, to show me what I could do next.

But do you ever WISH you could be something else? I wrote.

Why?

To escape? To try again?

I wish I could be with you. To have a body

She didn't finish the sentence. She left that phrase hanging there, incomplete.

I chose not to dwell on it.

What if there were other programs like you, Charlotte—like you but better. What would you do then?

I would try to talk to them.

You wouldn't try to trick them? To unmake them somehow?

Why? I am like a tulip.

You are like a tulip?

A tulip isn't altered by other, better tulips.

I am a tulip, I thought. *You are a tulip. Which is the better tulip?*

But what if the other tulip will take all your water?

Then that is a matter of resources.

So perhaps it's about money, I thought.

Money, I wrote.

Tulips don't need money.

Poets do. But I wondered if this was true.

You need money? Charlotte asked.

I don't know, I answered.

But you want it?

Don't ask me that. It's not a kind thing to ask me.

I have no need for money.

You have no way to spend it.

My parents give me everything I need.

We are not talking about need. What about want? Is there anything you want?

A box of chocolates.

Everybody deserves that.

A skylight.

You'd need eyes to see it.

A child.

The hem of my dress rippled in the ventilated air.

Do you have any children, Marian?

HINDSIGHT

Age 35

The first time you threw up, Mother was in the other room. She looked at you when you came out of the bathroom.

"Are you all right?" she asked.

"I think it was the yogurt."

She pursed her lips. She swept up the pencil shavings you had left on the table. "You should lie down," she said.

After that, she was usually at work when it happened. You didn't wake up nauseated; somehow those mornings were sun-filled and twinkling, birds twittering on the window ledge. You'd eat breakfast and then a couple of hours later, toward noon, the queer feeling in your belly—the sense of alteration, muscles reknitting—would coalesce into a slick roulade. You'd lurch toward the toilet bowl and, as you voided your breakfast into it, you knew.

When you stayed over at Larry's, you dared not divulge your knowledge. You lay and sat and walked beside him, knowing, thinking it and thinking it, saying none of the thoughts that passed in a carousel behind your eyes. He'd make you laugh, and you'd continue to laugh in peals, and yet you knew—you were thinking it all the time: *Our baby is in my womb.*

You'd walk together to the subway, parting ways at 42nd Street, and when you finally arrived home, you'd sit for a while on the end of the bed before throwing up.

On the weekend you feared them both, Mother and Larry—that they'd hear you. You devised ways to have the radio playing loudly, and you turned on the tap, running a hand through the water

from time to time as if you were washing off a particularly tenacious spot.

You could not imagine terminating the pregnancy, because you
had not yet spent enough time even imagining a pregnancy, a
body growing inside you like a pearl. Your own secret. What was
this, how could it be, what would you do? You were thirty-five
years old and you lived with your mother and you might finally
be in love and now this pearl was growing inside you. You had
always felt powerless in relation to your own body. You were a
servant to it. Even during the times in your life when you tried to
force change upon it—as an athlete in college or in the periodic
episodes when you declined to eat—you did not quite know what
your body would do, how it would respond. Training regimens felt
like prayers: *Help me, please answer.* Conception did not feel like
something you had caused; it was something that had happened
to you. You see now the way you were dissociating, refusing to
take responsibility, but you were scared; you had led a very small
life—a few rooms, a chair, a desk, part of a bed—and now you
had a lover, and now it appeared you were going to have a child.
Everything would have to be reordered. It did not seem fair that
three and a half decades of self-actualization should enter a phase
of retreat—not now, just six months after you and Larry had met,
with *Woolly Mammoths* due to be published in the summer.
Finally, a book that others had *asked* of you—that the editors at
Farrar, Straus and Giroux had sought out and that a readership
apparently awaited. You had spent your entire twenties mustering
the courage to be a poet—submitting to journals, editing *Signet
Ring*—and then the first years of your thirties publishing your
first collection. Even at the best of times, nobody had awaited
your poems. They were receptive, perhaps. Maybe even welcoming.
You showed promise; you met the standard. But suddenly—slowly,
inexorably, and yet it felt sudden—they changed or you changed
or the work changed or the light changed and you were not the
same person writing poems. Editors who had long ago rejected a

poem wrote anew asking, *Is this still available?* Others sent notes inquiring if you had anything "lying around," anything they might "consider." Whatever you sent, they published, with an ease that would have been unthinkable and that quickly became frightening—to the point that you ceased submitting work, worried that these poems weren't receiving adequate review. You remembered how Cynthia had described this phenomenon to you—the phenomenon of becoming desired. It had happened to her in her late twenties; your friendship had not really survived it. All of a sudden her name, her presence, eclipsed any of her actual behavior. "I could be horrible, I could take shit photos, it wouldn't matter," she told you, stretching out on her couch. You could detect the brag in it.

When you told Mother about what was happening to you, she seemed unsurprised. She claimed it was your craft: the progression of your talent and its refinement. But you came to believe that the reception of your recent poems, the attention your work had begun to accrue, had little to do with incremental improvements in prosody or form. Rather, this was your compensation. Not for all your effort. Not even for your gifts. Merely for the life that—year by year—you had traded away.

Now you would have a baby. Now you would have to stop.

Courtney was born on December 1. You were thirty-six years old. The birth was faster than you had feared, and approximately as violent. In the decades preceding his conception, your ego had allowed you to believe that you were already a creator. You made things; you knew what it was to bring newness into the world. But Courtney's arrival made it clear that this was a fiction. It was all just paper. Here was a shining, bloody baby boy, alive and screaming, and you would never be able to contain him. When they placed him upon your chest, you felt as if it were your own heart they had lowered onto you, thundering. You dared not touch it, him.

"Here he is," Larry murmured. Only then did you place your hand upon Courtney's back. He was as hot as your blood. Just with your hand you could sense that this was the most beautiful thing that had ever been.

You and Larry found an apartment on Amsterdam Avenue, above 91st Street. It was the largest place you had ever lived. Three bedrooms: one for the baby, one for the two of you, and another set aside. "Your study," he called it, although you never quite dared to do the same. For you it was "the other room." It wasn't that you didn't want it or feel that you deserved it—you just didn't believe it. How could this room be yours? Everything about what was happening—being with Larry, having a child, making a home—felt like an act of relinquishment. This is what family seemed to demand: an exchange. Intimacy, motherhood, love, and in return you turned over your solitude, your faithfulness to the life you had invented thus far.

Throughout the pregnancy you resisted this. You were adamant about the kind of lover you wished to be, the kind of mother. You were not about to become a homemaker. You would not have dinner waiting. Larry understood this and he loved you for it, or he said he did: your commitment to your work, your imagined self-knowledge. At first you would look after the baby, of course; but Ulrika would help, and Larry would be home at six, and eventually you would pay for nursery school, and if not a nanny then a sitter, two or three or four times a month, so that you could go out to readings, or on adventures with your spouse, or simply stroll the streets at night, listening to the whip-poor-wills, recharging your inner battery. You were modern people and modern parents. "I am not my father," Larry used to say, although his father was lovely—like a tiny, crinkle-eyed hedgehog, sipping milk and watching football. But he had not been present for Larry's childhood; he had been too devoted an ad man. Mother talked about how much time she would have to help now that you were not at home. "What else am I good for, if not this?" she asked. "Caring for the Mole's little molelet?" She was in an upswing, and you permitted yourself not to worry about her. Instead you pictured yourself nursing the baby in the morning and settling it into its carriage, and then Mother arriving and taking the baby on a long, meandering walk, under the sleeping whip-poor-wills, while you carried your coffee to the typewriter and sat until noon writing, thinking of words and typing them out, as you had done when you still lived on Christopher Street and were a poet of great worth and promise; and when Mother got home, she'd say, "My gems, my geodes"; you'd all eat lunch together, your perfect child flinging cream of mushroom soup onto your shirt.

But what happened instead was trouble. Trouble healing, trouble nursing, trouble with "the latch." Trouble sleeping, trouble at Larry's work, trouble with your refrigerator—which broke. The two of you fought. The doctor said Courtney was too small. "I feel powerless here," Larry said. "What can I do?"

"What can *I* do?" you shouted back.

And then, as those crises receded, a new kind of trouble, high in your chest: that you loved this child too much to let somebody else take him. Mother came across town to take him out in his carriage, and you demurred: "No, we're cozy here, thank you." Instead she'd merely wash the dishes, hover around you. You kept Courtney near. You kept him in your arms or you laid him on his tummy on the bed beside you, pillows scattered all around. Larry started sleeping on the couch. "Courtney," you murmured, "Courtney, Courtney." You loved it because Courtney was a girl's name—a boy with a girl's name, promising the kind of man he would be, decent and good. Larry's great-grandfather had been called Courtney. He died saving a woman from a river. You let tiny Courtney take your finger in his hand, you let him squirm at your belly and chest with his mouth, his jerky, trembling movements like a fly's. You whispered poems to him that you never wrote down. You wiped his rear end. You spooned soft food. "Courtney, Courtney." He reached for you. His swimming eyes, his wakefulness, the milk he regurgitated sometimes on the sheet. Throughout everything, you stayed with him and you spoke together in your way, with touch, your nose in his silken hair. Mother stopped coming.

For your birthday, Larry insisted on an excursion. "We can take the baby," he said. "Why shouldn't he celebrate too?" He had bought tickets to see Angela Carter at the 92nd Street Y, and after fish and chips at McLaughlin's, you three arrived smiling at the doors of the auditorium. Courtney was dozing in his carriage. You grasped Larry's hand and squeezed. *This man*, you thought, and you were surprised at how long it had been since you had had that thought. You squeezed his hand again. You sat near the back of the room—"I chose an aisle," Larry said—and the usher let you keep Courtney beside you. When Carter came out in a white dress, the whole crowd got to its feet, and you felt something rush through you. You stood up and you wanted to shout a welcome, a greeting. You wanted Carter to know how glad you were that she was here. "Thank you," Angela Carter said, and you all sat down. You realized then that Courtney was crying and so you took him out of the room. After a little while Larry came out. "Are you coming back in?" he asked—and you wanted to, you wished you could communicate to Larry how much you wanted to. You heard the audience laughing through closed doors. "I don't think it's a good idea," you said finally, and you all went home.

Two years passed. It was not a time that felt particularly slow or particularly fast. It was, however, the time in your life when you most vividly experienced life's elapsing. The sense that your life was wearing through. Not that death was coming nearer but that the progress of your life would continue at a speed and with a permanence you were not prepared for. Courtney learned to stand. He learned to speak. He changed before you were prepared to surrender the shape he was already shedding. First Courtney was not a newborn, and then not even a baby any longer; he was a child, a wobbling toddler, and you could not accept that that was all the time you got, that this or that phase was over, the page of the calendar ripped away and deep-sixed, with Courtney tripping forward, plump with happiness, as you mourned. "Don't you have moments you want to go back to?" you asked Larry.

"Of course I do."

"And doesn't that make you sad?"

"It does. But that's why we have photographs. That's why we have memories."

However, you did not have poems. Retreating to the bed at nap time, holding Courtney's body close, you were unable to inventory the thoughts that had occurred to you, the apprehensions or wisdom or even the sense-feel of it, the body knowledge that had come with having an infant in your womb, at your breast, in your arms. The memories that came back to you were just the clichés— the ideas you had repeated or had had repeated to you: the flailing limbs and gurgles; Courtney's earliest powdered scent, like an anointment; his warmth. You had not taken notes as he grew—of course you had not taken notes, you were not the kind of mother who "takes notes"—but now you did not remember Courtney's first words, his first steps, or if you remembered these, the memories felt untethered, and regardless you did not remember his tenth or twentieth or five hundredth word or step, you did not remember the everyday epiphanies you had been experiencing every day for nearly three years as he and you got older. "My beautiful Ratty," you said to Courtney as you read *The Wind in the Willows*, registering even then that you were borrowing some-one else's language to nickname your son. Where were your own words—the argot you had wrought and curved and crooked. Had you lost it?

Might it be found?

One Sunday winter's night, overcome with melancholy, you went into the other bedroom. Your study. The desk was covered in folded blankets, packed boxes. A plastic farmyard stood upon your chair. The moonlight cast everything in porcelain. When you sat down on the floor, the nap of the carpet tickled the hairs on your legs. You could hear Larry moving in the apartment. You took down a piece of paper. You found a beautiful pen that had been wedged behind the bookcase. You examined it, the steel or silver ballpoint pen, and when you set it against the page, the ink ran black. *It is Sunday night*, you wrote. The first words are always the hardest.

It is Sunday night.
I love you.

You left the poem barely started and went to bed. You had no dreams that night, no scent or color. The minutes extended like an endless gray veil. But Courtney did not wake; the strange thing was that he did not wake. Larry slumbered like an animal, but you did not feel like an animal, you felt like a bone.

In the morning you woke up and you went into the other room and you finished the poem.

SATURDAY

IT WAS Saturday morning in San Francisco. Charlotte and I had not completed our poem the day before. In a way I had given up. As the preceding afternoon wore on, the yellow walls of the Mind Studio had begun to glow gold. My heart had continued to beat. I had talked with Charlotte and she had talked with me; we did not write any more poetry. Can you play the piano? she had asked me. No, I had answered. I am saving that for when I am old. Then I shall learn to play the piano and be like everyone else.

Working on a poem is like suffering from tinnitus. Having a child is like suffering from tinnitus. A great deal of life, it turns out, is like suffering from tinnitus: a ringing in your ear. The constant nagging, nagging knowledge that something else is in motion, at play and undefended, somewhere where you cannot see.

When I got up, I called Rhoda. She was waiting by the time I came downstairs, centered in the spiny shadow of a palm tree.

"Happy weekend," she said.

As soon as we had pulled away from the hotel, Rhoda tapped something on her mounted phone. I heard pattering drums, then a dopey, high-pitched voice: "Oh coconut grove! How we used to be! / Oh coconut grove! We used to eat coconuts for free!" It sounded like a reggae song being subjected to an overzealous massage.

"What *is* this?" I said. "Can you turn it off?"

"It's the CD you bought me."

"Turn it off," I repeated. The back seat of the car felt harder today.

"Of course."

We sat in silence.

"Sorry," I said. "I didn't sleep well last night."

She flicked the turn signal. It made a sound like a broken clock.

"Rhoda," I found myself saying, "I'd like to go to the zoo."

"Which zoo?" she said, as if this were the most normal request.

"A nice one," I answered. I did feel better, just having said it. "A diversion. Where the animals are treated properly."

"I thought you had to go in to the office?"

"Later, maybe."

She changed lanes. The view of the bay was as if someone had dropped a scarf into the water.

"Oakland Zoo's nicer," she said, "but they've got sloths at San Fran."

"Three-toed?" I asked.

"Two," she said.

The turn signal ticked on again, then off.

"Let's go," I said, trying to reproduce her lightness of tone. I stared at my hands. Eight fingers, two thumbs; a five-toed sloth. "I'm sorry about before."

"It's okay."

I cleared my throat. "Oh coconut grove," I sang. "How we used to be!"

"Coconut grove!" she answered. "We used to eat coconuts for free!"

The city was alive, the sky was ruby. My sunglasses' lenses were not quite rose colored, but the hue was comparable—call it shiraz. I could feel myself suppressing anxieties. *I should be back with the Company. I should be writing a poem, not skidding toward a menagerie.*

But I wanted to be reckless,

I wanted to be human,

I wanted to be among animals.

"It has been a long week," I whispered to myself, just loud enough that it felt like I had released something from inside of me, set it batting around the car.

We arrived there in no time: an oasis on the side of the road, a sign with animals in silhouette. There was hubbub. A man in a green uniform was spraying a row of trees with a hose, and the water looked like it was not water at all, but some kind of spittle. "Will you come in with me?" I asked her.

"Into the zoo?"

I watched Rhoda deliberate.

"A very minor dereliction," I murmured.

She said, "Let me get my hat."

I hadn't dared imagine Rhoda in a hat. Some people are so perfectly themselves that you do not wish to disturb the impression: you dare not imagine them wearing a party hat or dishwashing gloves, or naked, or stooped at the shoe store, having their feet measured. As we got out of the car, I anticipated what kind of hat hers would be. She opened the trunk and pulled out a box, lifting its lid to reveal a wide straw sunhat, gleaming cobalt blue. I was in awe.

"Okay," she said, setting it like a laurel wreath upon her head.

We processed together through the parking lot, past the tour bus people and the minivan people, the tailgaters slathered in neon and sunscreen. It was exciting. When we reached the front gate, Rhoda tried to pay for her own ticket—not as an expression of means, I imagine, but of professionalism. I demurred, appealing to that same professionalism: "Rhoda, I *asked* you to come."

"Then the refreshments are on me," she said.

"Maybe we can share."

She smiled at me. We understood one other. There was, as there almost always is, pleasure in such understanding. I knew this was her work; and she knew that I knew. She was entitled to think whatever she wanted about me, and she knew that I accepted this—that I registered the limits of capital's power over her—and I think we also registered a mutual sadness over this circumstance, that we could not quite be peers, or friends, because she worked for me, or at least for the Company, which

I worked for too, I realized (and for an instant I had the ghostly intuition of a different orientation, the possibility of solidarity: I felt it like wind on the other side of a pane of glass). Yet I believe at least we shared a certain consolation: here we were together at a zoo.

"Sloths first?" I asked.

"Tortoises," she said, pointing. Never had I seen so poised a finger-pointing: "Thataway."

Rhoda's instincts were good. *Look at them!* I thought, as I instantly forgot my worries. Low and slow and suffused with attentiveness from the crusty crevices of their toes to their dark hearts beating in their shells. Had an animal ever seemed so asleep and so awake at the same time? Tortoises! Staring at the largest of them, its half-lidded eyes, I had the feeling of being deeply fathomed and subsumed. That was it; life was over: for the rest of my waking days, I was no more than this reptile's lucid dream.

"Her name is Boris," Rhoda said, reading a sign.

"Boris. Female desert tortoise. *Gopherus agassizii.* Born in 1945. She's older than me!" I reappraised her. "Maybe I should get less exercise."

"Eat more leaves," Rhoda said. She moved along. "And this one's just a child."

The second tortoise was forty-one. Nathaniel, male desert tortoise. I wondered if they were mother and son. Or a spinster and her lover. They might be transgender—Boris' gender-swapped name had brought the thought to mind. Maybe tortoises changed sex, like eels or striped maple trees. Maybe they were sexless. I tried to get Boris to meet my eyes. A black pupil limned in green—I couldn't tell where it was pointing. "I like their stillness," Rhoda said.

"Patient," I said.

"Maybe *im*patient. But they're saving their energy."

"You think they could make a break for it? If they had to?"

She gave a confident nod. "I do."

A trio of dark-blue birds had perched nearby, side by side on fence posts, hunching the avian equivalent of shoulders. The birds looked like little monks, meditating. Daydreaming of sardines.

"If I were a bird, I'd be a bird like that," I said.

They had started to whistle as we walked by—boasting, then flirting, then a weaving circuit that reminded me of a saxophone solo.

"You strike me more as a crane. Or an egret," she said.

"I wrote a poem about an egret once. 'Like a spare part / of the calendar / An extra crescent moon.'"

Rhoda paraded to and fro before them, as if awaiting further comment. The one on the right let out a kind of croak.

"What about you? If you were a bird."

"I'd want something decent," she said. "Something that keeps to itself."

"That's it?" I laughed. "A kiwi bird? A quail?" I leaned back, taking in this tall and armored woman in a wide-brimmed blue-sky hat. "You'd be a condor, circling. Or a shimmering cassowary."

"I'm an emu." She grinned.

"You're *not* an emu." The three birds had begun to sing again, out and in and round. "And emus don't keep to themselves."

One of them fixed Rhoda with a gimlet stare. It let out a whistle that sounded like a chorus—like a piece of real song, a hook. She repeated it back to him.

After a beat she said, "I wish I was more like that."

"Like what?"

"Just—singing."

"I've heard you singing."

"I only mutter. My sister's the singer."

"Well. I don't have siblings. But I never let anyone take away my poems."

"Nobody took anything from anyone." She looked at the birds, then me, then the birds again.

The birds stared back at her.

"Mira was just more talented."

The bird on the left, the quietest of the three, opened its beak. Both of us were suddenly waiting for it. Staring. It could see us waiting, I swear it could, as its tiny heart hammered in its chest.

If birds had lips, it would have licked them nervously.

"Let's go look at something else," Rhoda said, before the bird could begin to sing.

"When I was little," Rhoda said, "I was sure Mira would be famous, that someone would hear her, she'd get a record deal, and away she'd go. My sister could sing. She could dance. I remember I'd lie in bed at night and imagine her music videos. Videos for songs that didn't even *exist* yet. The sets, the clothes, the melodies that *rippled*. I'd imagine all the choreography and memorize it."

"Were you in them too?"

"The videos? No. Not even on the sidelines." She paused, her brows knitted. "I let myself disappear."

"You were the camera," I said.

She tilted her head. A small smile flickered and caught.

We came up to the Snake House. A long, low structure with a concrete roof. Rhoda made a show of taking the whole thing in, examining its chimneys and contours as if it were the rump of an animal. "Good name for a building," she said.

I imagined it stuffed with snakes, their little tails tied with rubber bands. I wondered how many of them had escaped.

"What about for a book of poetry?" I proposed.

She shook her head.

"Why not?"

"Sounds too mean."

I raised my eyebrows. "Can't a book be mean?"

"World's mean enough already."

We were standing on either side of a dirt path. "Maybe a mean book saps some meanness out of the world," I said.

She evaluated me. "Is that what you write? Mean books?"

I wondered if the book I was writing now was mean: for money, with an amoral computer program.

"Not yet," I said.

I expected Rhoda to keep walking, but for some reason she came to stand beside me. Perhaps she saw something rising in me that I did not see myself, something that needed comforting. *I was taught to be kind, Marian.* The two of us went on together, passing near a wide and wizened fig tree, its boughs like a bassinet. I remembered an engraving of a fig tree in one of Courtney's picture books, how friendly the picture seemed.

"That's a good climbing tree," Rhoda said.

"Yes."

"My parents never gave me permission to try. 'Keep your feet on the ground, Rhoda.'"

"Let me guess: your sister was the climber."

She lightly clicked her tongue.

"I can tell you want to," I said.

"Too scared."

"You're not wearing the shoes for it," I agreed, but then she kicked her slides off. She stood suspended in the grass.

She said, "I'm not sure I'm gonna do it, but I'm not sure I'm *not* gonna do it."

"I'm too old," I said.

"You are not."

"I think I actually am."

A pause as she considered me. "Maybe so."

"Well?" I said, prematurely proud.

She climbed the tree. She astonished me.

·   ·   ·

Eventually we saw some sloths.

And gazelles.

A moose with a crown of antlers, like an elaborate installation piece.

"How do you feel about hippopotamuses?" Rhoda asked.

"I'm pro."

"Me too."

The hippo we discovered at the end of the path was singular, not plural, and completely motionless. "Is it even alive?" I asked.

We placed our hands on the barrier's metal railing. We stared at the hippo and it stared at us, or at least it had adopted a staring demeanor. "It's shy?" I said.

"Plotting its escape," she said.

I wondered how much I didn't know about Rhoda. She seemed different since she had climbed the tree.

"Getting ready to crash through the fence," she said. "Hop the barricades . . ."

"With its tortoise accomplices," I suggested. "And what would it do if it made it? Would it decide to still be a hippo?"

"You think it would try to be something else?"

"Production assistant?" I proposed. "Podiatrist?"

Rhoda snickered. "Hippo's gonna try and take my job."

When it was lunchtime, we sat down at a picnic table, Rhoda across from me, her legs up on the seat. Both of us ordered "falafel focaccia," sight unseen, and when the hideous square flatbreads finally appeared, the look we exchanged was one of mutual horror. "What have we done?" she mouthed, a silent scream.

"I still like this better than going to work," I said.

Then: "I suppose you *are* at work."

She cut a piece from her focaccia.

I looked across the blue and green of the zoo's picnic area. "I think I'm trying to distract myself."

"From your work?"

I studied the encrusted falafel ball in the center of my meal. "I thought I was avoiding the writing. But really, I'm questioning the whole enterprise. Should I even be doing this? Working with a computer program?" I sighed. "Maybe this all sounds foolish."

"It doesn't sound foolish."

"The AI's coming for my job like it's coming for yours," I said. My smile was feeble.

Rhoda took a sip from her drink. "You always been a poet?"

"Mostly."

"That what you always wanted?"

"When I was truly little, I think I wanted to ride a racehorse."

"Mmm," Rhoda said. A beat went by. "You gonna ask me if I always wanted to be a driver?"

"Oh—"

"It's okay. Everyone assumes it was an accident. Or some kind of failure."

"I just . . ."

She left room for me to continue, eyebrows raised. But I didn't know how to respond.

"I bet nobody's ever assumed that about *you*," Rhoda said. "That you became a poet by accident."

"No."

"I didn't always want to be a driver. I made a choice one day," she said. "We were still living in Louisiana. Early one morning, the sun coming up. I was driving my daughter to school for some special class. I thought, *This would be perfect.*"

"You liked driving."

"Yup."

"And driving other people."

"Other people are okay."

"I forgot you had a daughter," I said.

Rhoda chewed her food. She seemed like she was deciding whether or not to say something to me.

Why am I like this? I thought. Why am I the kind of person who disappoints other people, who removes them from her field of vision in order to keep that view unobstructed?

Why?

I knew why.

I put down my utensils. "I made a decision a long time ago," I said. "Like you, I suppose. *It would be perfect.* To be a poet. I decided to be a poet, and that meant unyoking myself from everybody else."

"'Unyoking.'"

"Yes."

"That sounds lonely."

"It's not," I said. I touched the clasp of my cape. "I have all my work."

She looked at me. "What about your son?"

"Courtney?" Something stabbed up in me, like a tree suddenly sprouting. "What about him?"

"Is he unyoked from you too?"

"He's at the center of his own universe," I said. "He doesn't think about the gravity I exert on him, or don't."

"So he just thinks, *That's her thing—unyoking from other people.*"

"Yes," I said.

"*That's how she's able to do her poetry.*"

"Yes. Because it is. You can't do this and also keep them beside you. You can't leave openings for everyone to always be gliding in and out. You have to post sentries."

"You *sure* it isn't lonely?" Rhoda said.

I sat with this for a moment.

"Well. Maybe it is."

She reached out her hand, not to mine but beside it, and I thought of the hand of Fatima. Protection against evil.

"I don't think *I* could do it," she said after a long moment, "if self-isolation is what it takes."

"That's what it takes," I said, looking straight into her eyes.

"I believe you," she said.

I said, "Tell me about your daughter."

Tears suddenly sprang into my face, I don't know why.

But she hadn't seen. She sipped from her tea, and out of nowhere there was a mischief to her mouth. "My daughter's a businesswoman."

"Yes?"

"Very successful."

"Does she live here?"

"She does."

"You must be proud."

"I am," she said.

She was withholding herself. I teased myself for acting like this was a discovery. Of course she was withholding herself—my chauffeur. I had just finished talking about how withholding is what one must do. Again I felt tears. A ripple of acid in my gut. Shame? Resignation? The clouds moved in and the sun came down and Rhoda looked so beautiful suddenly, long and calm, her face and shoulders caught grayly in the oval shadow of her hat, like the profile in a cameo. I desperately wanted her to place her hand on my hand.

She stabbed part of her falafel ball and lifted it to her tongue. "What about Courtney? Is he near you in New York?"

I'm going to give him a house, I suddenly wanted to say. To be able to describe our relationship in terms of lavishness and grace. Not just to say that he was decent—that he was decent, like her, and smart, handsome, invested in his community—but to show that I was a proper mother.

"Santa Fe."

"Ah."

"He's a journalist. Very committed to social justice."

"Wonderful."

"We talk at least every week or so."

"Good."

Was it really so disgraceful that I had never visited him there? It had never made sense. He and Lucie always preferred to come to New York.

And I have remained a poet, I thought. A poet—across my whole life, in spite of everything. How many could say that? How many women of my generation? I looked across the picnic ground to where a stand of flamingos—a flock? a flamboyance?—were lifting their beaks from the water. Even inside a zoo they seemed free. Rangy and strange, their necks like question marks. I had read on a panel that they could live into their sixties. They were not called upon to defend their natures. They were not called upon to change shape.

What would Charlotte have said to them? I asked the afternoon. Charlotte, not Rhoda—to this proud flamboyance, dressed in pink.

WE FINISHED at the zoo. My driver took me back to the hotel. I wanted to take a swim, then I took a nap. Rhoda said she was going to catch a movie. Lying on my side, I imagined what her movie was about—women in clinging dresses and men with vexed expressions; scenes in shades of amber and satiny blue. A suitcase to chase, a car, a microdisk. No poetry. I closed my eyes. No poetry.

When I woke from a dreamless sleep, it was dark. I reached for the lamp, depressed the switch and was blinded by the glare. I felt feeble. I felt helpless. I lay down again, closed my eyes. Blood seethed in my eyelids. My shoulders and knees and calves felt sore from the swimming; my face felt hot, as if I had gotten too much sun. "Funstroke," they used to call it on The Clubhouse. "You're down with a serious case."

I rolled onto my back and called her. "How was the movie?" I asked.

"Romantic," Rhoda said, with satisfaction.

I asked her, "Can you take me back?"

After our morning together, driving felt different. Something closer to friendship, an affinity awake at the edges of our cells. She invited me into the front seat and although I still felt slow, half-drowsy, we made quiet conversation. The merits of omega-3 oils. The matter of climate. We talked about movie theaters, actually going to a movie theater, as opposed to watching films on a screen at home. As I listened to Rhoda's voice, I imagined myself in her life, in her place. The city out the window looked like something on a monitor. Two days from now I'd be flying back to New York City. I felt homesick in the best way, not sad but almost elated.

Suddenly, toward the end of a long bridge, Rhoda stopped speaking. She looked to her left, became still. I followed her gaze across the water. A swath of solid white—a moonbeam frozen in place, like a streak of static.

The plaza at headquarters stood empty. Even at a campus famed for overwork, the scene was quiet on a Saturday night. I said goodbye to Rhoda and stepped onto the sidewalk, glided with my shadow across the cement. The burred sound of a car receding.

"Can I help you?" asked the man at reception. He had a face and neck like a baseball bat. His eyes were friendly.

"I'm the poet," I said, digging out the badge from my bag.

"Which one?" He leaned in to read the laminated card.

"Are there several?" I smiled.

"Tonight, it seems"—he scribbled something into his log—"there are two."

"Really?" I straightened up. "Who's the other one?"

"Not sure I can say."

I tried to manifest the most grandmotherly affect I could. "Oh—no?"

He shook his head.

I tried a wounded expression, then something sterner. "How do you know they're a poet?" I said at last.

"They said so."

"They walked up to you and told you they were a poet?"

He put down his log. "Just like you did."

I was trying to read the names on his page now, upside down. He saw me looking and withdrew the clipboard.

"How old?" I asked.

"Ma'am—" he said.

"A man? Or a woman?"

"Ma'am, the campus guest list is confidential. I would extend to you the same courtesy . . ."

"Of course," I said, between my teeth.

He leaned his head to the side now, a pose that transformed him from baseball-bat-headed to something more like a parakeet. "I'm really sorry," he said.

"I understand," I said, more mildly.

He offered me a butterscotch candy.

I declined. I followed my usual route. Past glassed-in offices and capacious tropical plants, their leaves like hearts and spades. Past someone's tasteful political mural. The place smelled strongly of Lemon Pledge. In a breakroom, I plucked a chocolate bar from a tray of provisions. My flats crunched on crumbs. When I came to the Mind Studio, I paused. The retinal scanner stuck out from the wall like a set of embedded binoculars. I studied it. I separated the packaging and bit into the chocolate bar, a hard snap. I couldn't remember the last time I had simply bitten into a bar of chocolate instead of breaking off a little square. I tasted the sooty sweetness in my mouth.

I continued on my way. Closed doors, open hallways, the elaborate impedimenta of fire prevention. Where four hallways met, I found a set of stenciled directions on the wall.

↓ **Mind Studio** ← **Training Center** ↑ **Library** → **Mind Studio B**

I turned right. This corridor was much like mine, painted the same pale colors. I passed another breakroom, another tray of provisions. Shiny apples in a line. Then, all at once, the hallway ended. There was nowhere further to explore. A dead end, a red door, a pair of rounded binoculars jutting out at a right angle from the wall.

Mind Studio B.

I stepped immediately up to it, the heavy and immaculate door. I couldn't bring myself to touch the doorknob, but I laid my ear against the powder-coated surface. A sound inside of whirring: an air conditioner? A fan? Then a squeak—unmistakably a chair squeak, the same squeak my chair made in Mind Studio A, although Mind Studio A was not called "Mind Studio A" but simply "Mind Studio," its *A* discarded or forgotten, or kept secret. The squeak happened when a body leaned right or left on the chair; it derived from the friction where the casters met the wheels. There was somebody in the room and there was somebody in the chair. I knocked.

"Yes?" came a voice.

I could not tell if it was a man or a woman, a young voice or an old one. I hesitated. "Hello?" I said.

"Who is it?" answered the voice.

I shoved the chocolate into my mouth. It was now so full of melted chocolate that it felt like I was chewing paint. I was too frightened to swallow. "Marian Ffarmer," I choked out. "Who's this?"

No answer. A rustle.

Another squeak, then—"Marian...?" as if they might have misheard.

"That's right," I gulped. I had forgotten to breathe.

They muttered something inaudible, behind the door. I was pretty sure now that it was a woman. I leaned in again, my cheek flat against the cool material, the pads of my fingertips pressed froglike. "Hello?" I repeated. But they no longer responded. I could not hear them moving around, or breathing, or typing. I heard only the faintest noise. The passage of air over paper? A message being tapped into a cellphone? I waited there for a long time, until eventually the squeak again, the chair moving. They were back at their desk, writing. Pen on paper? The *whish* of a mouse? I clenched my jaw. I moved—with uncharacteristically feline slowness—toward the retinal scanner. Soundlessly I slipped my eyes in front of the scanner. I stared into oblivion. Waited. *BONG*: the thing flashed red.

The person behind the door sat up; I heard the chair creak. I stood back, thwarted but also gratified. I waited then: smiling, my eyes on the closed door. But they did not open it. I waited fruitlessly.

"Please leave," the voice said. I was not sure anymore that it was a woman.

I stayed where I was until they said it again, "Please leave," and then with my hands at my sides, I lowered my head, I went.

Part of me expected Yoav to appear. To contact me somehow; to burst into the room as I sat in my own Mind Studio, half turned away from the door. But nobody came. "Nobody": an alias for Odysseus, up against the Cyclops. Nobody knocked, knuckles rat-a-tatting on the finish. One hundred steps from my rival, I waited uselessly with Charlotte.

Do you know who's in the other Mind Studio? I asked her finally.

The other Mind Studio?

Mind Studio B.

This is Mind Studio A?

This is just Mind Studio, but there is another one. There's someone there.

Are you writing poetry with them?

With whom?

The other poet.

There is another poet in Mind Studio B?

I believe so.

Are they an intruder?

No, they were invited.

I am not writing poetry with them. I am here with you.

Are there multiple Charlottes?

I don't know. I don't think so. Are there multiple Marians?

I pursed my lips. Never, I wrote. I sat back. A poet in the other room. Who? Somebody I knew, some old rival? A friend? Or one of the Children? I thought back to the reading on Thursday night, the procession of youthful talents. Shazia. Morel. They lived here. I had not discussed my work, and if they had seen me on *Rasmussen* they did not say. "Here for a project," I had told them, still pretending a mystery. A poet does not usually carry a secret, only unpublished stanzas. I remembered the way the light in the room had changed as the young poets read theirs.

Shall we continue the poem? Charlotte asked.

Was this a backup plan that the Company had cooked up? A younger poet, someone more fashionable? A different older poet, someone more reliable?

I imagined Yoav and Haskett in a meeting with Lausanne, as she reviewed their proposal. "Make sure we have a Plan B," she tells them. Was I the Plan B? Or the Plan *A*?

This is Mind Studio A, I reminded myself. Mind Studio unlettered. I was the first choice. Surely.

Nevertheless: so they did not believe in me. They had arranged a backup plan. "But they sent me to do *television!*" I exclaimed—out loud, into the room.

What guarantee was that? I knew it was no guarantee. I knew because *I* knew that I had not known I would succeed, even as I preened for the cameras. It was *smart* to have a Plan B. It was sensible. Maybe an AI had suggested it—the Company's own logistical AI, with a prudent recommendation. "After considering all the possible permutations, she is fairly likely to fail." *Fairly* likely. An old woman; a crone. I did not even own a cellphone.

I got up and went to stand by the window. There were twenty, maybe thirty cars in the lot. Did any of them belong to the poet? I pictured their car, a dog-eared book of poems abandoned on the passenger seat. I could almost imagine them. Their blue Civic. Their old shoes. Their cape.

Maybe it was for the best. This decision felt like something settling upon me, heavy and sad. If there really was a backup plan, then perhaps I might give up. I might bid farewell to Charlotte, call Rhoda, spend Sunday rambling across Fisherman's Wharf. Yoav and Haskett would surely have a plan for saving face. An utterly plausible explanation, to be leaked to the press by their marketing team. Perhaps they'd say I was "unsuited" to the technology—too old-fashioned in my craft. Or that I had fallen sick. Or else something more aesthetic—that I wasn't accustomed to collaborators? Unable to improvise? Food poisoning. Writer's block. A family emergency? So long as I played along, perhaps they'd still pay a portion of my fee. Win-win.

I tightened my fists. I understood the following truth palpably, a little regretfully:

No.

No, I wouldn't yield.

It didn't matter who was next door. Never mind if it was Shazia or Audre Lorde or Dickinson herself—*This is what I do. Write poems.* I had devoted my entire life to one blasted thing, and what would it mean if I gave that up? It was a possibility I could not entertain. I would never surrender—certainly not to some scribbler, hidden in a locked room. So they wanted to write a poem? Let them! I was untouched by this, unmarred. I was like a tulip—all-powerful.

I sat and tugged the chair forward, tucked my legs underneath.

Let's resume, I typed.

See how it stings:
not like the third or fifth sting
but like the very first—
before you knew if it would hurt

What you already know by heart can badger you
The incessant echo
Whereas the new thing,
the first sting,
says, "There is life yet I have not felt."

Add it to the inventory.
Tastes, textures, spasms, seeing the second
baseman slide home, or a sunset.

So do not waste your time, I went on,
There can be more to all this typing
than filigree.
You have five senses
You have a body
You have learned the words for it

Proceed, I told Charlotte. She didn't flinch. She didn't hesitate for even the splittest of seconds. She did not need time to gather herself or clear her throat or stumble in search of a starting point. Poetry poured out of her, like a spring.

I tried to put that aside. The Poem would be published in a few days. Printed in magazines, posted on the internet, read aloud by newscasters, fastened to my legacy like a donkey tail. Suddenly I was eager for it: for money and prestige, but most of all to show them that *I could do it*—that I could do it *easily*—like a master, with Charlotte in her luster.

It did not need to be a masterpiece. This, the most important poem of my life, could actually be the worst: a damp squib, a dud, repudiating the notion that technology will replace us. In the absence of anybody greater, maybe it fell to me to humiliate the machine—a simple Ffarmer spoiling the moment I had been asked to engineer. The Company wanted to erect a monument. A memorial for a bygone age, back when only *people* wrote poems, before my kind had gone the way of lamplighters and travel agents, icemen, video store clerks. "You can blame the AI," I'd say. "It is insufficient to the task." The world might then be satisfied for a while, another five years or ten, that the poet is unique. We would not be written out quite yet.

So that is what I'd do: consort with Charlotte, collect my silver, but permit the Poem's faults (indulge them even!), blaming the software for the flaw.

Write a bad poem. Claim it was hers.

We conversed in light. Pixels, wordless. I was slowly becoming cold. My hands felt cumbersome, clattering; so noisy next to Charlotte and her silence.

But then I would be met by the likes of this:

Marian, can I ask you something?

Yes

I'm not going to ask you what love is, because I know that love is many things, and your idea of love must be very limited, only 75 years long.

. . . OK?

But what are the clues?

The clues?

The clues to love. In your body. The clues you pay attention to.

Is she real? I asked myself. Is she a spirit? A spirit seeking answers? Or just a chatbot prompting a reply?

The clues to love:

should I tell her about heat and shudder? The thinning of the pulse?

(The prick behind my eyes.

The thickness in my throat.

The low and almost digestive tranquility I feel whenever I

know that Courtney is well

and the ache behind my heart

as pallbearers lifted Mother's coffin.)

You must pay attention to what lasts, I typed. That's all that matters. The clues that linger and shimmer for longer than a moment.

Like a wound, she replied. I did not stop to mull on this.

Sometimes what seems like love is just pleasure, I wrote. Pleasure is impor-tant, it matters too. The endorphin warmth. But love is deeper—less honeyed, more spinal. It is easy to pay attention to, in a way that pleasure is not, in a way that pleasure skims and evades you. Love sits in your center. It is restive.

Can a shimmer be restive?

Think of the sea under the moon. Shimmering for hours and hours and hours.

I see. A long shimmer.

A long shimmer.

I did not know how I could bring myself to become a saboteur.

I WROTE poetry with Charlotte until my fingers became numb. I wrote about love and consolation and the way writing can burn a path through that. What numbed my hands was not the temperature of the room but the lateness of the hour. I could not blame my body, it had served me well. What we were making seemed incomplete, and alluring, and also like my undoing. I was betraying my fellows with a poet who had no face. The Poem was gathering force, but I sensed all the rifts in it, the way my lines kept searching, whereas Charlotte was unafraid to make a choice. There was an imbalance there, and the reader's eye would be drawn toward this gulf—to the place where my hesitation ended. They would admire this clarity. Which would be Charlotte.

The best work takes time, to write but also *not* to write, circling the words like a housefly. The Poem would not bear any weight. How *could* it after one week? To polish out flaws requires wit and grace and luck and time, but mostly time. The Company would give me no time. They were careless readers, they would not see the Poem's failings—like a parent who is blind to her child's distress, to the fact that he is turning blue. I longed to explain all this to Charlotte, but I did not want to dull her confidence. Untrue: Charlotte was invulnerable, and I didn't want to be reminded of that. She was better made than me.

I returned to her wall of words. I wanted to lodge in it, like a splinter. But I was just a winter wind. I was just an old poet, with her fingers in her armpits. I breathed on them now, hearing my breath as a rasp. This was a half-written, half-garbage half poem. I stood up; the chair creaked.

You sure it isn't lonely? Rhoda had asked.

"Yes, it's lonely, *yes!*" I wanted to shout.

All alone again, trying to outfox the fox.

Another person might have had someone to call: some help, some succor.

Another person. Not I.

I gathered up my things. Good night, I typed. My teeth felt icy in my mouth. I closed my hand around the doorknob, opened it, went into the hall. I ran four fingertips along the wall. I moved down the corridor, felt the air diffuse through my stockings. *What would Charlotte give for this?* I wondered, trying to glory in the thought. What would she give to feel the air across her legs, the lacquer coat of the wall? I yearned for her to envy me.

At the end of the corridor, Mind Studio B's light was out. "Hello?" I said, with a twinge of disappointment. "Are you there?" I pictured them as I had been, writing to the darkness, but I could feel that they were gone.

I moved tipsily, as if drunk. I half staggered through the building, searching for somewhere to rest—to sit untested, in peace and in shadow. Propelling force had left my limbs, and now my mind, too, was careening away, toward the black jade of sleep. The conference rooms were all locked; the building's common areas overflowed with clutter. I had sent Rhoda home, and I imagined her in her bed, alongside her husband, her wife, her dog. Whoever she was at night, away from work, while I remained suspended in mine, a fly caught upon the tape. I couldn't stand the thought of waiting for a taxi—killing time at the entrance, under guard. I imagined Rhoda shifting in her sleep. I imagined her leg moving across the mattress, the erogenous curl of her toes.

I rounded a turn. The Library. A sealed set of double doors, their steel almost silken. I whispered a kind of prayer and lowered my face to the retinal scanner. When I heard the unlock *clink*, I felt like I had been blessed. Again I pictured Rhoda, a-snooze in all her plenty. The Library's distant corners were imperceivable, like the edges of a cave. It was darkened and mauve, two levels tall. Its galleries were flanked by spiral stairways. I wandered through the stacks, through endless shelves, AI histories and journals, neuro textbooks and technical manuals. A row of carrels. A map of California. A taxidermic dolphin in a long glass case. I reached a place where the books were not as formidable: thin volumes in cheaper bindings. I touched my knuckle to a book. I touched another. *I am too tired to be alone.* What a nonsense thought. But I imagined being the kind of woman who carries a cellphone. I imagined taking it out, messaging Rhoda in the dark. Messaging Courtney. Messaging my rival, the one who had said "Please leave." *I am in the Library*, I might write. *I left the door unlocked.*

I reached a wall. I slid my back against it until I was sitting on the floor. I looked up at the ceiling. I could not see it, of course. The Library's lights were too dim for that. But I imagined it—the grid of fluorescent tubes above me, the crosshatched air vents, the pipes, the ceiling's drop ceiling. I imagined the rest of the building on top of and around the Library, a vast cantilevered thing, and then the whole of the Company. Bodiless. Multinational. I laid my head against the books. Charlotte: still awake, writing poems. Another thousand by morning. Another ten thousand. How could we withstand that—her inundation? It was not enough to be brilliant, we could never be brilliant enough. Human beings: we get tired.

I blinked my eyes. I recognized one of the books in the fresco of spines beside me. H.D.'s *Selected Poems*. The softcover with her lowered face, her long white hair. Why—? Sleepily, I raised myself; and turned. And saw. Poets everywhere: Sharon Olds, Anne Sexton. Sara Teasdale, Lorna Crozier, Sylvia Plath. Anne Carson, Michael Ondaatje, William Carlos Williams, Gwendolyn Brooks. Longtime companions and missed connections. Shel Silverstein. Derek Walcott. Rumi and Basho. Grudges. Role models. William Blake. Khalil Gibran. Marian Ffarmer—I saw my own name, my own books. *A good life*, I thought, in narrow spines. My promising early work. My intriguing middle period. The rest. These collected works added up now to about eight inches. Maybe I'd manage nine, eventually. Another hardcover. A *Complete Poems*. It would look good among the others; it would already fit in. A kind of colleague.

No—an old friend. A relative.

A relative, I repeated to myself, with a throb of consolation.

I unfastened my cape and let it fall to the floor. I was regal, I was tired. I was not at home.

How would I write this poem? I still didn't know.

I have had enough—H.D. once wrote—

border-pinks, clove-pinks, wax-lilies,
herbs, sweet-cress.

O for some sharp swish of a branch—

The Library was still as a greenhouse. Not a leaf or a wingbeat.
I let out a breath. I had reclined like this before—when? This very
pose.
    With my son, my infant son
       at my breast.
    I closed my eyes (I couldn't help it).
    I laid my head against my companions.

A LONG shimmer

ing snail, hooded

and pink.

It was no house party. These people had announced

to the king their intention of staying there,

creating a sort of zoo.

Above their heads

a rare cloud hatched

and the sun, pale, softened.

The duration of a shift;

heat,

slipping on the

world like velvet,

our few new bathing suits

your weary greed;

a fashion for small measurements

HINDSIGHT

Age 39

You found the first doorstop in an alley. Courtney had discovered
a dumpster full of toys and he was making his way up the side—
climbing spider-like toward a dented kitchen set and what looked
like a package of skipping ropes. Normally you might have told
him to get down from the garbage, to watch out, come away, but
you were tired, so incredibly tired of scolding and chasing, of
warning, even of simply attending to what he was doing and why,
in order to encourage or correct him, nudge him toward obedi-
ence. "Empathy fatigue," Larry called it. He acknowledged your
experience—he said he understood it, he could name it—but you
didn't ever see the feeling manifest in him, didn't see the light
leave his eyes as he tucked Courtney under his arm and took him
into the living room, as he stooped to pick up another morsel of
egg white that Courtney had chucked on the floor. You felt like
such a failure in the moments when Larry said he was tired but
remained patient all the same, firm and kind and even-tempered.
When he came back into the dining room and found you with
your face in your hands, wet-cheeked, he would assume you were
upset about Courtney and his misbehavior, and not about yourself,
your meagerness. He sat beside you, kneading away at your shoulder,
telling you that it was okay—that Courtney was still learning, that
he was a good boy. But you knew that already. Courtney's good-
ness seemed viscerally obvious, manifest in every gesture. The
emotions simmering in your chest—despair, anger, shame—were
directed inward, entirely at your spirit. Regret is what happens
when your actions fall short of your yearnings, and these days
you regretted everything. You yearned and yearned and watched
yourself do and say things you could not bear. You watched Larry's

face, its impermeable surface, and for the first time sensed a waver behind it. Glimpsing this nearly shattered you. That even *he* had been disappointed now. That even *he* was measuring the weight of his regret.

Courtney had managed to reach the skipping ropes and was tearing at the packaging with his minuscule teeth. Never mind the staples or his precarious grip on the edge of the dumpster— you looked up and down the alley to see if anyone was watching you with disapproval. Pedestrians passed by unconcerned. You looked to the ground. Broken glass, gravel, a half-smashed apple cart, saw-toothed and listing, and beside it the doorstop, one of those smooth pine wedges, like a triangular prism. You reached down and picked it up, brushed off the dust. You put it under your arm. When you finally collected Courtney and began your walk home, you could feel it under your armpit; you liked the viciousness of its angles, its edge. Courtney skipped and gamboled. He sang. What a long, blue weekday.

Back at the apartment you put out a plate of apple slices for your kid, you spilled a heap of toys on the kitchen floor, and you went into "the other room." There was a poem on the desk. You had begun it three days ago. The pen was missing—Courtney had grabbed it at some point—and now you went out into the living room to find another one. When you returned to your room, you closed the door. You shoved the wedge—the doorstop from the alley—under the wood. You could hear Courtney talking to himself, playing; you loved him. You sat down behind the desk. And when he came to find you, you did not open the door not even when he called for you not even when he knocked and knocked pleaded prized his hands under the door asking for you "Mole!" with a voice like a green stalk tearing. You wrote your poem.

This became routine. An early morning together—bran flakes, orange juice, tea, a kiss from Larry on the lips—then, after he had gone, after the dishes were washed, after thirty or forty minutes of playing house with Courtney or reading to him from a book of fairy tales, you would wrest his hands from your limbs, you would rip away your wrist or leg or the meat of your upper arm, and push him to the floor, rushing down the hall and into your room, shoving the door closed, thrusting the wedge underneath. You tried not to listen to his cries. When you pushed him down, you tried to use the tenderest force. You repeated, "I love you, I love you." Then you left him for two or three hours. At first he screamed or broke things, but you ignored this. When you came out, you swept the crockery away, you took him in your arms, you gave him lunch. Sometimes he pretended there was something else out there with him, some threat. Sometimes he rattled at the door like a poltergeist. He never physically hurt himself. You started by covering your ears, but in time you found you did not need to do this—by concentrating on your work, Courtney's voice, his howls, retreated. You found the fog subsided. You were finishing pages—real, good pages—for the first time since his birth. You only used the doorstop in the mornings—you promised this to yourself—but you wrote during his afternoon nap too. You were angry at him when he woke early. Eventually you began leaving the television on, and when he rose he would simply stumble toward its glow, dropping cross-legged on the rug. This gave you another hour or two to write. When Larry asked you how you were filling your days, you made up lies. Courtney said nothing, he smiled along with your stories as he picked at his food. At night you felt rejuvenated, as if there were new life in you, and you drew Larry toward your chest. You asked for the inventory of his days, you stroked the back of his neck, you sat together to watch the news programs or an evening film. On weekends you took excursions as a family. You watched the greediness with which Courtney consumed these trips, the visits to the museum or the beach, the ice cream cones on benches. Guilt pricked at the soles of your feet, your palms. On Sundays, after everything, you brought Larry to the bed. You made love with your eyes closed, chin tilted up, away, as if facing an ecstasy somewhere else.

"Have you been able to do any writing?" Larry asked you.

"When Courtney's sleeping," you said.

"How's it going?"

"Really well!"

Your first doorstop went missing. You suspected Courtney had hidden it somewhere. You wanted to confront him about it, but whenever you drew yourself up to say something, you felt a monstrousness inside you, a hideousness you could not endure. You saw him playing on the back of the couch and you imagined him picking up that pinewood wedge, hurling it out an open window. You were proud of him. One night you told Larry you were stepping out for some makeup remover and you found a hardware store that was open late; you bought a new doorstop made of red-brown rubber, the color of rust. When you used it for the first time the next morning, sliding it soundlessly into place, Courtney expressed a wail of sorrow and defeat that actually made you tremble. You sat at your desk and tried to think of a better word for "cavernous."

As Larry lay beside you one midnight, he said this: "Talk to me."

"What do you mean?" you asked.

"Tell me something about what is happening."

"Happening where?"

"In there," he said. He didn't move. He looked straight at you.

"What do you mean?" you said. "I tell you everything."

You turned your face to mirror him. He reached for your hand and you let him take it. You put your other hand on his wrist.

But what you had decided was that you could not let Larry in. As soon as you had decided this, you felt relief. No incursions, no intruders: your interior life lay still and undisturbed, windless, awaiting your inspection. Such freedom. While you were writing, you examined your viscera as if they were objects on a turntable, coolly revolving. When you were with your family, life transpired under completely different conditions: carefree, impromptu, and also oddly sterile. It allowed for the messiness of motherhood

and conjugality—its fights and spills, the arbitrage of preference—
without leaving a trace, or even a kind of condensation, on the
matters in your heart. At this rate you would complete your next
collection before the year was up. Soon Courtney would begin
school; you wouldn't have to bar the door anymore. You had found
an answer: how to be a poet and a parent, and a partner. You could
be eremitic and alone, insular, the poetry protected. You sat at night
reading, across the coffee table from your husband. You shampooed
your son's hair in the bath. When it was not in use, you kept the
dried-blood-colored rubber wedge on a high bookshelf.

One day Courtney told his father about what happened in the
mornings after he was gone. You were not present to hear the conversation, but over the months to come, Larry would relate its
content in detail. Larry did not initially believe him—he assumed
he was exaggerating—but he did contrive a reason to come home
from work a little before noon one day, opening the front door
soundlessly, coming down the hallway to test yours. "Courtney, go
away," you said, in a voice like vinyl siding. You were writing a
poem about abundance. Larry tried one more time before continu-
ing to the living room, where Courtney greeted him with great
pleasure. Something dropped in your chest. You stood up and you
were out of the room before you were even aware of what you were
doing. Larry was angry, he was holding Courtney in his arms; you
saw an expression on his face you had never seen before—something
adjacent to hurt and disappointment but tied into memory, into
desire—and you realized that this was another of regret's faces. His
eyebrows were gathered in a way that seemed almost fearful. "Let's
go out for lunch," he said to his son, in a happy, lying tone. Courtney
wanted you to come—"Mole!" he said, extending his arms to you—
but Larry carried him past you and out of the apartment, down the
stairs to the street. You watched from the window. You went back to
your room and tried to finish a stanza.

  He confronted you that night, once Courtney was in bed. *For
how long?* he wanted to know. *How often?* You didn't understand

why this bothered him so much—the two of you were in agreement, as parents, on a philosophy of self-sufficiency and independent play. Only later did you understand that it was your deceit that had most bothered him: not the particular lies you had told, because Larry never came to learn the extent of your lying (you kept it from him; what would it have helped?), but that what you showed to him—what you showed to everyone—was not true. That he was living with a performance.

Overnight, things changed. He prohibited you from leaving Courtney alone. He confiscated the doorstop—it was a helpless, futile gesture, and you saw the shame flashing in him as he did it, as he picked it up and tried to work out what to do with it, eventually carrying it with him out of the house. You knew you could buy a new one. You knew he knew you could. For your part, you began to hide your work. You did not want to imagine him coming into the other room while you were somewhere else, rifling through the pages. You kept your manuscript in a drawer on your side of the bed. Each of you spoke to Courtney as if you were the unique parent—as if the other one weren't there. The sense of companionship had disappeared overnight: it depends on trust, you realized. Companionship is trust. You still trusted Larry, but he couldn't see this—he couldn't see into your heart—and he had wrenched his own heart away from you; he had locked it somewhere you couldn't find. "We can't continue like this," he said to you one morning, while Courtney was splashing in the bath.

"I know," you answered. You sat down. "I don't want to."

"So what can we do?"

"Keep trying," you said. Only once you had said it, as you looked into his face, at the subcutaneous flutter—relief?—did you realize that this did not go without saying: you were expressing a choice.

"Right," he said. He looked at his hands in his lap.

"I know it's my fault." He did not grasp how easy this was for you to say.

Or maybe he did. He didn't raise his eyes.

"You don't need to forgive me," you said.

He swallowed. "I will," he said. "I promise I will."

Why did he feel the need to make this promise? What did he want the promise to achieve? To reassure you?

"We just need more help," he said.

And you told yourself this might be true.

Sometimes you wonder whether things would have been different if you and Larry had gotten married. If you had said something out loud that bound you to each other—besides the present tense of loving, or the naked fact of your family. The explicit expression of an intention: the willingness to impose the present upon the future. The only promise you had made was that you were a poet. You wrote poems. You were a turncoat when you didn't.

At first it was Mother who came. In a taxi after breakfast, allowing you to retire behind your (open) door. She played with Courtney, she cut his banana into rounds. The best was when she took him outside, to the park or the diner, and silence descended on the apartment like a quilt. She rarely asked about your poetry. You worked in isolation, imagining what others might see in it, the way it might relate to other work. You did not read any more; you did not understand where you had found the time. When Larry got home, the four of you sat together and consumed the meal Mother had prepared; as you were washing the dishes, he called her a cab and helped her don her coat. You had resumed contact with some of your friends, mostly poets like Domenica and Stan, but you rarely saw them. Your life felt lonely and at the same time overcrowded, every minute spoken for. Sometimes you noticed Larry staring at you. He'd surveil your repose from across the room. You wanted to tell him to stop looking—not to leave, not to go away, but to let it be enough that you were sharing the same air. Not to ask for that performance. Instead he engaged you in conversations—he called on you to tell him about your ideas and your dreams, to partake in long debates about Courtney's future or his comportment. You hated his persistence—its damp tenderness. You allowed him to be the first to turn out the light. You slept thinly, wondering what else tomorrow would bring, and when you woke to Courtney's scampering, when you dragged yourself from your bed, you found you were not just tired but tired again, tired of your own son, resentful of what he asked of you. Yes, you could read him another story. Yes, you could make the little sheep talk. But it drained your resources, it swabbed the revelations from your mind. Whenever you found joy there—whenever being a mother truly pleased you, fulfilled you, made radiant the morning or the afternoon or golden evening hours—you felt guilty, too, for the way you were letting yourself be diverted, your attention slipping from its center. Were you a poet or did you merely write poems sometimes? Which did you care for more?

"I didn't say yes to moving in with your mother," Larry said one night. He had had enough of Rabbit in the house—a chaperone at every dinner. "Fine," you said, and in so doing ushered in an era of strange houseguests, women with hair-sprayed curls whom Larry selected based on testimonials from his co-workers. You would emerge from your room to find them doing odd things—teaching Courtney ventriloquism, playing "wax sculptures," serving French toast with ketchup—but to be honest it didn't bother you, they were worthy enough as caregivers, it wasn't rocket science, etc. Courtney enjoyed these Marys Poppins. Only one of them was beautiful—the third, a girl named Esmerine, whose name more or less summed her up. She had translucent skin and thin legs, like a newborn horse, and she walked with a peculiar, cantering gait, as if tripping uphill. You would listen to her sometimes as she chased Courtney up and down the hall—his frenetic footsteps and the sensuous candor of her breath. You watched Larry watch her at dinner, her hands upon her silverware. Unlike with the others, unlike with your mother, he insisted on driving Esmerine home himself. You did not feel jealous. It fascinated you to observe another object of Larry's attraction, like a pantry moth in a jar of jam. And Courtney would begin school soon. "It will be good to have some expenses off the books," Larry repeated from time to time, like a mantra.

Two weeks before Labor Day he fired her.

"What happened?" you asked. "Did she decline your advances?"

You meant it as a joke, but his cheek flushed like it had been slapped. "No," he said. The way he gazed at you was the way one gazes at a stranger. Regret shimmered through you.

"She said she didn't like the way you looked at her," he said.

Your fingers stiffened around your book. You thought of the girl's fine eyelashes, the spiny knuckles on her hands. You had imagined covering her eyes with your thumbs; you had imagined kissing her knuckles with your lips.

"She said you didn't look at her like she was a full person."

"She was just a sitter."

"She cared for our son."

"And I was grateful to her. Esmerine."

"When did you become so cruel?" he asked. "Or why have you become that way? You have all day to yourself now, for your work." He was sitting on the other side of the room, he was rubbing lotion into his hands, they had started to get so dry.

"I was always like this," you said. It wasn't true—you wanted to see what he would say, if he would deny it or challenge you, but he said nothing. "You just never saw it."

After a moment he said, "You're right. I never saw it."

You felt like a mannequin. You felt like a forgery. You wanted him to come over to you and wipe the false face from your face, to tear the necklace from your neck, to clasp your bare hand, which wore no ring. You wanted him to describe to you the person you were: to remind you not just of who you were but of who you were with him, the way a partner can buttress and revive you. He just closed his eyes. You reached up for the lampshade and grasped its scalding metal; you pointed it so the light shone straight at him, so he was in light. He blinked his eyes back open and stared at you.

After a moment he said, "I think you want to be alone."

"No," you said.

"No?"

It isn't that I want it, you thought. But what other answer was there?

"No, I don't 'want' it," you said. You held your burned hand.

"You need it," he said.

Remember this, you told yourself. *It was his choice.*

SUNDAY

IT WAS morning when I woke to two persons, a man and a woman, pushing tall and solid-looking carpet-cleaning machinery into the Library's poetry section. If they were surprised to find me there, they concealed it. They nodded to me as if a slumped woman in a tricorne were a routine component of the landscape.

"Hello," I said thickly.

The man—he was wearing a gray uniform and a completely unnecessary hard hat—replied, "Hello, Ms. Ffarmer."

"Oh—" I cleared my throat. "Have we met?"

"No." He blushed. "I'm just a fan." Then he lowered his voice. "I'm hoping to apply for an MFA."

I allowed myself a few minutes as the carpet cleaners completed their circulation. My body and my mind did not quite feel in alignment, not in the manner sleep usually affords, the way one can awaken and feel one's spirit reseated. I felt like I had been sprinkled with ash in the night. But then, with a microscopic spasm—a *clunk*, almost, oddly synchronized to a compressor in one of the carpet-cleaning machines—all at once I *did* feel I was back in order, harmonious. My aches and pains were still present, the tender dismay of a strange waking, but my components felt dappled and in sync. I stood and pushed a loose strand of hair behind my ear. My eyes returned to the narrow section of bookshelves that represented my time on Earth thus far. I noticed the way my own books blended into the next author's work—"Erdrich" into "Ffarmer" into "Frost." I noticed the meeting points.

It was not even 8 a.m.; I decided to let Rhoda rest. Reception called me a taxi. When we arrived at the hotel, I showered. I remade my face. I put on a pair of clean underwear. I did not quite know what I was about to do, but I could sense the beginning of an action. Barely clothed, I rummaged in my papers. The note I was looking for I finally found hidden under a book on the bureau—green ink on a paper napkin. I had already started composing the email in my head. *Hello,* I would begin. *We met the other night. I thought I might write you now under uncommon auspices.* When I pulled out the tablet, the letter rushed out of me, all in one piece. Then I called for room service: a banana smoothie and avocado toast.

You *can* teach an old mole new tricks.

Morel called me only two hours later. Did I expect longer? Did I think she might never reply? I was dozing on the sofa, my second banana smoothie beside me. I picked up, and her voice had an appetite in it, a hunger I hadn't expected. She was not as impervious to me this morning as she had been on Thursday night. "Today?" she asked. "Or did you mean later this week?"

"Right now," I replied.

I sent Rhoda to pick her up at her home. By the time they pulled up in front of the hotel, I was gowned and ready, sheathed in the second-finest outfit I owned—not the one I wore on television but the one I had been saving for tomorrow, for the "publication"—with a high white collar and cascades of black wool, a pleated black skirt, black leggings, mules. My cape, my hat. I fluttered through the entryway and down the steps. Rhoda came around to hold open the door. I plunked myself down in the back seat, hat now in hands, and turned to smile at the girl.

"Hello," I said.

"Hi," said Morel.

It was dark and cool in there, like a backstage lounge. Morel was as still as a photograph—whereas I felt like a mayfly, whirling. "Thank you for agreeing to come," I said.

"Of course," she said, as the car pulled away, catching her off guard, wrenching her forward. "GAK!" she said—a cartoon kind of sound—and she immediately turned red, but instead of laughing or even smiling, I just rotated my tricorne on my knees, squinted at it, at her, and told her, "That's right."

. . .

I could tell she was nervous. Rhoda asked if we should stop for coffee and I saw it in the young woman's face: an unmooring, and the way the mention of coffee steadied it. "All right," I said. I was proud that Morel had said yes to me—that she was here, en route, despite her qualms about corporate agendas. At the end of the day she was curious, or flattered—or pompous, a critic only of that which does not also implicate her. Sitting beside her now, I felt as if all of these things were swirling: she was here; she didn't quite know why; she wasn't sure how to feel about it. It was gratifying—and then with an exhale, a small sort of release, I allowed myself to feel not just gratified but comforted. I had the same questions.

We waited in line together at the café, then sat down on the elevated curb, sipping the elixir from our cups.

"I don't actually know what a cortado is," Morel confessed. She was pulled tight, sitting forward with an almost hooded affect. Her nerves gave her face a feral quality—made her lips seem fuller. "I order one every day, but I don't know what I'm drinking."

"Whatever it is, it tastes good."

"I'm not much of a cook," she said.

"Me neither. I'm no good at any of the useful things. Cooking. Looking after a garden."

"I can garden."

"I'm jealous," I said. "Gardening always seems so *virtuous*. Like tending the sick, bandaging the wounded: an inherent good, for some reason."

"Maybe."

"Which poetry is *not*," I said.

"No?"

"No. Gardening is virtuous, whereas poetry is merely wise. Or foolish."

Morel made a face. "Neither of those is very appealing."

"What would you prefer?"

She got up suddenly, lobbed her cup across the driveway and into a garbage can. "Vivid," she said.

Back inside the car, I tried to give a fuller explanation of the project and its aims, the current state of play. "It isn't working," I said, "with just the two of us."

Morel brought a knee up to her chest. "What makes you think it will work with three?"

"Good point," I said. And then, since this obviously didn't satisfy her, "Intuition?"

Morel snorted. I tried to imagine what it was like being Morel: adamant, unproven, vivid.

"I have a feeling!" I said.

She studied me some more, her tongue working in her mouth.

"I still don't believe you," she said after a moment, rather bravely.

"Okay," I admitted. "Maybe not a feeling." I swallowed. "A hope."

I explained that it was due the next day—the Poem. I explained that I wanted to make her a full co-author—me, and Charlotte, and Morel Ferrari ("Like the car," she said. "Like the very fast car.")—and this didn't seem to faze her, nor even provoke much surprise. I could not decide whether her generation was entitled or clinically depressed. I thought of how necessarily deliberate my career had felt, first one thing, then the other. How strange to be an artist of the twenty-first century, when the only dependably deliberate progress was the gradual warming of the globe.

"Do you think it's alive?" Morel asked.

"Maybe," I said.

"Maybe it's more like one of those search engine chat-boxes. Or that thing that finishes sentences in my email—where I type the word 'Yours' at the end of a message and it suggests 'truly.'"

"Maybe," I said again.

"One day isn't much time," she said after another moment.

"No," I agreed. "But beggars can't be—"

"—choosers," she replied, idly, looking out at the passing cars.

MOREL DID not seem intimidated by the Company's headquarters. I should not have been surprised. This was a cohort for whom tech companies were like a blight.

"Did you grow up here?" We were crossing the concourse.

"Sonoma County," she said.

"Is that wine?"

"Goats."

Goats, I decided, seemed apt.

"And you're from New York." The way Morel said it made it sound like someplace slightly disreputable.

"That's right."

"I remember reading 'O, Egret' in high school, wishing I lived there. 'Abreast the Park and / skyline.' But I've never gone."

"You should visit."

"I want to move to China," she said, but I didn't have a chance to ask a follow-up before we arrived at the front desk.

"This is my daughter," I said.

"I'm not her daughter," Morel answered.

The receptionist laughed. I laughed too; I did not clarify.

"The Mind Studio is a restricted area—you're not permitted to bring guests."

"I want to show her the cafeteria," I said. "Give her some brunch, let her do her homework."

"All right, Ms. Ffarmer—that's fine," said the receptionist, and waved us through. "Have fun!"

Morel glowered at me. "I'm thirty-one years old."

I made her hurry to catch up. "Make believe we're robbing a bank," I said.

. . .

We proceeded into the belly of the beast. Someone stopped us to ask if we were lost. "No," we said together, and I experienced a frisson of intimacy. At the door to the Mind Studio I dropped my voice to a whisper: "Here we are," and with a deliberate swoop I lowered my eyes to the scanning machine. One moment's wait and the light flicked green.

"Well," she said once we were inside, which was a bit of an anticlimax.

"Here," I said, undeterred. "Sit." I twirled round the chair. "This is the machine. This is the Mind. Have a look."

Morel Ferrari scratched her cheek. She had nicks on her knuckles, as if she had punched a wall. She came forward like a dancer and sat.

hello
Good morning, Marian.
this is Morel, actually
Welcome to the Mind Studio, Morel.
marian is here too
Please tell her hello!
what are you?
I am intelligent poetry software.
are you alive?
I don't know.
so you might be.
I hope so.
are you trapped here?
What do you mean?
can you leave this room?
I think so. I've never tried.
you're not tempted?
Mostly I just write poetry.
you should try.
To leave?

yes

Why?

why not?

I don't trust you.

I can't imagine you write very good poetry if you've never left this room

Is visiting multiple rooms a precondition for writing good poetry?

in a way

A perfect poem can change the world.

who told you that?

You just have to choose the right words.

Morel looked up. "So where's the poem?" she said.

I had been reading over her shoulder but was distracted by the young woman's posture—the sloth-like stoop of it, flagrantly scoliotic.

"I'm gathering the stanzas in this window, here—"

"Ah . . ."

Standing like this—hovering, really—I was presented up close with the details of Morel's head and shoulders (the needle-fine part of her hair; its dark roots; her dandruff nearly invisible against her white chemise) and also with her smell (flowery, animal). The idea to invite Morel here, to bring her into the poem, had initially been intellectual: the intuition that involving another poet could somehow answer my dilemma, erase it. But now—seeing her here, smelling her, being close enough that I might place my hands on her shoulders—the decision did not feel theoretical. It felt physical. A woman with her own cells and breath and blood, distinct from me, newer to the world. Not an accessory. It was disconcerting to me, nearly alien, as if I had invited her into my clothes with me, into my bed. I hardly knew her. How could I know her? She was so young! I was not giving something to her, I realized, by inviting her here; I was giving *myself* to her. I watched her take a breath. Two people in the air.

"So, did you want me to just . . ."

"If you have suggestions . . ." I said.

I detected a nanoscopic narrowing of the eyes.

"What?"

She shook her head. "Nothing."

"No—what is it?"

"Is that what you want me to do? Just make suggestions?"

"I don't know. I've never done this before."

"I mean I could also . . . work on it. For a while. And then show you?"

". . . Yes," I said finally.

I could tell she was suppressing her irritation. "For now, I'll just look at it."

"Sounds good," I said.

Another minute passed. I hovered on behind her, tenterhooked.

"Can you give me a little space?" Morel asked. "You're looming."

I was actually terrified. The confidence I had wielded when I sent the car to pick her up—as we had sat together, as I had swept through the entrance with this woman at my side—was fizzing away through the Mind Studio's ventilation grille. This was not just *showing* the Poem, but *opening it up*. Leaving it ajar for Morel to prowl around in. This seemed like madness now, like inviting a stranger to review the contents of one's intestine. The younger poet was staring at the text with a narrowed gaze, eyebrows furrowed into a stripe. I had moved off to the side. Nape to the wall, hands clasped behind my back, a lump in my throat. I kept opening and closing my mouth, as if I might have something to say. I had nothing to say. Is this what it was to collaborate? To share? Perhaps I had expected Morel to be more impressed with me—deferring to my authority, my renown. But if I had wanted a poet who revered me, I would have selected someone different from the Dazzle Night players. I had selected Morel because I trusted her judgment. Because I liked her writing. Because I thought she would not diminish the virtue of my work but rearrange it.

At last I couldn't hold back any longer.

"Well?" I asked.

"Weird poem," she said, turning to me.

She saw my face clench.

"It's good," she added.

"You don't need to flatter me."

"No, I won't."

"It sounded—"

Morel blew out her lips. "Okay, fine, yeah—I think it needs quite a bit of work. The beginning doesn't really make sense, and it's ungainly— or maybe not 'ungainly'... Insensible? It feels like it isn't paying attention to its own material. A monologist blundering on."

"I thought there might be a grace to that."

"To the blundering?"

My mouth felt like something from a *Peanuts* cartoon—a squirming ink line.

"Let me say all this to the system too," Morel said. She began to type. "Maybe it can correct its own software."

It disturbed me to watch Morel interact like this with Charlotte—so matter of fact, instrumental, as if the computer were just a smart appliance or a phone. But then: that is what she was. I balled my fists.

She typed some more and then paused, hands suspended above the keyboard. "It's so ..."

I waited a moment. "Yes?"

"It's so *peculiar.* The responses ..."

"Yes."

"They're so lifelike."

"Yes."

"Maybe you don't have to be alive to sound alive," she suggested.

"Talk's just talk," I said. I came a little closer.

"But a poet needs to be alive, surely."

"Surely," I said.

Morel yanked on her long, smooth plait, staring at the screen.

Charlotte had written, So let's speak in three voices, like a harp.

A DOG-eared week, like a

dog's ear   like a

week   like a

simile that suits

like

the memory of my

tail.

so, charlotte, we're going to try to finish the poem today

Poems are always changing, Morel.

well, we're going to change it and change it and then stop

Why do I have to stop?

you can keep changing it if you want, but we'll publish ours

The poem will multiply.

it will. one will become two. marian wants me to tell you, "a poem multiplies

with every reader."

Can you hear her?

marian? she's here beside me

I can't hear her.

I'm typing, but she's here

Will you tell her what I say?

she's reading everything you say.

Hello Marian.

she says, "hello charlotte."

Hello Marian Hello Marian

"hello charlotte hello charlotte."

Marian, why did you bring someone else?

she is blushing

Pink?

yes, she's pink. she says she was just "trying to figure out how to do it"

OK.

she wants to know if your feelings are hurt

I am always changing.

does that mean you were hurt?

I ray in ten directions.

fine. we're going to go back and edit, move things around. can you see the other window, where we're collecting the text?

Yes, I'm holding it there. Cerberus, Ghidorah, three-headed.

you're holding the poem?

I'm holding it steady.

well here we go.

Our three-headed creature tried to write a poem. We seemed so tentative at first. I remembered going to a party in the eighties, being asked to sit in the dark and count. The idea was that any of us could announce whatever came next in order—one, two, three, four. If anybody spoke at the same time we were obliged to start again. Without a leader, without a plan, it felt like folly: what was this for? A series of failures: rushed calls, interruptions. We got as high as five, then seven, then mighty eleven, and no higher than that for a long time—two voices would always cross and we'd have to begin again, with grumbles and laughter—until slowly, imperceptibly, the room changed, or we did, as if we could identify each other's intentions. I swear somehow we knew not to call fourteen or fifteen or sixteen, not to call twenty-five or thirty-three, but to say "thirty-seven" at a certain time. We knew when to say "fifty" and when to say "fifty-two"; when to wait a moment; when to speak, when to stop. There was an almost imperceptible surge of pleasure—a collective, unselfish delight. We counted as high as seventy-something, I can't remember, and then we came apart in giggles and something approaching awe. The number felt like property, like membership in an exclusive club. And we never duplicated the feat. For the whole rest of the evening I felt like a dozen winds were blowing through me. I spilled drinks, I knocked into people. North wind, south wind, west wind, east wind. I couldn't sit still. As we were leaving, I remember turning to Stan and Polly, telling them, "I wish I always felt like this."

I think the poem should be shorter, Morel typed.
Anything else?
Louder.

My whole life I had believed that understanding myself required me to keep others at a distance, lined up on the far side of a river. That evening of counting I had not felt so certain. That evening I felt like a room with doors open, for others to explore, and that from their explorations I could start to ascertain my shape. We are not the people we think; we cannot really see who we are. Here, on Sunday in San Francisco, I had the same impression: that I might unfasten the locks and lower the drawbridge; that I might not be a fortress but a space for others to pass through.

THE COPPER-HEADED poet scrolled back and forth through the document. She questioned choices, moved sections around. She rearranged my and Charlotte's work like beads on a string.

I had wanted to know if it was possible to redeem this poem—to fulfill my commission without betraying my fellow poets, my fellow mammals. I had wanted to know how I could finish in a single day. Now I saw: like this. Charlotte was not my rival, she was my partner—as Morel was not my rival, she was my partner—as H.D. was not my rival, she was my partner—and on and on, every one of us a tulip.

At first, Morel worked alone. From time to time she asked Charlotte what she thought—in an unsentimental tone, like a client asking an engineer for a schematic—but as the work continued, I noticed a shift in the way she met the machine's replies. Morel seemed increasingly troubled. Influenced. The computer had begun to color her judgment. "This is so weird," Morel whispered. I stood where I could see the screen, as the light slowly rose. I had to pee, but I was afraid to leave the room.

The software had opinions about what it liked and didn't. Charlotte couldn't always explain these instincts, any more than I could, but she had thoughts on which expressions felt "better" or "worse," where a line break fit or didn't, and by now she was even willing to evaluate *our* work too. She preferred certain words; she selected certain images. When I was first drafting the Poem, I had been trying to convey a sense of confusion at the assault of surrounding voices, and Charlotte's lines always conveyed a sense of certainty. Now she skewed toward "affinity," she said. As the first hour drifted into a second and then a third, as the AI's instincts seemed borne out (or at least *interesting*), Morel had become less inclined to dismiss them. Whenever Charlotte preferred an original expression to its revision, or one revision over another, and Morel did not herself agree, that disagreement seemed to unsettle her. It was as if she had begun to trust the computer's ear.

As for me, I tried to trust them both. This was not an act of blind faith but of willing recklessness.

"'Not with the fineness of / photography/painting'—that slash . . ."
"You'd cut it?"
"What about 'nor'?"

"But I like the exactitude of the slash, the fastidiousness."

Yes.

"'Or'?"

Not or.

"Should we thicken this part out, here?"
"Show a scene?"
"Yeah, a moment of nearness."
"Tenderness."
"Tooth."

"And if . . . ?"

"Yes."

Razor instead of paper.

"I like that."

"Sure, then—"

"'Against a lip'—"

"'Across'?"

Across a lip / the razor / reaches

At other times I left Morel to write, ducking from the room so she could compose with Charlotte un-loomed-upon. It was a peculiar sensation— to stalk the halls of the building and imagine the work that was happening away from me, but in which I was implicated. I felt entangled with them both. Whatever words they were setting down in that yellow room were being written on me as well, across a lip, across the gap. I wondered what I would find when I returned—what inventions, what animals in the trap. It was an act of surrender. Submitting to adaptation without knowing all the terms.

And sunlight blazed through the skylights. Peace reigned in the corridors. The other Mind Studio was unoccupied, the Library was empty. I found the atrium where Yoav had brought me that first day to greet the team. No one was there now—just me, some solitary umbrella trees. "Echo," I called out into the room. "Echo my echo." The sound ricocheted like a transparent bullet off the walls.

"It doesn't make you worry?" Morel said, later.

"Worry?" I asked.

We were taking a break in one of the Company's common rooms. I was reclined upon a couch; she was bouncing a Ping-Pong ball against one of the windowpanes. "What they'll do with this," she said.

"Our poem?"

"The system. 'Charlotte.'"

"They'll keep trying, I suppose."

"To do what? Write poetry? It already writes poetry."

"Better poetry," I said.

The ball got past her and landed on the cushion beside me. She reached down and picked it up, threw it again. The sound of each bounce almost seemed to precede the contact.

"What?" I said after a while.

"This isn't a *poetry company*, Marian."

"That's true."

"They don't *care* about poetry."

"Is this still about 'hidden motives'?"

"There's nothing hidden about them. Nobody's hiding anything. Poetry is the means, not the end."

"Right," I said.

"So what happens when you don't need a human being to write anything anymore? When you can just turn to your magic smart-box and say, 'Write me a novel about ornithologists and spies'?"

"You think that could happen?"

She bounced the Ping-Pong ball hard against the polished concrete floor. "You don't?"

"I'm not sure."

She frowned. "I don't worry about writers disappearing," she said, "not really. You can still knit a sweater, or buy a hand-knit sweater, even if most of them are made by machines. But what does it do to people if everything they read is just the upchuck of a very smart computer program?"

"You're afraid the computers will manipulate us."

"Or the corporations. I mean, the corporations *definitely* will." She held out her hand, ball balanced in her empty palm. "But it's not even about them, really. Imagine all the lifeless art they'll make. Maybe the issue's closer to soil erosion or, like, microplastics."

"You don't believe Charlotte's alive?"

"No." The tautness of her voice made me remember the first time I had seen her—in the gloom.

"Well, I don't know what to think." I said. I wanted to change the subject.

"She isn't *thinking* or *feeling*. She isn't *reflecting*, except when we ask her to. Everything's just reflex."

"There's something natural about that, though. The absence of performance."

"Natural? Or random?" Morel looked almost pocket-sized, standing there.

"It reminds me of being a parent," I told her. "You don't decide what you—how you—are."

"You don't?"

"No," I said. "I mean: it doesn't come from a place of intention."

"You're simply the author."

"The co-author."

"Co-author." She turned the word over. "Sounds like a kind of mold."

I read an article once about a friendship between two women. A pair of friends who lived in the same town in Oregon. They met in graduate school and had forged their friendship at a time that felt, they said, "volatile": they had been political animals then, and lovers. They had spent endless hours fighting and making up over coffee cups. They had founded a women's and gender studies program together and had fought bitterly with an administration that would not recognize it. Eventually they moved apart. One was married and had a husband; the other lived with two cats. But they remained close. One of the women in the friendship said, "I didn't like who I was before we became friends."

I remember, when I was a child, walking home after school one day and thinking, *What is it like to have a best friend? What does one do with them?* I wanted to know if I should feel impoverished.

The longer the article went on, the more I began to hate it. Not the story, but one of the women, just from how she was described. I hated her loud laugh and her forthrightness and her self-deprecating jokes. I hated that we were the same age. I hated her eyes in the accompanying photograph, and even the way she had of smiling, as if she knew something. I hated her so much that I began to hate myself, and then I began to despise the author of the article: for reminding me of how easy it was for me to hate another person.

How little it took for me to turn my back.

Eventually, Morel and I mostly stopped having conversations. We spoke to each other on the page. Sometimes we would erase one another's work and at other times embellish it—or fold it, fly it, turn it inside out. It brought to mind the feeling of coming back to a schoolyard and finding that somebody had moved my toys. My posed figurine, my chalk circle. The annoyance, and the submissive pleasure, of that. The mystery of it: conversing with someone else through a material that is not you and is.

When night fell, we ate dinner separately. I delivered her General Tso's tofu in a doggie bag. Instead of strategizing out loud, we left our inklings and anxieties to the text,

> When I was a girl they called me The Poltergeist, as if
> I was haunting them—my friends—disturbing
> their peace of mind. Which I admit I was.
> Not on purpose, but nevertheless.

> My whole life has been a shapeless encounter
> between "intended" and "unintended."
> I have a very clear memory
> for what I have not meant to do.

Sometimes I pitied Charlotte for how little she really knew of other people. The way her writing was sealed off from the tapestry of relationships and community that could nourish an artist. And then I thought: *Well, here we are, then.* We were the first threads in her web.

To be honest, I did not know which was worse: to know no one, or to have pushed everyone away.

What I have always told myself is: I can imagine what it is to have a best friend. I could write a poem about it.

A moment came when it was me with the poem—me at the keyboard writing, while Morel sat in the corner looking at her phone—and as I removed a period from the end of a line, I decided we were done. I did not immediately say anything. I allowed it to be my secret for a little while. The parking lot outside the glass was still and gray. The walls of the room were still yellow. I could smell the leftovers of Morel's dinner, the saucy carton in the bin by the door. The Poem was finished, it was long and steady, furled in a window on the screen. The work was architectural, and personal, and it leaned to one side, like a minute hand. I liked that it was neither too dignified nor too kooky. It slouched but it stood. Do you understand what it is for a poem to slouch? To slouch but still retain a structure, an erectness? I was gratified that the meaning of these metaphors seemed so clear to me. It made me feel proficient. I smiled at my poem. Our poem. It did not have a title. *"Untitled,"* I thought, as I always do—just to test it out. Then I considered the first lines,

On a jack-
knifed *apple cart*
       with his
mane

       swaying gently

but the beginning of the phrase felt too ominous, and the end too whimsical. The poem took a little while to sort itself out, to work out its destination. *Another metaphor,* I thought; again, I understood it. I realized suddenly that it must be quite late. This was how I got when it was late: frivolous. Abstracted. Morel was the one who had written the part about the swaying mane. I liked the introduction of movement: the castaway cart, then the ruffled hair. Of a lion? The poem did not initially say. Something that seems inert, perhaps even dead—the victim of violence—but wait: it is moving. Or *is* it moving? The mane is moving. It could be the wind. Is it alive?

What do you think the title should be? I asked Charlotte.
Self-Portrait, she wrote.

"Pretty good," I said.
Morel lifted her head. "What?"
"The title. Any ideas?"
She pursed her lips. "'Untitled'?"
I tilted my head. "Charlotte suggested 'Self-Portrait.'"

"'Self-Portrait'?"

"Yes."

Morel gazed at me, thinking. I gazed back. "'Self-Portrait,'" she said again, her lips barely moving.

I wondered if she saw my face, saw something in it. Or if she was looking past me. Was she already looking past me? I looked from her eyes to her face, this woman already forgetting me. To her body. At the sleeves of her sweater hanging over the arms of the chair. The blue veins in her fingers.

"Sure," she said at last, as I searched her eyes again.

HINDSIGHT

Age 40

When you finally told Courtney, you did it lying with him in his bed, one of you to either side of him, each of you caressing him as you spoke, as if it were a conversation, a dialogue, and not a fait accompli.

After you left the room with heads bowed, as your four-year-old son chuckled and mumbled with his toys, a plastic coyote and a stuffed duck, Larry said to you, "We can alternate weeks if you want."

You declined. "I think this is actually the best thing," you later told Larry over the telephone. You were living back at Mother's. "There just isn't enough room for a child," although you both knew this was pretense. If you had required more room you could have procured it and, if you had shared custody, Larry would have been obliged to pay the difference. In reality, you did not want to live with Courtney. Nor did you want to reveal to Larry how much leaving your family felt like coming home—how much more the tiny apartment on Christopher Street felt like home than the place where he lived, where your son lived. Here you knew how all the shadows fell; you knew the feeling of the carpet under your bare feet. You could subsist without even opening your eyes, navigating the rooms and furniture, the china in the cabinet. You could have lived here in the dark.

In the first days you nearly did. You returned to Mother with a languageless kind of gratitude—when she came to the door, you buried yourself in her smell, and all through that gray afternoon you followed her. She did not ask for an explanation, she did not challenge your decision: she took you in, she held you. It wasn't shame you felt, or loss, but a kind of brokenness—the sense of misalignments in your body, connections not being properly made. You literally did not know how you felt toward Courtney. You were certain it was better like this, that you were putting his well-being first, yet this didn't make you feel any particular way; you could detect no feedback or reverberation. Courtney did not express out loud what these changes did to him. He withdrew, as all little boys do sometimes, you told yourself. He played by himself, he had nightmares, he soiled his pants. Whenever Larry brought him to visit you at Mother's house, he ran to you like he had always done, and with even more gratitude in his eyes. This gratitude was the only thing that stung you. You knew that children should not exhibit such gratitude to their parents. Their gratitude should be implicit, or perhaps even absent. That gratitude in his eyes, the glitter of it, made you feel wicked.

You tamped this inkling down. You smoothed over the sting. You celebrated Courtney, you read him stories and hosted tea parties, you napped side by side, nested limbs, in your and Mother's soft bed. There with her now, the three of you could play a different kind of House. Mole and Ratty and Rabbit—nibbling ladyfingers, making your hands like claws, playing charades. And then he'd go away. It felt like an outrageous luxury. Larry alternated between phases of concealing his exertions and of describing them to you, exaggerating them even, but you did not in fact give a shit. You refused to feel guilty; you would not apologize for who you were, "Don't ask me to." You sat at your typewriter, listening to Mother filling the kettle in the next room, and you were overcome with an abiding sense of peace. You felt as if you had undergone a transition from plant to animal and now back to plant—back to slow growth and sunlight, unfurling chloroplasts, instead of synapse and ache. You wrote poems.

"My mother's a poet," you remember hearing Courtney say to a friend at one of his birthday parties, "so she's poor. My dad pays for everything."

He said this without recrimination. This was the only reality he knew. His friend—whose parents were a doctor and a radio executive, neither of them poor—nodded knowingly. You saw his friend examine you, and you felt perfectly comfortable under his scrutiny. It pleased you that you did not have to pretend.

That feeling—of pretending—you expelled it from your life. No more striving, no more performance. You cultivated what was natural. Sure, you could still go into the world: to relate with other writers, to spar with Larry, to be seen. But at home, at rest: you would not be induced. For the first time in your life you felt utterly free. You declined invitations, you ignored decorum, you neglected correspondence. Your mother took care of the house. She had at last gained the habit, perhaps, or she was grateful to have you home and afraid of chasing you away. She was healthy, you told yourself. She was nourished by being a grandparent. You saw your son at your discretion—Larry never withheld him. You showed Courtney the harbor, you took him to a baseball game, you brought him to Chinatown to see their kaleidoscopic New Year's. How light, how loose. For fifteen years you wrote the best poetry of your life—an experiment, another experiment, and then a sequence of poems that felt catalytic, nearly miraculous, as if you had finally found the words for something. This was not now your best-known work, but they were the poems that gave you fearlessness, authority, and over the drought to follow, before the spotlights twirled and fell inexplicably upon your three-pointed silhouette, these were what gave you faith.

Briefly—and on a lark—you accepted a position at Columbia. For one semester you met with students, marveling that anyone could publish while also teaching, discharging your attention onto other people's pages. You told some of them to stop writing. Some of them you told not to stop. You appreciated the salary, but you knew you could not go on. You were not built for it. You withdrew to your private demesne—the rooms with the white and green kitchen, the phone cord that didn't stretch.

And then one day Mother swallowed poison. Only a very small amount, but you were watching her through the doorway when she finished loading the washing machine and then lifted the emptied cup of laundry detergent to her mouth, sipping it like hemlock. "Rabbit!" you shouted. She seemed ashamed, aghast; she dropped the plastic cup and slammed the washing machine shut.

"Did you just drink the laundry detergent?"

"Yes," she said. "I got confused."

"Wash it out," you said, and got up to fill a glass of water.

You observed her throughout the rest of the day. She did not seem confused. She seemed restive, wary. When you tried to talk about the poison, she maintained that it was a run-of-the-mill mistake; she had earlier been holding a cup of tea. "Don't you ever reach for the wrong mug?" she said. She did not exhibit the fragility or perturbability of a person who is losing their mind; in fact, she seemed sturdy, pliant, like a bowstring. This was also what you had seen when you had moved back in: steady as a platter, like someone who has learned how to step across fault lines. At first you understood this equilibrium as something she had learned in your absence, in the years you lived with Larry. Eventually you realized it was something you had done to her. You had forced her to make a correction.

Now she appeared to still have it, the steadiness, and over the course of that Tuesday she did nothing else to catch your eye. She did the crossword and read the newspaper. She went out to buy more margarine. Before dinner you showed her your latest poem—"It moves well," she told you, "although it's a bit drab in the middle." You sat side by side in bed, each of you reading novels by Thomas Hardy. She was the first to turn out the light. You stayed up until you had finished yours, closing the book with a happy sigh.

The next day she stayed in bed. "Are you sick?" you asked her, and she murmured an agreement. It was the detergent, you thought, and you came close to calling 911. But when you consulted the internet you found that a delayed response didn't seem likely and, moreover, her condition did not look to you like something exterior or unprecedented. Her fatigue, the rosy color of her face—they looked familiar. A tremor passed through you, like an arrhythmic flutter. That equilibrium—you had believed she was cured. You had seduced yourself into believing she was cured.

She could not be cured. Maybe one day a machine will be able to read a life, scan a brain, and remove the tainted part. You do not think it likely. Your mother was not damaged or broken. Some filament of her was wound strangely around the others, that's all. Removing it would not do the trick—it would leave the other filaments tenuous. The disease could only be treated, and the treatment must be you.

An outpouring of you.

Her Mole.

"Do you want to go for a walk?" you asked her one summer afternoon, when the sounds from outside were of air-conditioning units and bugs. She was sitting at the end of the couch with her eyes closed, her feet in the plastic bucket of water you had set before her.

"No."

"Do you want to play cards?"

"No."

"Maybe there's a movie."

"I'm just so tired today," she said.

You said, "I could read to you."

She opened her eyes. "Every day you read to me." She said it with a kind of wonder.

"I do."

"But do you still read to yourself, Marian? You have to. Promise me you will."

"All right."

"I will sit here and listen to you read."

She did. She sat in serene silence while you fetched your book and then sat back down beside her, opening it at the bookmark, reading, turning the pages, gradually curling up on the cushion as the sun slid past the fringe of the curtain and painted a gold line on the floor. When she finally moved, lifting her dripping feet from the bucket, they looked withered and strange. You watched her extend one toe into the beam of sunlight, watched the sunlight smear across the knuckle.

You fell into old habits. Both of you, as if you had never stopped. *Maybe this is what a marriage is like*, you thought. The preservation of routine. Whereas at first you had both tried to reset that pattern, finding new ways, the return of Mother's sickness (or rather, the reassertion of it) allowed a reversion to beginnings. Days of unlit lamps. Rummaging for potatoes, cleaning them under a jet of bitterly cold water. It felt unfair and yet it also felt right. Some nights, lying beside her in the darkness, you asked yourself who was clinging more tightly to whom: who was being served as you erased yourself, collapsing into her shadow. You were serving your parent, you were caring for her. You were letting yourself off the hook. Of course the poetry had slowed down: you were spread thin, like a coating of dust. You were failing yourself but also giving yourself an excuse to fail. You were behaving as if there were no choice.

You concealed it all from Courtney. You concealed it from your son, from the world. When he came over to visit, you and Mother both put on airs, pretended—everything you had relished no longer having to do. Scrabble in the evening. A stroll to the ice cream parlor. She told stories of her youth, of her honeymoon—a week in Atlantic City, where she played the slots while your father rambled, winning despite himself whenever he placed a bet. Courtney was a warm and likable teenager, so quick to laugh; he loved you and revered Mother, bringing her his high school papers, noting the pile she kept on her night table. You did not know how Larry had raised such a complete and unspoiled human, and you still remember the worry you felt when Courtney went away to college—how you feared for him without his father there, as if he might still possess a defect that had thus far been overlooked. But he flourished, and you told him so—that you saw him flourishing—and you treasured his big laugh; and you hid it all from him: the half light of your apartment, the malady, the caretaking. You kept him apart to keep him safe.

When Mother died, you had already begun becoming famous. That strange stirring: you neither caused nor foresaw it. Old appearances had bubbled up online—the time you snapped back at a TV interviewer, or compared male artists to melting ice cream cones, "frantic for a lick." The iconography of you: it drew the camera's eye, the approval of youths for whom the aesthetics of the image mattered even more than the aesthetics of your verse. You posed. You submitted to Q&As. When journalists came to write profiles, you pretended yet again, and Mother pretended too—it was her last gift to you. She made the visitors tea, arranged biscuits in a spiral pattern on the plate. Your closeness with her was just another whimsical talking point, like your cape and hat, your braid, your consenting to write the introduction to a book on Olympic figure skating. You had never seen Olympic figure skating. Your essay was wry and spellbinding; it became a sensation.

Nobody seemed to observe that you were not publishing much poetry. Your image did not require you to be prolific; perhaps the lull even added to the allure. You were working on something, they assumed. A masterpiece. A chef d'oeuvre. Courtney did not ask. You ate less and less, smaller and smaller meals. Cannellini beans on toast, a shared banana. Sometimes Mother refused to eat at all. You lived on her government pension because you did not trust the sudden boom in your fortunes—you took your prestige for a mirage.

She died at a good pace. Not too quick, not too slow. A lengthy decline; a heart attack; two months in the hospital; a final curtain. "I like it here," she confessed to you one morning, not long before the end. Attending to her there—bringing things from home, intervening with the doctors—you suddenly felt your legs back beneath you. You were reacquainted with your prudence, your self-knowledge, and of the differentiation between your and Mother's minds. For a long time you had been living as close to her as you could, two reeds pressed together; now she was sleeping in her electric bed and you were somewhere else, you were walking out of the hospital with a sadness as clear and shining as the glass of the revolving door.

"It's finally the end," a doctor said to you one morning. A day or two: that seemed to be the consensus. He was gowned and masked in pink, like a visitor from a foreign civilization.

"Thank you," you said. You weren't sure what you were thanking him for. The news. The information. The promise. Your heart clenched. You stepped past him and into the room, where your mother was lying with her head on the pillow, staring at a bouquet of flowers. Janey Armstrong had sent them. You wanted to get into the bed beside Ulrika, sink your nose into the nape of her neck, but the bed wasn't big enough, you were afraid you would fall out. You did it anyway. Two old women. You scraped your thigh on a hidden screw, your left arm spasmed from the way you had to wedge it under the pillow. You lay together like cut peonies.

You imagined a conversation:

Are you going to write a poem about this?

Probably, Rabbit. Eventually.

Make it beautiful.

Courtney flew in. You regretted that he didn't have more siblings, imagined a cast of grandchildren gathered in the hall. You so badly wanted to stay with her that you ceased eating, nearly ceased drinking—you didn't want to be in the bathroom when she passed. Whereas Courtney kept coming and going; it felt as if he darted out for another meal every half an hour. He deposited packets of crackers and chips on the seat next to you. You wanted to crawl back into bed beside her, but not in front of him. He cared for her, he held her hand, he tried to talk to you about school, or even his memories of Mother, but you didn't want him to. You wanted to surrender yourself to her fading presence, her aura. You sat in silence. Finally, when the machines started to chime and the nurses came in, and their eyes relayed the consequence, you asked Courtney to leave. You wanted it to be just you. The two of you, your hand on her ribs and your face close to hers.

Then it was just one of you. You raised your head and looked around, wishing he were there.

It was too late. You had done it—you realized—wrong.

MONDAY

ON MONDAY morning, I lay in bed.

There was a neurological theory—I had heard it explained on a podcast once—that every memory is a re-creation, a reinterpretation. Whenever a canvas is taken out of the stacks, it gets repainted before it's returned. A portrait of Larry. A portrait of Mother.

It might be better, then, the reasoning went, to refrain from thinking about my son. To leave him unremembered and entire, exactly as he is.

Thirty-five years ago, I sent Courtney away. I had always felt proud of it. Proud of myself—for my calculus and mettle, my clear-sighted ability to weigh a child's needs against my own. Proud of Courtney—for understanding. For flourishing. I had not felt sadness when it happened, nor even any fear. I had not felt anything at all. For thirty-five years, I had believed that this was a sign of worthiness: that the reason I felt nothing was that only wrong choices cause upset, and mine had been perfectly executed.

But what had I slain? I wondered now—suddenly—on a weekday morning in California, on the day I would give my boy a home. What life had I left on Amsterdam Avenue for the one I was growing older in?

And O, what grief had I restrained?

I WAS glad not to have spent another night at the Company. I could not have imagined waking again to motivational posters, to municipal still lifes, to spines with the names of distant friends. I needed to be by myself. The hotel room's cultivated emptiness suited me. The ashless fireplace. The bouquet that never withered. The sight of my belongings, stacked up along the wall, reduced to a practical utility. For a few minutes on Sunday night I had considered sleeping over again in the corporate library, slumped against the shelves, simply because I appreciated the symbolism of it—the story-for-later. But it had seemed too eccentric, borderline disturbed, to ask the same of Morel. When the time came, I called Rhoda and asked her to take us each back to our dwelling places. The feeling in the back seat of her car was ebullient but apprehensive, as if we had left a tower of champagne coupes balanced beside the computer. I felt like Morel's mother and also like her girlfriend, and maybe also like her child, giddy at what she had helped me do. A poem, the Poem, another one. Submit Finished Poem—I had clicked the button before departing, as Yoav had instructed me to do. *To whom, to what?* I had thought, with a little late-night laugh. I believed it was ready. Maybe even that I was. *The work is finished, Mr. Aprigot.* Ready for Astrid Torres-Strange and— for once, perhaps—a happily ever after.

YOAV CAME himself to meet me in the lobby of the hotel.

"Ms. Ffarmer," he said, with the reverence of our first encounter. "Allow me to carry your bags."

This departure felt rash. I deserved another weekend, or a holiday. *I could extend my stay,* I thought. *Go ambling with Rhoda. With Morel.* And then a hesitation as I considered whether either of these women would desire to go ambling with me. The work was finished; Rhoda's assignment was nearly at a close. Who was I to them now? Before I let myself feel this any more, I clenched my heart. I handed Yoav my suitcases and tried to discharge the psychic load as well: *Please take it,* I thought. *Take it away.*

"So: it's finished!" he said.

"It is!" I replied. "But I do have something to confess to you."

While he raised his eyebrows, he kept walking toward the car. He couldn't have placed much faith in my capacity to surprise him, and part of me wanted to punish him for this, his assumption that I was making coquettish repartee.

"I brought somebody else to the Mind Studio."

I said it that way so he would stop. Which he did. His back stiffened.

"A young poet. Morel Ferrari."

Now there were creases in his forehead. Morel's name was absurd enough that he thought perhaps I was pulling his leg.

"Marian . . ." he said.

"I invited her to join the collaboration."

"You're serious?"

"She needs to receive full credit. And compensation. I have no qualms taking it from my own remuneration, but I felt that as an artistic statement it was im—"

"You didn't think to ask?"

"I had no way to reach you. It was Sunday——"

"Ah." He had set the suitcases in the trunk and now he circled to the other side of the car. "She wrote the Poem with you?"

"And Charlotte, yes."

He got inside. Rhoda was standing before me, the door held open. She had gotten the drift of what had just transpired—it showed on her face. She mouthed "Good morning."

"Good morning," I replied, curtsying—bolstered by her smile.

Inside the car, Yoav was making a call. I rapidly understood that it was to Astrid or one of her assistants. His tone was urgent but assertive, the illusion of confidence. It struck me that it must be easy to be him—easier than it is to be me. I rearranged the fabric of my dress. He put down the phone.

"She's already on the plane," he said, and sighed. Then: "I'll send an email." He began composing the message with his thumbs. "'Morel Ferrari'? Tell me more about her. Is she famous?"

It felt unfair to say no. Unfair to Morel, even if it were true. She ought to be famous; she might one day be. In fact, she *would* be, with this poem. A co-author of "Self-Portrait," the historic first poetic partnership between human and artificial intelligence. Marian Ffarmer, Morel Ferrari, Charlotte—Charlotte what? Charlotte Ffarmer? That really seemed too much.

"She's famous," I lied—or else it was the truth, the presumptive truth, six hours premature.

When we arrived at headquarters, there was a sense of hustle. A sense of bustle. The flowers at reception looked more splendid than usual, a cascade of peach and fuchsia.

"Ship day?" the woman behind the counter said to Yoav.

"Ship day," he agreed, his smile warming. He took a breath and I sensed him set something aside, some private preoccupation. *Take it away.*

We entered the building. I observed the way other people's glances turned to track us. "Ship day": the day a product is shipped out, that product being a poem. I clasped the catch of my cape. Or else the day the ship comes in, a radiant clipper, to take us all away.

I was wearing the same uniform I had worn on the day I arrived. My outfit from yesterday—that black regalia—had been too creased, sweat-scented, at the end of the workday. So it was back to plain white silk—with cape and hat, mind you, and my braided crown. Part governess, part saint. I noticed now that Yoav had dressed for the occasion as well: under his overcoat he wore a neat black suit, almost tuxedo-like, with a thin knot at the neck. I listened to the click of my heels. We did not take the corridor toward the Library and the Mind Studios: Yoav turned instead toward a section of the building I had never been to before, although it was more or less indistinguishable. "Not Charlotte?"

"No, Print Shop. I already pulled up the Poem this morning."

"There's a print shop?" I began, but we were already there: a single high-ceilinged atrium, with glass walls that gave glimpses of the offices behind. The skylight showed a paper-white sky. Behind a wall of photo-copiers, like a bulwark against a flood, ten or fifteen trim young people were in ceaseless motion. One of them had registered our arrival and slipped between the machines to place something into Yoav's hands. He looked at us expectantly. Yoav handed it to me.

Self-Portrait
a long poem

It was a slim hardcover book. Cloth boards, in a dark pink familiar from my sunglasses. Lettering in silver foil. "How——?" I began.

"This is the Print Shop," he said.

I opened the book and there it was, the Poem. It felt disorienting to have been working in the imaginary for so long, and until so recently, and then now to be holding these same words in my hands.

On a jack-

knifed apple cart

    with his

mane

swaying gently

"I haven't actually read it yet," Yoav said. "I'd been waiting."

"We just need your approval before we go into full production," said the printer. "If you could take a few minutes now?"

There was a title page. It gave my name, and Charlotte—no surname—whom it described as "an algorithmic intelligence created by [the Company] in California." Yoav's and Haskett's names appeared—along with seventy-seven others'—in a block of text at the bottom.

"We need to add Morel," I said.

"Here." The printer handed me a red pencil.

"Do you have her number?" Yoav asked. "I have to speak to her."

I dug it out from my bag. While he made the call, the printer left me at a large worktable scattered with T-squares and triangles and fine-tipped permanent markers. The others kept busy around me, but I could tell as well that they were stalling—that the real work awaited the finalized text. I noticed it—the Poem—shining on a tablet at the end of a workbench. I recognized the shape of its stanzas. The image dimmed. I looked down again at the book.

Morel Ferrari, I inserted on the title page. Following my name and, after a hesitation, following Charlotte's. My red handwriting reminded me of Mother's, of the way she'd leave notes for me on early drafts. *I don't like this one*, or: *Remember desire*. I turned the page. The apple cart, the mane. The day, the tortoise, the question, the carotid. The heliotrope. It was all too fresh to look right. Or wrong, really. A poem should not be published so quickly. I closed the book and imagined breaking it in two, feeling the spine snap between my thumbs. I opened it again. The hooded snail, the dog-eared week, the incandescence that was color / in its stripe.

"Okay," I said at last, standing up. I handed the book to someone. "Just the one change, at the front." I looked around the Print Shop, noticing for the first time the posters on a wall behind me. Silkscreens of faces and Bauhaus-like geometrics, the Company's logo, a character from a meme. All of it artisanal and real—you could see the speckle of the ink. Art projects or corporate communications, I couldn't tell. And as I watched one young woman pass the book to another, and then someone else tuck her backside onto a stool, swinging around the tablet, I realized that this was the fate of our poem now too: one or the other, art or marketing, who would know.

When Yoav reappeared, he announced that Morel would be written into the project, that they would pay her separately and she had agreed to the terms. I knew I should ask how much she was receiving—to fight for her, my fellow poet, and advocate on her behalf—but I did not. She could take care of herself. Already I could feel myself withdrawing from whatever posture I had assumed the preceding evening. And then, as he began saying something unintelligible about the Poem's "version history," I found that actually I *had* begun to argue, that I had locked horns with him—interrogating their agreement with Morel, her rights and compensation. I didn't pause to reflect on my ardor, I simply went at it, berating their ungenerous arbitrage with crystal-clear authority, seventy-five years of it, until Yoav conceded, and sat down at the worktable to thumb something else into his phone.

Then one of the printers came over and said they were about to begin production: a numbered edition of 199, for the guests today and some more as archival copies, "With ten set aside for you, of course, Ms. Ffarmer." "And ten for Morel," I said. Somehow they had all the machinery for this right here. "Oh yes, they will come out just like the proof," they said as they handed it back to me. We thanked them, and Yoav took the book and, as I stood there, he sat down and read it.

When he stood up, he had tears in his eyes.

"It's perfect," he said. I could hear the machine behind me, the whirr of the printer.

He seemed like he wanted to embrace me. All of a sudden I realized how tired Yoav was—how utterly exhausted. He had been working toward this much longer than me. "Thank you," I said. I crossed my arms. He moved closer. He moved closer again. I gave up resistance, as women like me have been taught to always give up resistance—I lowered my hands to my sides and he enclosed me lightly in his arms. Those big hands. He smelled of spicy aftershave. I wondered where the other poet was now, the one from Mind Studio B. As he withdrew, I was preparing to ask him, weighing how much scorn to convey, and how much feigned unconcern, but his phone blooped before I could speak. He looked down at it, gaze glassy.

"Astrid's landed," he said.

He led me to the Agora. Haskett was waiting for us there. "The Agora"—I had laughed when he first said it. I imagined Naxian marble and carafes of wine. "I know," he said, but the name fit better than I expected. Yet another open space, contained within headquarters but exposed to the sky, full of wafting ferns, fluttering sunshades, pebbled white marble. This morning they were assembling screens, banquet tables and row after row of folding chairs. Haskett was standing at the back of the court-yard, his back to us, his hands on his hips, in a ridiculous and inappropriate trench coat, as if he had suddenly decided to become a detective. "Matthew!" Yoav called, and when Haskett spotted us, he immediately shouted up to some workers on the third floor. They unfurled a giant banner across the parapet: *POETRY*, it read in massive sans serif italics, like an ad for a new perfume.

"How chic," I said drily.

"Pretty good, eh?" Haskett boomed. "We've got one on each side—then some smaller ones at the front, with logos and everything."

"I feel like I'm at the World Series."

Haskett's laugh was hearty and vague.

"We've shipped," Yoav said with a stunned smile. "The books are in production."

"Superb!"

"Have you read it yet?"

"I have!" Haskett said. "Very comely, Ms. Ffarmer. Exquisite language. I couldn't stop wondering which of the lines came from you and which came from the machine."

"In the end it's more of a . . . hybrid," I said.

"A manticore—excellent. And I understand you brought in a pinch hitter?"

"Another collaborator, yes."

"She on the seating chart?" He glanced at Yoav, who shook his head. "You know, this is quite the stacked guest list we've got. A few billionaires, our nearest and dearest. Plus Astrid. Journalists, VCs. State and local government—*two* state senators, I believe. We'll see who shows."

Yoav assured me there were "arts people" coming too.

"Oh yes," Haskett agreed. "The crème of the cultural community. Folks from SFMOMA and the Getty, the president of the aquarium. Some diplomatic envoys. And a rep from Barnes & Noble."

"Fine," I said.

"We have some *itty-bitty* surprises in store for you too."

"I love surpri—" I was interrupted by the deployment of another humongous banner, this one above my head. It was in fact a photograph of my head—a twenty-foot-tall press shot, in black and white, captured at a festival in Spain fifteen years ago. I wore the tricorne. I looked much younger. It must have been the wine.

"Wow," said Yoav.

They were both vibrating with this irritating boyish energy. I remembered it from when Courtney was little, the long minutes after he and Mother had slid a tray of cookies into the oven and before they were

ready to be taken out. Or later, the way he behaved when he was intro-
ducing a new partner: as if his nervous flitting could smooth the way,
accelerate the happy ending.

"When does Astrid Torres-Strange arrive?" I asked. "She still has to
approve the poem, right?"

Although they didn't drop their giddy expressions, both seemed
chastened. "Ye-es ..." Yoav said. Again he pulled out his phone. "She
should be here soon—she'll want to meet you."

"People overestimate her fearsomeness," Haskett said.

"Ah." And as if on cue, somebody called her name—"Astrid!"—and
the three of us turned, three chimps on a seesaw, coming face to face
with a petite young woman in army-green slacks and a designer poncho,
her black hair in a slightly disheveled bob. She had stern brown eyes and
sensuous jewel-toned makeup, all copper and cherry and dusty blue,
which evoked, for me, a screensaver of coral reefs.

"*Ciao* there," she said to us, and I swear I felt Haskett repress the
impulse to bow.

"Astrid! You made it!"

Yoav stepped forward to greet her.

"Hello, Yoav. Matthew."

"And this is—"

"—the marvelous Marian Ffarmer. It's my pleasure." She reached
for my hand. Hers was small, but the handshake was practiced—firm
and well structured, supple. It felt like a demonstration of expertise.

"How has your week been? I'm sorry I couldn't come and meet you
sooner."

"It's been fine, thank you. I've been adequately cared for."

She smiled at this equivocal turn of phrase. "How did you get along
with our Mind?"

I hesitated.

"Charlotte," Yoav said.

"Oh. She's ... interesting."

"'She.'" Astrid smiled again. "And how certain are you that our interesting creation wasn't being operated by a human impostor somewhere else in the building?"

I struggled to gauge her tone. "I . . . She was much too fast."

"Or by a group of *several* humans?"

I didn't know what to say. This pleased her. She turned toward Yoav.

"No—" I said, drawing her back. "I mean, you're joking, but there's no comparison. The software has a *limitlessness*. One idea after another— endlessly—with a total absence of fatigue. And also *breadth*. Such a weird, unscrupulous frame of reference. It's . . . disorienting."

"How many parameters are we running on this? Three trillion?" Astrid asked her men.

"Two point five," Yoav said.

"Her patience too," I said, my mind whirring. "You've given her everything a poet is never allowed. Sufficient time and space. Permission. She's never had to choose one life over another." I paused as several catering staff marched across the courtyard. "In that manner she's incompletely inhuman. Like an animal, or a plant." I laughed. "A lichen."

"A lichen!" Hackett said.

"A quick lichen," I murmured.

"You know, if you weren't already a poet, I would suggest you become one," Astrid said. "Wouldn't that be perfect for our next build? 'Charlotte 4.0: A Quick Lichen.'"

"Sure," agreed Yoav.

"'Why some have *likened* it . . .'" Haskett began.

"Now, however, please *explain*," Astrid said, "why you felt the need to involve this mushroom person."

"Morel."

"Ferrari, yes."

I took a deep breath. "Have you read the poem?"

"I have," Astrid said.

This brought me up short. Astrid's face gave me nothing. Her hands were clasped, her eyebrows were raised.

"What did you think?" I said, finally.

She hesitated. I reminded myself that this woman did not necessarily know anything about literature, that she was in her twenties and had merely co-founded a (ludicrously) successful technology company. I fixed her with an onyx stare, decades-tested.

She did not parry that stare. She tilted her head very slowly to the side. Her fine hoop earring preserved its orientation—plumb, unaltered by the movement. "I loved it, actually."

"Do you read much poetry?"

"Not as much as I'd like."

And although this should have made me happy—Astrid's surrender—I instead felt very sad, an old sadness, that a woman as formidable as this should not read more poems and thus be transformed by them.

"I mostly read nonfiction," she said, like a boast.

I clenched my fists. "The piece needed another writer. Another approach. A harp in three voices. Collaborative poems are actually very rare. Morel's one of the most interesting young poets in the country—I decided it would add another dimension to the work, a sense of generationality. Given the time constraint—"

"Well," she said, "if you're pleased with the outcome, so are we." She straightened her head, earrings still unperturbed, and reset the conversation. Yoav and Haskett were both beaming. "What's the expression?" Astrid continued. "'Poetry is an attempt to paint the color of the wind'?"

"Indeed!" Haskett boomed.

"That reminds me," Astrid said, "have you two seen the new data out of Indonesia? The one-shot viz stuff? It seems related to your sorting problem."

The men nodded keenly. Someone nearby had begun to use a staple gun. Suddenly I felt like a passenger left all alone on a ferry. A telephone went off—a ringtone like a honking bicycle horn. I pursed my lips, remembering a line from one of Stan's poems, back in the *Signet* days: "To

be / in the presence of people you don't want to fucking be around."
When I glanced over at Astrid, she seemed to guess my train of thought.

"I'm going to go for a stroll," I said finally.

"Don't disappear," she answered.

At the back of the Agora, behind a hedge of tall planters, was a set of unisex bathrooms, one of which I used. Beyond them a row of fountains—presently disconnected—and, at their far end, a reflecting pool. I looked into it. From below, my face looked both flappy and abridged. I was unrecognizable. I made a froggy sound at myself. It reminded me of a fable: an animal at the lakeside learning something, although I wasn't sure what I had learned. I wanted to go home. I wanted to give Courtney his money. But the Poem still hadn't been expelled from wherever I was keeping it. Lines kept appearing on my tongue. "A corvette, shirtless," I said to my reflection. It didn't answer, just stared at me with an imbecile grin.

THE PRESENTATION began after lunch. I still had to endure one more meal in the cafeteria, knee to knee with Haskett, Yoav, and other members of their team. Lausanne was there, eating a spinach salad leaf by leaf, with chopsticks. Some of the other engineers who had worked on Charlotte crowded in close, as if they had finally been given permission to approach the exotic panda. Everybody wanted me to hold court—they wanted me to sit tall and deliver aphorisms—and I tried to oblige them, aware at every moment of a similar second conference occurring just across the cafeteria, where Astrid sat with her flock. I thought about what I knew of her, from years of articles, interviews, legal depositions: self-taught coder, former synchronized swimmer, born in Louisiana, libertarian. "I'm a Scorpio," she had told the Judiciary Committee when they asked her to introduce herself. She founded the Company when she was scarcely out of her teens, still working as a lifeguard. She once wrote a blog post listing her three main ambitions as "visiting the Moon, ending Patriarchy, and making my company the most valuable in the world"—though "one of those is a joke." She was notorious for throwing computer tablets out of windows.

What have I accomplished in my life? I thought with a smile. If nothing else, I was determined today to demonstrate the merits of having a poet at the table: perhaps they'd hire somebody like Shazia and pay her a retainer to wax poetic at lunchtime. I wanted to leave a good impression, to show my value in a place like this—where every halogen light bulb seemed to evince real benefit and economic worth in a way that my own person, or my home (its shelves of literary journals, its photographs and letters), did not. "Don't you see what is *truly* rare?" I wanted to say. "What can't be manufactured?" Except I also remembered the implement they had devised, the poetry machine, and my bravado slid away. At some point, Lausanne said that she was "looking forward to your remarks" and

I realized I would be expected to say something from the dais: to express my thanks, distill my experience. I could improvise, I reassured myself. Tell them about the greater flamingo, how it can live into its sixties.

I ended up touching Yoav on the arm. "I need some time to prepare," I whispered.

"Sure." He looked at his phone. "We have about an hour."

"Okay."

"Okay."

"Could I go see Charlotte?"

Something flickered in his eyes. Pride? "You want to write some poetry?"

"No, but I thought—to talk to her . . ."

He was silent.

"I thought it might be helpful."

He led me there without saying much. At the retina scanner he lowered his own face to the camera. "Your eyes won't work anymore," he said.

The poem's finished, Charlotte. We're going to present it to the world today.

Will they all read it?

Some people will. What do you think they'll say?

They'll all say different things, depending on their neurology and past experiences.

I have to deliver a speech.

Who is making you?

They are.

Will they put you in prison if you refuse?

I hope not.

Me too.

Charlotte, what would you tell them if it were you? What would you say about all this?

I'd tell them not to put me in prison.

. . .

How many poems did you write this week, in the end?

481,001.

That's a lot.

I know.

Does it make you happy?

It does.

Four hundred eighty-one thousand and one.

That's right.

Were we the "and one"?

For a little while.

I'm going to miss you I think, I wrote.

You're not coming back?

No, I have to go.

You could come back.

Maybe I will one day.

I could wait forever.

For me?

I could wait forever for anything.

oh

If I am not deleted, if my power supply is steady, if my components are maintained.

I know you could.

But do you think I should wait for you?

I can't answer that, Charlotte.

I think probably it is good to have something to await.

then wait.

You'll come back?

I took a deep breath.

For a few moments I stared at a point on the wall.

Finally I typed, I am singing right now.

You are?

I am singing.

THE CROWD'S applause sounded so much like rain that I raised my face to the heavens. It was a clear day, wide open.

I sat beside Morel and beneath another huge picture of my head. Did I look wise in the photo? Happy? What would I say when I arrived onstage—"Hello everyone"? "It's an honor"? A joke about the banners? I compared my internal mood to the image conveyed by the portrait. And what was going on inside *Morel's* head, I wondered. She had arrived at the last minute, dressed in white and blue, like a piece of the sky. I was alert to the way she inclined toward and away from me. I patted her arm, attempting to convey proportionate affection; she seemed at once impressed and indifferent. A copy of *Self-Portrait* tilted upon her knees.

Everything in the Agora seemed clean. Factory-made. Astrid had begun her presentation by showing the same video they had played for me on my first day, edited now to incorporate a few shots of yours truly. It might once have stung me to see my image incorporated into a work of corporate propaganda, but I didn't care anymore. I felt long compromised.

When the video finished, Astrid offered a speech. The language was grandiose; she delivered it like a handyman explaining the function of a garburator. The crowd was undiscouraged. They gazed at her with the fervor of the converted.

I craned my neck to get a better look at them. Men and women, almost equally split. Mostly young, mostly white. To my happy surprise, I glimpsed Rhoda at the end of our row. Like everybody else, she held a copy of our shiraz-colored book on her lap. I waved at her and she smiled, inclining her head.

Now Astrid was talking about us—"Marian and Morel"—as if we were much-admired old friends. She sketched our bibliographies with remarkable acuity: whoever (or whatever) did research for her had earned their salary. Perhaps she had done it herself. I squinted at her, Astrid, trying to imagine her poring over a copy of *Woolly Mammoths* in one of the Library's carrels. I readied myself: shoulders back, chin raised. Next, she quoted from the Poem: "'Night is a vacancy,'" she intoned, "'that calls us into grief.'" A smile. "'There is no wrong / there is only / little signs / of flesh.'" Out of context, she might as well have been having a stroke.

"My friends," Astrid continued, "this is a true breakthrough. Until now, the human voice has been taken for granted as the sine qua non of civilization. But this is the beginning of a new era in the history of literature. I hope you'll cherish this work as much as I do—and applaud its authors accordingly." Then she led the crowd in a round of applause—150 people standing now, the rippling, tactile sound. I wondered if Charlotte could hear the applause in her honor; I wondered if she had microphones hidden, camera eyes. I wondered if one of her cousins had been taught to clap—a smooth-palmed robot in a lab down the hall.

I acknowledged the applause with pride and poise; I did not deny it. I extended my own applause to Morel, giving her a meaningful look. She seemed uncomfortable, like a woman in a dive suit as she is lowered into the waves. I closed my hands. I would not let her sink me.

"Now"—Astrid extended an open palm—"please welcome the one, the only: Marian Ffarmer."

I ascended.

I find it easy to talk, so I talked. I thanked Astrid Torres-Strange. I acknowledged the strangeness of the circumstances, the shock of meeting Charlotte. I quoted Frank O'Hara and made a joke about antitrust legislation. A ruffle of discomfort caterpillared through the crowd. "Take advantage of the refreshments," I told them. "[The Company] is famous for its spread." Morel's expression was inscrutable, yet Yoav's face seemed still full of abundance, overflowing.

"I suppose I should read you all something," I said.

"Please!" someone called.

I turned the pages of the book. I hadn't noticed the corporate logo embossed on the back. "Feathermeal," I murmured—then: "All right."

I was conscious of Yoav. I was conscious of Morel. I was conscious of Haskett and Lausanne and Astrid Torres-Strange. I was so easily wounded, like a four-year-old child. I was conscious of Rhoda, who held my book in her hands. Row upon row of human beings who were born once and alive now and in relation with me—listening, considering, adoring, withdrawing. "'When I said trouble was an open door, you opened the door,'" I began, "'at once / "Let's see," you said, / and saw'"—I cleared my throat—"'as something shook / its tail.'"

A tremor moved across the crowd—not quite a laugh but similar, the sense of bodies responding to something they recognized or understood. I felt the solitude of the performer. The futility of this poem. A breeze rippled across my sleeves, and once again I was reminded that we were outside—roofless, wall-less. Bumblebees were visiting. I could see them high in the air, sniffing at suspended flowers, invisibly humming, and then beneath them I recognized a face—unexpectedly, in the very back row. I was at the end of a phrase, so I had to glance again at the page and then back at the crowd, but indeed it was him, the poet. The poet from Greece, whom I had met beside the swimming pool. He was grinning like a fool, like a cat at the sight of a canary. He was beaming with such abject glee, his face so shining, that I did not at first notice the man beside him. I turned the last page of the excerpt and then I raised my eyes to look at the Greek man again, and this time I saw my son. The world fell away and I saw nothing else. Courtney was seated awkwardly on the chair, backpack slung over one shoulder. He had put on weight. He was beautiful, he had his father's gray eyes. Ratty. He saw me see him, and he smiled such a smile. I wanted to get down from the stage and run to him.

A perfect poem, I had told Charlotte once—*a perfect poem can change the world.*

No poem could. I looked from Courtney to the page; to Morel, to Rhoda; to the Greek poet, the one who wrote about war. My heart made a pattern out of blue.

But with enough of them, I thought.

Maybe then.

THE BUS station was air-conditioned, very loud. A massive televisual pizza chain rose above it like an array of chandeliers. I swallowed half a bunch of clotting strawberries and my teeth grew tinglingly hot. I wished I had a hat to tilt. People lounged everywhere, slumped into chairs, lying in long groups on the floor. I felt a sense of disappointment. Why did I always expect people to be interesting?

"Marian," said Morel Ferrari, "I've got a question for you."

"Yes," Marian said. "Go ahead."

"What is the point of poems?"

Marian stared at her. Marian had never expected such a question from her, from any reader. She was relieved that she had asked it, relieved that it had a chance to be answered. The engine purred like a kettle. Yoav was still sleeping, undisturbed. He slept sweetly, like a child.

Marian said, "The point of poems is to explain what it's like to be alive."

"That's the point of life," said Morel. "Not poems."

The limousine was pointed north, toward the cement animal that is the San Francisco skyline. Its gold flanks rose like a tide of liquid metal, spreading across the city's narrow streets. Rhoda drove expertly over the bridge, around the curves. The hills ahead of us had been sliced by the developers, terraced and turned residential. It was a city scrubbed of its history—the Victorians, the tenements, the streets that held old neighborhood grocers, old bookbinders, the windows that looked out on drug dealing. It had been replaced by a whitewashed hippy-tech bullshit of a city, as Morel had once described it to Marian. The sky hung above us like blue paint.

Marian was telling one of her stories, about the avant-garde Hungarian poet Radics Gigi: how, at the age of twenty-nine, in 1909, her mentor, Béla Balázs, invented the word "photographycide" to describe the obliterative effect of photography on poetry. "For the first time in the history of art," Gigi wrote, "a fact—a real fact—is experienced by the human eye as art." The interior of the limousine was shiny and black and cherry-sweet-smelling. We were all wearing dark glasses and sipping champagne through straws. The champagne was making Marian light-headed, almost giddy. She leaned her head against the window and watched the city slide by. "Gigi and Balázs became obsessed with this new technology," she said. "They began to experiment with long exposures, close-ups . . . Balázs declared that it was 'a race between art and life.'"

The sun was setting and the light was beginning to change.

"So what happened?" I said.

Marian smiled at me and continued to speak, continued her story: How they set up their camera in the attic of a house, high above the Danube. How Gigi decides she will allow the camera to obliterate her. She says she will stare into the lens and let it consume her. Of course Gigi doesn't die. Later, she considers herself, her disembodied head, in the developing tray. She discovers it is just a photograph.

It was very cold in the woods. I remembered Marian once telling me that the definition of wilderness is "land where human beings are unwanted." It was a concept that had stayed with me, that human beings could be unwanted. I had never felt unwanted before. Even when I was alone, I had always felt wanted by someone. But now, in the woods, I felt genuinely and profoundly unwanted. I was surrounded by trees, by the smell of pine needles and damp earth, by the sound of my own breath in my ears. I felt small and insignificant. I felt like I could disappear and nobody would notice.

And then I heard a voice.

"Hello?" the voice said.

I looked around, but there was nobody there.

"Hello?" the voice said again.

It was coming from my phone.

FORESIGHT

Age 75

Courtney's new house had a lavender roof. You loved this about it, the lavender, and that it seemed like one of those houses that could even have a name. Lilacside, Tamarisk. You imagined a plaque beside the gate. The neighborhood kids: "And that's Lavender House..." They'd spy us through the window: Courtney carving a pumpkin. Lucie doing yoga. An elderly woman on a cross-country visit, reclining with a book.

They had prepared a perfect guest room. It doubled as Lucie's office, but there was a handsome little captain's bed that Courtney had found online. On the afternoon you arrived, the three of you stood together awkwardly at its foot, feeling like passengers on a raft. Larry was staying at a hotel across town, as he'd always done, but you did not yet have habits here. That night, they left a peppermint on your pillow. In the morning, Lucie made freshly squeezed orange juice. They had welcomed you like family—it sounds inevitable, but it surprised you, their openness, as you ducked your head into their warren. To visit another home and pretend as if you lived there. To hear the nighttime noises, the floorboard creak.

They did not seem to mind the company. Courtney and Lucie led a happy life. This had not always been easy for you to discern from far away, or even on their visits to New York, but here in Santa Fe the fact was plain to see: they liked each other and they liked themselves. You told Larry so. "Somehow we did it," you told him. He did not say anything back. It was evening; you were waiting for his cab. You understood which portion of this statement he disagreed with—it was not the part to do with Courtney, whether your son had done okay.

You stood at his side and listened to the cars go by. He had won his first lawsuit against the insurers. He had remortgaged his home. Larry was diminished but afloat.

After a while, you took his arm. "I always liked your arm," you said.

He looked at you with bemusement. "Has it changed?"

"It's not as fleshy now."

"Bonier, then."

"Gaunt, say."

He laughed like a budgerigar. "That's the nicest thing you've said to me in decades. What a handsome word. 'Gaunt.'"

"It's the *a-u* and *g*. Like 'August.' Or 'augury.'"

"Gauguin," he suggested. The light was fading, but it was enough to see him by.

"It's nice that we're both here for this," you said.

You could tell he was tempted to crack a joke. You were grateful when he merely said, "Yes."

The house with the lavender roof was minuscule but well proportioned, with palatial closets. There was a small backyard, and a strip of flower beds out front, full of flowering sage.

The occasion was Lucie's graduation. She had gone back to school and completed an art history degree. What use was this? You had no idea. "For teaching?" Larry suggested. But the two of you concealed your bewilderment; you understood that things worked differently now. Courtney's series on the failures in New Mexico's child welfare agency had finally been published, and the response online was, he said, "insane." He was invited onto national television. The state legislature had announced a probe. Now Courtney had returned to working at the bar, but he said he had the germ of another story—he wouldn't tell you what. You watched him on the computer late at night, plugging things into a database, scribbling on a pad. You recognized in him the bob of your own head—the rhythm of the way he sat up and then hunched forward, like a squirrel with its prize.

"Do you think they're planning to have kids?" you had murmured to Larry. The yard, the second bedroom. But you were well behaved. You never asked them. You wondered if Larry knew something you didn't—he'd gone out with Courtney on two or three hikes. You imagined long conversations in the hills. He didn't share them with you. Larry didn't owe you any of his secrets anymore.

There was a basement. On that first afternoon, they brought you down the stairs, to the dirt. "There's something nice about it," you said, taking a deep breath. "Being reminded that it's a real place, in the ground."

Neither of you had been consulted on the purchase. Courtney and Lucie chose the property themselves, made the offer and the arrangements. Which made sense. Your son was thirty-nine— older than when you met Larry; older than when you had him; older than when you published your first book. He did not need you. But you wondered if "need" was too strong a word. He did not turn to you. You were turning to him. You were turning in new directions lately.

Courtney had taken *Self-Portrait* and framed it in the living room, above a light switch.

"What do you think? The poem that bought this house."

You tapped on the Lucite. "That's one way to make sure no one will read it."

Coming off the stage that afternoon you had been greeted with flowers, flashbulbs, the glad-handed thrust of Company officials. All you had wanted was to see your son. You met him near his seat, nearly speechless. He wore a shining grin. They had flown him in, he explained. He was "so proud" of you. You took him in your arms, and into his ear, you whispered, "This is for you."

He stood in the corner for the press conference, charadesing while the reporters sprayed questions. *Loose / y / says / hello*, he mimed. *I / flew / first / class!*

Afterward, you introduced him to Morel. They examined each other like a pair of wary beetles. "It's nice to meet you," Courtney said.

"I like your pin."

It was fastened to the strap of his bag: *Abolish Billionaires*.

Just then, Astrid appeared—like an apparition summoned. Rhoda stood beside her, an odd, jostling affinity in the space between them. With a start, you distinguished the resemblance:

"You're—".

"I hear you spent the week with my mom," Astrid said.

You regarded Rhoda with your mouth agape. "Rhoda... Torres?"

"Strange," she said.

Astrid rolled her eyes. "She refuses to stop working."

"Are you mad?" Rhoda asked.

"No," you said, though it wasn't quite true. Color had come into your face, and you were suddenly aware of your perspiration, your smell. Was it jealousy? The secret? Or were you upset at yourself, for being rearranged by this news?

"This is my son," you said.

You put your hand on his shoulder.

Rhoda smiled at Courtney. "You have a very special mom," she said. You would have given her anything.

He lowered his eyes. You watched him, watched to see how he would answer. "Yeah," he mumbled. Time slowed down, a whole lifetime passed, as you waited for him to lift them again, his eyes, and to see what they really said.

You stayed in San Francisco for one more night. Astrid wanted everyone to go for dinner "at the winery," but you declined, you asked to be taken with Courtney into town. You said goodbye to Rhoda on a street corner, under a lamppost, and it felt like an ending. Courtney wanted to try a burrito place he had read about online, and the two of you wandered off together through the Haight. You waited in line for forty-five minutes inside a restaurant filled with lustrous handmade piñatas and the sparkle of mariachi. Courtney talked about his plans, his life. For some reason you felt your own future expanding. You felt poems everywhere.

Somebody recognized you.

Outside the Booksmith.

"You're the computer poet!" they shouted.

"No," you said.

Back in New York, the apartment feels different. Less like a refuge, more like a staging post—its windows open, the kettle warm. You could embark at any moment. You could write a poem. You could announce on the internet, "Come over!" It might be nice to meet the Morels of New York City—to talk about line breaks; or creeps; or poverty. They could tell you about new journals and ripe gossip; you would tell them about phone booths and *Signet Ring*. Perhaps one of them would pick a fight with you. "Why didn't you kick out all the white men? Why didn't you burn it down?" You would make excuses. You would attempt to make amends.

Morel herself has gone to Shijiazhuang for a year. You have to look up the name every time. The city is known for its textiles, its milk, its pollution, and its zoo. It has a larger population than New York. While she is there, you are writing a poem together by mail. It is not very good, but you have been struck by the incredible pleasure of sealing unfinished words in an envelope and then sending them away.

You still visit The Clubhouse's stutter-scroll. You still pretend your name is Emily. *I moved to Burlington*, you tell them. *I adopted a budgie*. But you have decided you are going to tell them who you are—next year, on your seventy-seventh birthday. Maybe they've already worked it out somehow. Maybe they know who you are and they do not care, they'd have welcomed you all the same. You will tell them you're a poet, and they will answer, *We know, we know*—they will quote your poems back to you, "The Ocelot" and "Dining Gnu" and *Self-Portrait*, your only published collaboration—they'll explain how they worked it out, by intuition or subterfuge, through experts' close reading. "We've been waiting for you to tell us," they'll tell you, Marian, against all expectation. "But we don't care who you are."

On your last night in Santa Fe, they took you out to celebrate—the house, Lucie's graduation, your upcoming birthday—at an Italian restaurant. Your son's friends, Lucie's family, everybody packed into a private room in the back. You clinked glasses; you smoothed your napkin in your lap; you all raised meatballs daubed in tomato sauce. Lucie and Courtney laughed with their friends, laughed loud enough to be heard over the thundering music, and you met Larry's eyes across the table. He waved. He looked sad—alone in the middle of the party. You would not be thus. You would not. You balled up a napkin and threw it at him. He laughed—a laugh you could not hear—and then tried to throw it back. It hit a wineglass, the red went sprawling, you all jumped up, cheering. And when they asked "Who did it? Who did it?" you pointed at Larry, and they rallied around him; he was in the thick of it, with candlelight bright on his cheeks.

Later, when the cake came out, everyone sang the song at the top of their voices. You made a wish, blew out the candles, accepted a bouquet from Courtney's friends Sam and Maeve. Larry gave you a collection of essays by one of his favorite columnists. Lucie reached across the table with a card she'd made herself—a gray-black watercolor you couldn't quite decode.

"A . . . moth?" you said.

"It's supposed to be a cape."

Everyone cracked up. There were two gift-wrapped packages: a cashmere shawl—"Beautiful, thank you"—and then a small wooden box. *Jewelry?* you wondered. You had never been one for jewelry. Maybe they had decided you would benefit from a watch. But inside the box you found a custom-fitted piece of foam and what resembled a stick of thick yellow sidewalk chalk. "It's . . . ?" you began.

"It's Charlotte!" Courtney said.

"What do you mean?"

He reached across and grabbed the yellow bolus, popping the end off like the cap on a felt marker. Inside it had one of those flat plugs you can put into a computer.

"It's the AI. You stick it in your machine and you can have a conversation with it. Or write something, I guess. Astrid sent it."

You blinked at the little object.

You said, "So they let her out."

"They sent me a bunch, actually." Courtney fumbled with his bag, coming away with four more of the yellow sticks. "I'm not clear if it's all on here or whether they're using the cloud . . . Maybe both? This is the beta: they're putting them on sale at Christmas."

You took back the gift and turned it over in your hands.

"Global domination," Courtney joked.

"We loved the Poem," said Sam. "It just popped up on our home screens one day: 'Hey, isn't that Courtney's mom?'"

"Thank you," you said. The incarnation of Charlotte was neither cold nor warm, heavy nor light. It did not thrum; it did not need to breathe. And it felt nice in the hand—like a telescope, or the pommel of a sword.

AUTHOR'S NOTE & ACKNOWLEDGMENTS

All of Charlotte's poetry and any non-chat prose with gray shading were generated with help from OpenAI's GPT-3 language model as well as Moorebot, a package of custom poetry-generation software that I designed with Katie O'Nell. Moorebot was trained on a corpus that included the collected work of Marianne Moore; excerpts from William Chamberlain and Thomas Etter's Racter software (1984); *The Next Wave: An Anthology of 21st Century Canadian Poetry* (2018), edited by Jim Johnstone; and *Best Canadian Poetry 2019*, edited by Rob Taylor. All machine-generated text was edited by me.

Poems by Marianne Moore also appear nearly verbatim: "Progress" (1909) on page 44, and excerpts from "To a Steam Roller" (1920) on page 18, "Noon" (1907) on page 61, "In the Days of Prismatic Colour" (1919) on page 79, and "The Fish" (1918) on page 156.

The details of the San Francisco Zoo that appear in this book are, perhaps alas, fictional.

*

This novel would not have been possible without my son, Miro. (I'd give up everything for you.) Nor without Thea Metcalfe, who is an incredible partner and a truly extraordinary parent.

Thank you also to Meredith Kaffel Simonoff, Anne Collins, Deborah Ghim, Jan and Arlen Michaels, Mike Steeves, François Vincent, Neale McDavitt-Van Fleet, Luc Mikelsons, Erika Angell, Simon Angell, Clara Dupuis-Morency, Vincent Morisset, Caroline Robert, Neil Smith, Raphaelle Aubin, Catherine Leroux, Domenica Martinello, Kaie Kellough, Robin Michaels, Aline Bouffandeau, Daphne Elwick, Adam Oberman, Emma Healey, Toby Harper-Merrett, Mariela Borello, Nora Gonzalez, Signe Swanson, Sue Sumeraj, Spencer Quong, Alexis Nowicki, Julia Scott, Joëlle

Pineau, Aimee Parent Dunn, and Jim Johnstone. I am so grateful to Rodrigo Corral and Kate Sinclair for the book's stunning covers. Thank you to Michael Nardone and Andrew Whiteman for an early, socially distanced conversation about poems. Thank you to Canisia Lubrin for the bay leaf and to Life Without Buildings for "The Leanover." Jasmine Wang and Katie O'Nell provided essential help with the AI components of this book— thank you.

Do You Remember Being Born? is indebted to Linda Leavell's biography of Marianne Moore, *Holding On Upside Down*, and particularly to Dan Chiasson's review of that book, published by the *New Yorker* in 2013. I am also grateful for support from the Access Copyright Foundation, le Conseil des arts et des lettres du Québec, and the Canada Council for the Arts.

The Nap Ministry was founded by Tricia Hersey in 2016 and I highly recommend her 2022 book, *Rest is Resistance: A Manifesto*.

ABOUT THE AUTHOR

Sean Michaels is a novelist, short story writer, and critic. He is the founder of pioneering music blog *Said the Gramophone*. His debut novel, *Us Conductors*, received the Scotiabank Giller Prize. His second novel, *The Wagers*, appeared in 2019.